M. LEIGHTON IS . . .

"FREAKIN' HOT!"   —*Nette's Bookshelf*

AND "SERIOUSLY SCANDALICIOUS."
                                          —*Scandalicious Book Reviews*

PRAISE FOR M. LEIGHTON'S BAD BOYS NOVELS

Down to You, *Up to Me*, AND *Everything for Us*

"Scorching hot . . . insanely intense . . . and it is shocking.
Shocking!"   —*The Bookish Babe*

"I definitely did *not* see the twists coming."   —*The Book List Reviews*

"Brilliant."   —*The Book Goddess*

"Leighton never gives the reader a chance to catch their breath . . .
Yes, there is sex, OMG tongue-hanging-out-of-mouth, scorching sex."   —*Literati Literature Lovers*

"Well, I drank this one down in one huge gulp . . . and it was delicious . . . Seriously *scandalicious*."   —*Scandalicious Book Reviews*

"Delicious . . . I stopped reading in order to grab a cold beer and cool
off . . . The twists and turns on the plot line are brilliant."
                                                  —*Review Enthusiast*

"OMG! It was freakin' hot!"   —*Nette's Bookshelf*

continued . . .

"Steamy, sexy, and super hot! M. Leighton completely and absolutely knocked [it] out of the park." —*The Bookish Brunette*

"Scorching hot . . . An emotional roller coaster." —*Reading Angel*

"I devoured it, and I'm pretty sure you will, too."
—*For Love and Books*

"Prepare yourself to be blown away." —*My Keeper Shelf*

"I loved it . . . Bring on the Davenport boys." —*Smexy Books*

PRAISE FOR M. LEIGHTON'S WILD ONES NOVELS

There's Wild, Then There's You

"Engaging and charismatic." —*Kirkus Reviews*

"Will leave readers enthralled by the intriguing and emotional infatuation Jet and Violet share. This story is hot enough to start a forest fire, yet will keep readers cool, calm, and collected as they attempt to decipher the characters' complicated personalities . . . This one is swoon-worthy." —*RT Book Reviews*

Some Like It Wild

"*Some Like It Wild* left me feeling breathlessly happy . . . the exact same feeling I had when I read *The Wild Ones*. M. Leighton has done it again—she's written the perfect, sexy love story!"
—*New York Times* bestselling author Courtney Cole

The Wild Ones

"This book is worth every second I spent reading it. Ms. Leighton is a phenomenal writer and I cannot give her enough praise."

—Bookish Temptations

"Hands down one of the hottest books I've read all summer . . . Complete with love, secrets, dreams, and hidden pasts! *The Wild Ones* is romantic, sexy, and absolutely perfect! Drop everything and read this RIGHT NOW!"

—The Bookish Brunette

"I can honestly tell you that this is one of my top books of the year and easily one of my new all-time favorites. I couldn't put the book down."

—The Autumn Review

"You will laugh, swoon, and even shed a few tears. M. Leighton knows how to write an amazing story. Get your copy of *The Wild Ones* today. You will not regret it."

—Between the Page Reviews

"This book was one of the best books I've read this year. It may sound like just a love triangle on the surface but inside there's so much more going on."

—The Book Vixen

"One of the best books I've read this year so far."

—Sim Sational Books

TOUGH Enough

M. LEIGHTON

BERKLEY BOOKS, NEW YORK

BERKLEY

An imprint of Penguin Random House LLC
375 Hudson Street, New York, New York 10014

Library of Congress Cataloging-in-Publication Data

Leighton, M.
Tough enough / M. Leighton.—Berkley trade paperback edition.
p. cm.— ("tall, dark, and dangerous" ; 2)
ISBN 978-0-425-27947-2 (softcover : acid-free paper)
1. Man-woman relationships—Fiction.   I. Title.
PS3612.E3588T68 2015
813'.6—dc23
2015025109

PUBLISHING HISTORY
Berkley trade paperback edition / November 2015

PRINTED IN THE UNITED STATES OF AMERICA

10 9 8 7 6 5 4 3 2 1

Cover art: "Couple" by Deborah Kolb / ImageBrief.
Cover design by Lesley Worrell.
Text design by Laura K. Corless.

Penguin
Random
House

Gratias autem Deo qui post pugnam.
Thank God for life after the fight.

PROLOGUE

Katie

Five years ago

Something is prodding me to wake up. Like an insistent finger poking my shoulder and someone whispering, "Wake up, wake up, wake up."

But I don't want to. I only want to hide. Hide from the light, hide from the world, hide from reality. I turn deeper into unconsciousness, but there's no rest for me there.

Wake up, wake up, wake up.

A dull pain begins to spread down my left side and sounds that were a distant backdrop only moments before come closer, closer, closer. One by one, I can make them out.

Sirens.

Metallic clattering.

Strange voices.

Screaming. Awful screaming.

It sounds so familiar, that scream. That voice, although I can't figure out why. The answer is fuzzy, like the face that swirls behind my eyes.

Distorted. Mocking. Cruel.

The face belongs to Calvin.

Panic swells within me, forcing me toward wakefulness. I don't want to go, don't want to wake. I claw and scratch. I dig in with my heels, with my hands, but nothing can stop my ascent.

Agony rushes in. It steals my breath and sweeps over me like flames, licking at my skin, turning the air to napalm.

More screaming, only this time I recognize the voice. I know it. I've listened to it my whole life.

It's mine.

And then I remember.

Just before the blackness welcomes me back.

I rouse again, despite a gut instinct that tells me not to.

I wake to harsh voices, shouted commands and muffled road noise.

The face is still there, still there behind my eyes. Taunting me, haunting me. Smug and satisfied.

Horrific pain radiates from the left side of my body. It sears its way across my nerves, gaining strength, gaining momentum until I can't fight the blackness.

So I don't.

My eyelids flutter open. I see white metal above me, the dark head of a man beside me. I'm lying on my back. He's sitting to my right. I don't know who he is or what he's doing. I don't even know where I am. All I know is that something is wrong. Terribly wrong. I know it. I can *feel* it, like frantic fingers picking at my consciousness, picking away the scab. Tearing away the blindfold. Luring me into awareness.

But I can't go back yet. Not yet. So I turn away. I retreat into the nothingness.

Seconds, minutes, hours pass. Time has no real meaning. It's only a series of disjointed sights, sounds and feelings. Fear. Dread. Pain.

Excruciating pain.

And aloneness, even though I know I'm not alone; I'm far from alone.

I hear dozens of different voices now. Sounds, too. Beeps. Thumps. Scrambling. And I can smell. Something awful, putrid even, mixed with the chemical scent of a hospital.

I can't focus on it, though. The pain is what overwhelms it all. It's nearly unbearable, like my left side is trying to secede from the rest of my body. Nerves tearing away from skin, muscle ripping away from tendon. Flesh falling away from bone.

So I run.

I run into the deepest part of my mind, the part that refuses to participate with the outside world. I hide there until the pain stops.

Only it never stops. It never stops stalking me from the shadows.

ONE

Katie

"You're not *the least bit* excited to be putting makeup on *the* Kiefer Rogan?"

Mona and I slow our walk as we approach my office. I use the term office loosely since mine is really just four thin walls that house a makeup chair, a bank of lighted mirrors and a wraparound counter. Two of the four walls are covered with shelves that hold the supplies of my trade—a wide array of everything from pancake makeup to prosthetic noses. It's not fancy, but it feels as much like home as any place does.

I turn my eyes to Mona's cornflower blue ones. She is the only person who might even *come close* to being called my best friend. "Am I excited to be putting makeup on Kiefer Rogan?" I repeat. Am I oddly nervous? Yes. Am I extremely uneasy? Yes. But am I *excited*? "Not even a little bit," I reply sincerely.

Her full lips fall into a disbelieving O. "Wow! I can't even imagine not getting excited over a guy like him."

"He's just a guy," I declare with a shrug. I wish I *felt* as casual as the gesture indicates. Kiefer Rogan *is* just a guy, but guys like him spell trouble. For that reason alone, I can't *really be* as nonchalant as I pretend to be. There's no point in dwelling on it, though, so I try to redirect her. "Besides, why should you care anyway? You've got a boyfriend."

She grins, which makes her look even more innocent than her platinum hair and eyes that are too big for her face. Physically, Mona is the perfect split between a Barbie Doll and a Precious Moments figurine, all with a touch of clueless porn star thrown in for good measure. She can work her assets like nobody's business, but she does it in such a way that doesn't make her detestable. That alone is quite a feat. She's very genuine, too, which is one of the things I like most about her. That and the fact that we are polar opposites in practically every way.

Mona is tall and fair and beautiful with a sweet, outgoing personality. I am none of those things, which is probably why we get along so well.

"White's great, but he doesn't look like *that*." White Bristow, Mona's boyfriend, is the executive producer of the show. He's fairly good looking, but nothing like the man I'm about to meet, Kiefer Rogan. White's as much of a player as Kiefer is alleged to be, but Mona loves him enough to overlook it. No matter what else he's doing (or *who else* he's doing), he always comes back to Mona. I guess maybe he loves her in his own way and that seems to be enough for her. "God, I wish he did, though."

"Looks aren't everything," I remind her softly.

Her expression falls into one of regret and sadness. She reaches out and smoothes the hair that I always keep swept over my left shoulder. It can always be found draped around my neck to hide my scars. She's one of the few people who know what lies beneath the swath of hair. And how sensitive I am about it. "No, looks aren't everything, but if they were, you'd still be one of the most wanted."

I smile. That's Mona—always seeing the best in me, whether it's accurate or not. "That's sweet, but you and I both know that's not true."

"Oh, but it is. Look at you, Katie. All this thick, wavy auburn hair, those big dark blue eyes and you're so tiny! I'd give anything to be petite like you."

"Mona, you're like a living, breathing Barbie Doll. If I were you, I wouldn't want to change a thing, not even your Amazonian height," I tease. She's not the least bit insecure about her five-eleven frame. In fact, she'd be the first to tell you that it's her unusual stature, replete with legs that go for miles, that helped her get the attention of White. And White is the person responsible for bringing her into the Hollywood world.

I stop in front of my "office" door and turn to face her. Mona leans up against the jamb, her eyes going all dreamy. "I wonder if Rogan likes tall women," she muses.

Back to Kiefer Rogan, I think with a deflated sigh. I won't be able to avoid him much longer, so why do we have to talk about him now?

My bitterness surfaces. A guy like him—beautiful, wealthy, had the world in the palm of his hand—showed me just how destructive men like these could be, and he left me with scars to prove it. Scars that won't ever let me forget it.

In an uncharacteristic show of emotion, I let that bitterness flow, secretly hoping it'll stop her from bringing the conversation back to him. "From what I've read in the tabloids, he likes anything with boobs. But I think he's into the divas mostly, which would count you out. Thank God!" I, for one, am glad that Mona isn't conceited about her looks or her position here at the studio. She's utterly guileless, happily clueless and I like her just the way she is—diva not included.

"I could be a diva," she says, straightening, her expression turning enthusiastic. "I could totally be a diva. If it meant having those flirty green eyes and that drop-dead gorgeous smile turned on me, I'd be whatever he wanted me to be."

Her little-girl giggle belies her words. She could never be a diva. "You don't have a diva bone in your body. Besides, why would you want a guy like that? He dates the most horrible women and he goes through them like water. I mean, look at Victoria," I say, lowering my voice as I scan the hall left and right to ensure we aren't being overheard. "What kind of decent person would date her? She's awful!" I go on cynically, finding some strange comfort in pigeonholing him, calling a spade a spade. Hoping that maybe if I build up my armor against him, I won't be swayed by his pretty face. "I bet he's a conceited jerk who only cares about what his arm candy looks like."

"Guys who look like him can be *annnything* they want, as long as they stay hot."

"Well, he's all yours, then. I don't have room for cocky, obnoxious, self-involved sleazeballs in my life." I glance at my watch. Six fifteen a.m. Mr. Rogan should be here by six thirty, but I won't be holding my breath. "I bet he doesn't even show up on time. Jerk!"

Mona sighs, tilting her head, a faraway look in her eyes. "I'd wait all day for a guy like that. He makes my special places shiver."

"Well, you and your special places are welcome to him. I don't see what the big deal is," I reply, turning into my office. "He's not even *that* good-looking."

I take two steps through the door and come to an abrupt halt. There, settled in my makeup chair with one ankle resting on his other knee, looking highly amused and as though he's been here for a while, is none other than Kiefer Rogan.

More gorgeous than words.

A rising star.

My first client of the day.

And the guy I just insulted.

TWO

Rogan

I sit in the makeup chair listening to the conversation happening out in the hall. I don't feel guilty. I'm not *trying* to eavesdrop. They brought that shit to my door. Literally. So of course I'm going to listen.

I'm curious to see what the two women who are talking look like. One is obviously very complimentary, while the other is anything but. I'm more used to flattery than dismissiveness, so I'm already working on a mental picture of the skeptic. I mean, yeah, I have an ass-ton of flaws, but I was lucky enough to be born with a decent face and a strong body, a combination that never leaves me without plenty of female attention. I'm not arrogant about it. It is what it is. I don't *try* to be handsome. I guess I just am. I mean, hell, I make a living getting punched in the face. Well, not anymore really. There aren't many who are good enough to land one on me these days. That's the beauty of rising to the top in the mixed martial arts arena.

I'm surprised when the two women walk through the door into the room where I've been waiting. I'm even more surprised by the way they look. One is a tall, blond goddess, the kind of woman I love to spend my nights with. The other is shorter and darker, but no less appealing. In fact, something about her immediately snags my attention. Holds it pretty damn tight, too.

She's staring at me with wide, midnight eyes, her deliciously lush mouth hanging open in shock. A long, thick rope of reddish hair is swept over one shoulder in a sexy wave and she's wearing a prim little dress that's the color of an apricot. What's inside that dress is just as appealing as the rest of her—two plump, more-than-a-handful tits pressing rhythmically against that soft cotton. They make my palm tingle to touch them, to see if they're as firm as they look.

When I make my way back to her face, I realize quickly enough that she was the one running me down. She doesn't have to say a word. It's all right there in her expression. The blonde looks dazzled. This one just looks . . . shocked.

Of course, me being the healthy guy that I am, *she's* the one I want.

The one who *doesn't* want me.

THREE

Katie

Even though Mona is still pressed flat against my back where she nearly ran me over because I stopped so quickly, I can't seem to budge. All I can do is stare, open-mouthed and embarrassed.

"Mornin', ladies," Kiefer Rogan drawls, dropping his ankle from his knee and crossing two thick arms over his impressive chest. He looks like a man who has not a care in the world.

And why should he? Look at him! I think.

Sweet Mary! His pictures don't do him justice. I knew he was a handsome guy. I mean, I'm not blind or dead. I've seen the tabloids. I've seen the news. But I had no idea just *how* handsome he would be. He's stunning. Simply stunning. Practically perfect in every rugged, manly way.

His short hair is dirty blond and his brows are just few shades darker. They hover in a dramatic slant over amazingly bright green eyes. They nearly glow in the tanned sea of skin that's stretched tightly across his angular face. His mouth is chiseled perfection, and his jaw and chin might as well be carved from a chunk of granite. He's not so perfect that he's pretty, though. No, he has flaws. Well, at least one that I can see. It's his nose. There's a slight crook at the bridge. Obviously it's been broken a few times, but it does nothing to detract from his looks. Not. One. Thing.

"Mr. Rogan," I finally manage to mutter. "You're early."

"Just Rogan," he instructs in a sandpaper voice. "I may not be that good-looking, but at least I'm a *prompt* selfish asshole."

Ohgod ohgod ohgod! He heard me!

I can hear Mona's soft whisper in my ear. "Shit!"

For far too long, that's the only sound in the room aside from the pounding of my heart and the crackling of the fire that I'm certain has engulfed my face. Or is that just my imagination?

"I didn't call you an asshole," I defend weakly.

"You might as well have."

"But I didn't," I maintain, starting to feel a bit prickly, like a cornered animal.

"Touché," he says with an acknowledging nod. As I watch, one side of his mouth pulls up into a grin that's so sexy, for a split second I worry about Mona's panties bursting into flames and burning us all alive in this tiny little square of an office.

I don't know how to respond, so I say nothing. I just stand here, sinking in the quicksand of his stare as the silence stretches between us like thick, stringy taffy. Unfortunately, that gives me too much time to notice how his smile makes my stomach feel shaky and how the sparkle in his jade eyes makes my skin feel warm. None of this helps my composure.

Mona recovers first. I hear her clear her throat just before she steps around me. "Hi! I'm Mona. Mona Clark," she says in her friendly way.

My best friend strikes out across the room toward Rogan. As I watch her, I'm a little deflated. I could never measure up to a woman like Mona. And I don't just mean her California looks, surgically enhanced figure and her loose-hipped swagger, the one she's using right now. No, it's something more than that. It's her outgoing personality, too. Mona's just the whole package.

And *I* am not.

I can see her from the side when she stops and sticks out her hand for Rogan to take. She smiles and I think to myself that there aren't many men who can resist Mona, least of all men like *this one*. But when I swing my gaze back to his face, I'm more than a little surprised (and *even more* disconcerted) to find that he's not looking at Mona—Mona the beautiful, Mona the charming, Mona who's standing right in front of him offering her hand. No, Kiefer Rogan is still looking at *me*.

Instantly, my tongue goes dry, dry like a damp cotton ball that's been left out under a hot sun all day. Only *this* hot sun is a hot *man* with a curious gaze.

With my breath coming in odd little bursts, I'm forced to admit that I'm feeling a little starstruck, which is totally unlike me. Yes, Rogan is probably the most attractive person I've ever seen, but that shouldn't matter. It's no longer in my DNA to care about things like that. About men *at all*. I'm the classic "once bitten, twice shy." Things like this don't happen to me.

Ever.

Or at least not anymore.

I frown, confused by his attention. My confusion seems only to make him smile bigger, though. I want to look away. I really do, but I can't. I feel like a fly trapped on flypaper, glued to this spot by his penetrating stare. Stuck until he decides to let me go.

Just a heartbeat before his disregard of Mona would be considered rude, Kiefer Rogan finally shifts his focus to my friend and takes her hand, grinning up at her. "So, *Mona*, are you the one who's supposed to cover up all my imperfections?"

"No, that's Katie. And don't get me wrong, I love her and she's one of the best artists in the biz, but I don't think God Himself could improve *anything* on you," she gushes with her most winsome, wholesome smile. *I* can tell she's about ten seconds from stripping and throwing herself in his lap, but I doubt *he* can see it. She's all calm confidence and cool beauty.

God, she's good!

I envy my friend's ability to be flirty and natural and unflustered in situations like these, whether she feels it or not. I used to be that way—poised and outgoing—but that girl, that *version* of Kathryn Rydale, got burned up in a fire a long time ago.

"I appreciate that, Mona," he replies in a surprisingly genuine manner, "but I think the hi-def cameras might disagree. Apparently, scars are a bad thing."

I cringe a little on the inside, even though I know it doesn't show on the outside. If I've learned anything over the years, it's how to hide. Emotions, insecurity, myself—hiding is the one defense mechanism that I've mastered.

"Why? Scars make a man . . . *a man*," Mona assures him with a cute wink. That's something else I could never pull off—cute. It would look clumsy and ridiculous on me. I don't know what *I can* pull off, but I have a feeling it would be more in the neighborhood of awkward or weird.

"Oh, I'm a man, all right. *All man*," he teases, shifting his eyes back to me. The instant they connect with mine, I'm unable to move or speak.

Again with the flypaper thing, I think in exasperation.

I want to avert my eyes, to hide from scrutiny like I've done for so long, but I can't. It's like I literally can't look away. Even though it makes me distinctly uncomfortable in my own skin, I can't look away. Maybe that's because it also makes me feel breathless and warm and nervous and . . . fluttery.

In some way, the bizarre apprehension I've carried all morning makes perfect sense now. My gut told me he would be trouble. I just never expected him to be *this kind* of trouble. No one affects me this way anymore. No one. It's been safer for me that no one has. And I liked it that way. Because this isn't safe.

I work to hide my unhappiness with this situation. After all this time, why am I reacting to Kiefer Rogan? Of all people, why *him*? Is it his looks? His attention? The position of the moon or a random twist of fate? And why did I know, deep down, that he was going to be a problem? I don't know the answers. What I *do know* is that my life is much less complicated when men aren't a part of it. And Rogan is not just any man. He's danger on two legs. And danger is something I don't need. I've had enough of that to last a lifetime.

"I don't doubt that one bit," Mona murmurs, drawing me back to reality and the conversation going on around me.

"So does that mean *you're* Katie?" he asks me, blatantly ignoring Mona, who is still clutching his hand, practically drooling all over it. "Are *you* the beautiful artist I'll be spending my mornings with?"

There's a silk thread in the gravel of his voice now. It soothes and it entices. It invites and it promises.

No wonder the world fell in love with him. He's flat-out hazardous! That smile, that friendly nature, that wickedly handsome face . . . It's a potent combination. It's even working on me! And, as damaged as I am, I didn't think any masculine wiles would be able to penetrate the thick scars I've developed. But, then again, I never expected to meet someone like Kiefer Rogan either.

"Yes, I'm Katie," I mumble when I finally find my voice.

Rogan unfolds his big body from the makeup chair. I catch and hold my breath, stunned into immobility for the second (or is it the third?) time in a few short minutes.

He's got to be over six feet; six feet of solid muscle and graceful lines. Wide shoulders, narrow waist, thick arms and legs, and it's all encased in denim and cotton that hugs him like a lover.

In a slow walk that practically screams SEX, he makes his way across the room to me, not stopping until I have to look up at him from my diminutive five feet, three inches. "It's a pleasure to meet you, Katie. I look forward to changing your mind about me."

I'm spellbound. As much as I don't want to be, I am. Not only is he gorgeous, which is bad enough, it's clear that he's charming, too. Good God, what a combination.

Up close, he's even more heart-stopping. I can see that, unlike his hair, his lashes are nearly black and sinfully long, framing his eyes and turning plain green into dazzling emerald. I can also see that there's a tiny scar marring the smooth line of his upper lip. I wonder what it would feel like to run my fingertip over it. I find myself inordinately fascinated by it.

I drink him in, albeit reluctantly. Kiefer Rogan is like champagne—undeniably delicious, deceptively light, and too easy to get drunk on. To lose your mind with. To make a mistake with.

That mouth quirks into a half-grin and my gaze flies back up to his. His expression is amused. Confident. Sizzling.

Not taking his eyes off mine, Rogan reaches for my hand, curling his warm, rough fingers around mine. He lifts and shakes my hand, each pump a leisurely, measured movement, like he's thinking of things other than the polite, innocuous gesture. It gives me a little chill to imagine what those things might be.

When I reply to his determination to change my mind about him, I'm proud that it's in a calm that belies my inner flux. "That's not necessary. We don't have to like each other. I'm just here to pretty you up for the cameras each day."

"Oh, I already like you," he claims in a low voice. Before I can respond, he continues. "But Mona here doesn't think I need much prettying. Do you disagree?" His eyes twinkle with mischief, and I can only imagine what a less scarred and backward woman might be feeling right now. Dazzled, flattered, lustful. All of the above?

"It's my job to make *everyone* prettier," I reply mildly. I know better than to stir up that hornets' nest. I'm used to stroking egos and protecting pride. I work with some of the world's vainest actresses. Diplomacy is practically a job requirement in my field.

One corner of his mouth curls into that irresistible, lopsided grin again. This time, he's so close that I can see a dimple appear in his lean cheek. "Then consider me your willing canvas. Do your worst."

I would take a deep breath, but my lungs feel like they can't expand anymore, like they're already near bursting. "Then have a seat and we'll get to work," I suggest breathily, hoping he'll take the hint. At this point, I'd say just about anything to get some space from his disconcerting proximity. If I'm to spend the next six weeks in his face, touching him and getting him ready for his part as Drago in the cable series *Wicked Games*, then I need for day one to begin with as much professionalism as possible. And at this rate, that's looking less and less likely to happen. I mean, I started off by insulting the guy within earshot. Not an easy opening from which to recover.

After a few seconds of staring at me with that bone-melting gaze of his and then giving me a full-blown smile, Rogan finally turns to head back to his chair. I carefully and quietly let out the breath I was holding.

"Captivating the crowd already, I see," a cool and cultured voice says from behind me. I turn to find Victoria Musser, actress, beauty, and witch extraordinaire, standing in the doorway behind me. She looks perfectly rumpled, as though she fell out of bed looking amazing and dragged herself in here to hypnotize all the cameras, with or without makeup.

Having worked for Cinematic Studios for two years, I've been assigned to her before, and I despised every minute of it. I was thrilled when Kelly, our key makeup artist, assigned someone else to fix her up.

Before anyone can comment, Victoria is sweeping me into a hug. Her arms feel like scrawny, steel traps.

Or maybe like spider pincers.

I'm stiff as a board. Even after she releases me and smiles down into my face. Her blue eyes are soft and her expression is warm. I have no idea what to think of her right now. Other than that she's possessed.

"Katie! I'm sorry I haven't been around to see you in a while. I've missed you, girl!" I'm not sure how I manage to keep my mouth shut, but I'm glad that I do. I just stare at her like she's sprouted wings and a tutu as she makes her way around me to accost Mona. "And, Mona, how are things with White?"

Although Mona is not only the girlfriend, but the personal assistant to the executive producer, just like me she is far, far, *faaar* beneath the notice of Victoria Musser. Well, until today, that is.

Mona looks dumbfounded as she, too, gets drawn into the cold-fish embrace of Victoria. I suppress a grin, wondering if that's what *my* face looked like when she hugged *me.*

"And, Rogan. God, it's been too long. How have you been?"

Like a slinky kitten, Victoria eases herself into Rogan's lap, wrapping her arms around his neck in that familiar way that says, "Yeah, we've seen each other naked a million times and it was awesome." When she leans back from her hug, her face still very close to his, Rogan returns her smile. Even from this distance, I feel the effects of it. Like a drug, which is what reminds me that men like him are toxic. Especially to me.

FOUR

Rogan

"Tori. I thought you were filming on location in Ireland for the next few weeks."

I hide my irritation behind a smile.

I didn't *think* she was filming on location; I was *assured* she was filming on location. That's the only reason I agreed to do this little project my agent suggested. Said it would open all kinds of doors for me. I'm not too concerned about that right now, but I'm a smart enough guy to realize that I won't be able to fight forever. At twenty-eight, my time as a viable champ in the MMA is getting shorter with every passing day. These acting gigs and paid appearances are just retirement for me. I've got more money than I should ever need now, but I'm not stupid enough to pass up good opportunities when they present themselves. So here I am.

And, damn it, so is Victoria.

She was fun for about a minute until I realized, like so many of the others, that she's a clingy, demanding princess who will use any weapon at her disposal to manipulate people. People being me, in this case.

She found out in a hurry that I'm not the type to be led around by some top-shelf pussy with nothing in her eyes but dollar signs and photo ops. Unfortunately, she doesn't catch on to subtlety very quickly, nor does she give up very easily. And now here I am, stuck in a six-episode contract that will put me within claw distance of this beautiful yet vapid vixen.

I glance over Victoria's shoulder to see Katie watching us, an odd expression on her face. If I didn't know better, I'd say it was a mixture of disappointment and disgust. And, judging by the rebellious jut of her rounded chin, maybe a little determination, too.

No idea why the hell her disappointment or disgust would bother me, but it does. Something tells me she's the kind that's the opposite of Victoria in every way, *including* her looks.

It's obvious from her comments to her friend Mona that she's not the least bit impressed by me. But even so, I saw a little fire in her eyes when I got close. It was reluctant as hell, but it was there nonetheless. It's that glimpse of heat, that tiny spark that makes me want to see her melt like butter in my hands. If she's determined to resist any attraction she might feel, then I'm *even more* determined to make sure she can't.

FIVE

Katie

"Change of plans," Victoria purrs, drawing Rogan's attention back to her face, only inches from his. "I'll be *very close* while you're here."

There's a long, tense pause during which I work to suppress my gag reflex.

"Well, I need to get upstairs," Mona blurts. She's possibly even less fond of Victoria than I am. "But I need coffee first. I'll bring you some on my way back by," she directs at me.

I turn grateful eyes to my friend. "That'd be great. Thank you."

"Any for you, Mr. Rogan?" she asks, raising her voice and purposely interrupting Victoria's assault.

Rogan leans around his vicious ex-girlfriend and smiles pleasantly at Mona. "Just Rogan, remember?" He winks at Mona and I think I can actually *see* her knees buckle a little.

"Rogan, then. Coffee?"

"No, thanks. I try to stay away from . . . *artificial* stimulants."

Rogan's eyes slide back to mine, bringing with them that undeniable heat. I don't know what he means by that comment, but my belly tells me that it was deliciously wicked, that it was meant to stir, to incite. And, sadly, it does.

Victoria clears her throat and slithers off his lap, standing at his side and putting her body between us. In my mind, her taking steps to block me from his view confirms that his comment was meant for me. And she doesn't like that one bit.

Mona's smile is enormous and excited as she sashays past me, leaving me standing awkwardly near the doorway of my own makeup room. I'd like nothing more than to leave with my friend, but I can't. This is where I work. I can't very well walk out when I've got to get Rogan ready for the first shoot of the day.

Luckily, he takes care of part of the problem. "It was good seeing you, Tori, but Katie's got to get to work on me. I'm sure I'll see you around the set," Rogan offers as he sits up straighter in the chair, suddenly a touch cool and very businesslike.

"Oh, we'll be seeing lots of each other." Victoria sounds smug as she bumps Rogan with a swing of her perfectly rounded butt before she turns to walk away. Her smirk is satisfied as she passes me. "See you later, Katie."

Holy cow, I hope not! I think this, but I don't say it. Like so much of what goes through my head, it stays firmly locked away. There, it's safe. There, it won't get me in trouble. There, it won't let anyone know what I'm feeling. See the real me. Or get too close to her.

Rogan is watching me in the mirror when I turn my eyes back to him. "Ready?"

I hope he only means am I ready to get started with his makeup. If he means anything else, the answer is NO! In no way am I ready for a guy like him.

No. Way.

"Yes, sir, *Mr.* Rogan," I say, just to be obtuse. I'm disgruntled and

I have no idea why. Surely this man, this *cocky, shallow man*, can't get under my skin.

Surely not.

"Just Rogan," he repeats.

I nod and smile, but say nothing as I sling a drape around his shoulders.

SIX

Rogan

Katie is quiet as she evaluates me with narrowed eyes, her gaze roving my face, pausing on my eyes and my mouth, on my scars and my nose. She then looks through first one drawer, then another, followed by another and another, collecting things as she goes. She glances back at me repeatedly as she decides what colors to use to . . . I don't know what. Camouflage? Highlight? Hide completely?

When she catches me watching her, she looks quickly away and tucks her chin a little. I have no idea why the hell a woman who looks like her might want to *hide*. But it looks like that's exactly what she's doing. Like she'd rather be invisible in front of me.

The more closely I watch, the more I discover. For instance, I think she has a couple of nervous ticks—the way she licks one corner of her mouth, the way she pulls that sweep of hair tighter around her neck, like it's a security blanket. I'd say she'd much rather I not notice things like that, but for some reason they make her all the more fascinating.

And, damn it to hell, I'm already fascinated enough.

Since becoming whatever kind of freakish sensation that I've become, all the women I've come across have been nothing but media whores. They *want* the attention. All the attention. They crave it. Crave the eyes and the notice and the limelight. But not this girl. She craves obscurity.

She's different. And I'm ready for different.

When she's finally ready to get started, I watch her swirl a brush in a pod of makeup. The action is so competent and smooth it's easy to see that she's done it a million times. She feathers something all over my face, giving simple, succinct instructions as she comes to certain areas, like my eyes and my mouth, when she mutters a soft, "Close."

When she's done, she sets down that color and picks up another, lighter shade. Before she leans in to me again, she tugs at her hair. Nervous tick.

She swirls this brush, too—a smaller one this time—into the packed powder before bending closer to my face. I get a whiff of her perfume. Clean and floral with a little hint of musk or vanilla. The cocktail is sexy as hell, like innocence with a sin chaser.

Just enough sin to make a man beg.

Katie's tongue sneaks out at the corner of her mouth, drawing my eye. Her lips are just about perfect. They're shaped like a lush cupid's bow, plump and moist. Ready to be kissed. I can easily picture what they'd look like afterward—red and swollen.

Just enough sin . . .

She concentrates on dabbing at the scar that runs through my left eyebrow. She makes no comments as she goes about her work, but for some reason I want her to. I want her to talk to me. Most of the women I've been with won't shut up, but not this one. Again, she's different.

"Bet you've never had to put makeup on this many scars before," I wager, eager to hear her voice again. It's got the same understated sex appeal that the woman herself does.

"You'd be surprised," is all she says.

Is she really so shy, or does she seriously find me distasteful? Does she truly think I'm the selfish, arrogant asshole she described? Or was that just blustering? I shouldn't care. But I do. I don't want this girl to think I'm a dick. I want her to talk to me, smile at me, tell me what her favorite movie is, how she likes her coffee. Random shit. I don't even care *what* she says. I just want her to say *something*.

Inwardly, I cringe. I sound like a damn woman. *Talk to me! Open up! Why won't you let me in? Whine, whine, whine.*

Bloody hell! There must be estrogen in this damn makeup!

Yet, it doesn't stop me from trying to draw her into conversation.

"I remember when I got that cut. It was during a fight for the middleweight championship two years ago. The guy pulled an illegal head butt that the referee didn't catch. Split my eye wide open and just about put me on my ass. Luckily, I've been hit a lot harder, so it didn't knock me out. I took a step back and planted an elbow strike to his face. Blew the guy's cheekbone out. Won the fight forty-one seconds later."

"And who says violence doesn't pay?" she mutters sarcastically.

"You don't approve?"

Finally, I get her full attention. Katie leans back and looks right at me. Her eyes are puzzled, but all I really notice is that there are pale gold flecks in the dark blue of the iris, like stars sparkling in a midnight sky.

She stares at me, her mouth opening for a second to issue one little noise before her lips snap shut. Whatever she was going to say, she thought better of it. Now I'm *even more* curious and determined to get her talking. Usually I don't have this problem with women. Quite the opposite, in fact.

Her face straight and serious, Katie proceeds to ignore me, leaning in and continuing her work. She carefully covers all my various scars and scuffs, which are a helluva lot. She brushes something under my cheekbones and then gives my eyelashes a dusting of some kind of girly shit before rubbing something on my lips. For all I know, I could see a drag queen when I look in the mirror. I haven't checked my reflection. I've been too wrapped up in watching the artist inflicting the damage, too busy wondering what that little pink tongue I keep seeing tastes like.

The longer I'm around her, the more I want to kiss her. Not that it's such a surprise. I mean, I'm a guy. With an above-average sex drive. And I like kissing. And what comes after kissing. The thing is, I'm getting ready to go on set with some of the world's most beautiful women, but something tells me not one of them will intrigue me as much as *this one* does.

I can tell she's finishing up. She keeps leaning back to look at me and then coming back in to tweak stuff here and there. "You're *really not* very impressed by me, are you?" I blurt, wanting to hear her answer before I leave her little bubble of cosmetics.

She goes perfectly still and her eyes dart over to mine. I smile when I see them widen guiltily, her reaction an answer in and of itself. She starts to straighten away from me, so I reach for one of the long, loose auburn curls that hang over her shoulder, tugging it to keep her close to me. "You should prepare yourself, then."

"For what?" she asks in a whisper.

"For me to impress you."

Her delicately arched brows draw together over her sapphire eyes. "I-I'm not like other women, Mr. Rogan," she says, her voice more soft than stiff, like she regrets that she's not.

"And that's a bad thing?"

She licks the corner of her mouth again, drawing my eyes back to those lips. I wonder if they taste like pink cotton candy. I force my eyes up to hers and lean forward just a little bit, testing the waters. Her pupils swell and I hear her suck in her breath. She looks like she wants to run, but she doesn't move. Not one inch.

I'm just about to do something very unprofessional when another voice intrudes.

"Coffee's here! Extra hot, extra cream," comes her friend Mona's announcement.

Katie jerks back like she's laid her hand down on a red-hot stove. Her curl slips right through my fingers. It escapes me. *She* escapes me. Just like this moment has.

SEVEN

Katie

Seconds after Mona's timely interruption, one of the director's assistants came to escort Rogan off to the set of his character, Diamond Drago's, steamy underground club. As I clean my station and get ready for my next job, Mona stands beside me, gripping my cup of coffee and staring at Rogan as he goes. Her mouth is still hanging open long after he's gone.

When I finish tidying, I ask, "Did you bring that for me? Or did you just need something to molest?" I tip my head toward the cup that she's practically massaging.

She glances down at the steamy brew and then grins up at me, handing over the mug. "Sorry. I just . . . I mean, I can't . . . He's just . . . Wow!" Her eyes round even more. "And ohmigod, Katie? It looked like he was about to kiss you. Did you notice that?"

Did I notice that? How could I *not* notice? But surely that couldn't have been what he was about to do. Surely not . . .

I frown. "Do you think?"

"God, yes! For sure!"

"I thought maybe he was just . . . I don't know."

"Well, *I* know. He was definitely about to kiss you."

"But . . . but that makes no sense. I mean, why would a guy like *that*, surrounded by women like Victoria, have the slightest interest in me?"

"I told you this morning, silly. Most. Wanted. You just don't see it."

And I still don't. Nothing Mona can say will change my mind. I'm scarred. Damaged. No man in his right mind would want me. And if Kiefer Rogan does, it's only because he hasn't seen the real me yet. The bad parts. The ugly parts.

Mona tilts her head to one side, her expression softening. "I wish you could see how beautiful you are."

Reflexively, I smooth the wave of hair that falls over my left shoulder, concealing the source of my unease, the evidence of my past. "I know *exactly* how beautiful I am and exactly how beautiful I am *not*. We work in a forest of exotic creatures, Mona, but I'm not one of them. I'm no different than grass or moss or the leaves on the ground. Unimpressive, something most people walk by every day and pay no attention to. I'm invisible."

"You're so crazy, Katie! You don't—" Mona argues, but I interrupt her, taking her hand and jiggling it to get her attention.

"Hey, I don't need a pep talk. You forget that I *like it* this way, that I *want it* this way."

"But why? Just because you aren't . . . Just because you don't look like every other bimbo around here, myself included, doesn't mean that you don't shine. Because you do, Katie. Maybe even brighter than the rest."

I smile at my sweet, well-intentioned friend. "That can be our little secret."

Mona sighs, her eyes a little sad. "One day someone will make you see how gorgeous you are. And that day might not be too far away."

I shake my head at my friend's unflappable optimism, irrational though it is. "You're such a romantic, but Rogan isn't interested in me, Mona. And even if he was, it wouldn't last more than a few heartbeats. Maybe he thinks I'm a challenge because I didn't fall at his feet. I don't know, but whatever it is, it won't take him long to realize that I'm not a challenge. I'm nothing. I'm not worth his interest. His time. His attention. I'm nothing special. When he sees that, he'll move on. *If* he's even interested at all, which I doubt."

She cocks her head and considers me. "You ever gonna tell me what happened to make you this way?"

"What's 'this way'?"

"So . . . alone. And so content with it."

"I'm not alone, Mona. I have you. And Dozer. And Janet, my nosey neighbor."

Mona pushes her bright pink bottom lip out in a pout. "Dozer's not even a person. He's a cat. And cats don't count. Besides, that doesn't make me feel any better."

"Well, it should."

"I just want you to be happy, Kitty."

Somewhere along the way, Mona started calling me "Kitty" as a term of endearment. She began with Kat, but I couldn't let her continue with that. It made my chest feel tight and the room spin every time I heard it. Kat was another girl from another life. A life that ended in tragedy. Kat died a long time ago and I want no reminders. Mona took it well, though. That's when she started calling me Kitty. I let her keep that one.

Kitty.

I shake my head.

Some days it makes me feel like a porn star. Some days it makes me feel like I should have a hip holster and a gun so I can go around shooting up saloons. But other days . . . days like today, it makes me feel loved, something that I haven't felt very much in the last few years.

"I know. And I will be. I mean, *I am*."

"I won't be satisfied until you can say that a little more convincingly. And with a smile."

I nod, desperate to change the subject. "I'll come get you for lunch."

She claps enthusiastically. "Lunch! Yay!" And then she turns and blows out of my space just as quickly as she blew in.

I twist the knob and gently push open my front door. I peek around the wooden panel to make sure my cat has moved before I swing it wide enough to get through.

Dozer likes to sleep on the rug right under the mail slot while I'm gone. On several occasions, I've seen curious scratches and puncture marks in the envelopes of a few bills here and there. It makes me wonder if Dozer attacks the mail when it comes through the flap. I can only imagine that it would scare the crap out of *me* if *I* were sleeping when it landed on me.

I smile as my black-and-gray striped cat snakes his way over to my leg, weaving in and out in a figure eight pattern, rubbing his sides against me and purring loud enough to wake the dead.

"Hey, buddy, were you sleeping?"

I bend to scoop him up and he immediately head butts me. That's been his greeting since the day I rescued him from a cat-eating dog gang that terrorized my neighborhood two years ago. I think he realizes he'd have been dead meat if I hadn't intervened. He's been my loyal companion ever since.

"You're the only man I need in my life, aren't you, Dozer?" I croon to him, aggravated that I'm *still* thinking about Kiefer Rogan.

Dozer jumps out of my arms, walks four feet and flops down on the carpet where he proceeds to groom himself. I stand on the rug, watching him, letting the peace and quiet and familiar smells of my home, of my *life* relax me.

I love my little house. It's nothing special—a cute cottage that has yellow siding, a white wrought-iron fence around the yard and cheerful window planters that are blooming with pansies this year. It's not a mansion, but it's mine. My hiding place. My sanctuary. The one place that I can be myself, whatever mixed-up blend of Kathryn, Kat and Katie Rydale that is.

I moved here right after I got the job with the studio. I needed to disappear and the small town of Enchantment seemed the perfect place to do so. And, so far, it has been. And that's the way I like it. I don't go looking for trouble and I can only hope that it doesn't hunt me down. I've had enough of it to last a lifetime already, and I'm only twenty-four.

Before I can stop them, flashes of flames and fists, of writhing and wreckage, of tears and emptiness spew through my mind like a spray of acid, burning where it touches. Relentlessly, I push those turbulent thoughts to the deepest part of my consciousness. I learned long ago that the less contact I have with them, the less they can hurt me. I learned that if I give them an inch, if I give them even a few seconds of thought, they take over. They incapacitate. They paralyze. They eat away at the carefully constructed person I've become, destroying the peace and security that I've worked so hard to achieve. And I can't let that happen. Not again.

I busy myself with the routine tasks I perform each day when I get home from work. I find comfort in structure, in the predictable. I thrive on being ordinary and living an ordinary life. The spectacular can only end in devastation. The bigger the star, the brighter the shine, but the more epic the explosion and subsequent death. That's something else I learned. The hard way. It's better not to shine too bright. Or, sometimes, not to shine at all.

At a few minutes before ten, I'm already brushed and washed and lying in bed with one of Mona's books. I refuse to consider why I picked up another of her silly romance stories tonight of all nights. I also refuse to consider why, when I hear a door slam outside, I think for just a fraction of a second that it might be Kiefer Rogan. And that a guy like him might actually be interested in a girl like me.

I ignore the niggle of disappointment and remind myself that I'm better off without men like that in my life—the kind who love beauty and glamour, the kind who gravitate toward the kind of girl that I used to be. That got me nothing but trouble and pain and regret, and I've got the scars to prove it. No, I'm better off by myself and I'll do well to remember that.

Why, after all this time, I'd let a guy like Kiefer Rogan get under my skin is strange, yes, but I have to keep it in perspective. Not let him get inside my head with his killer smile and charming wink. Letting him in would be a disaster, plain and simple.

I snap the book shut with a definitive thud, glaring at the beautiful laughing couple on the cover. Life isn't a romantic comedy. It's more of a light Shakespearean tragedy. Or a cruel joke. At least that's been my experience.

EIGHT

Rogan

Because Enchantment, Georgia, is a small town—like such a small town that the one restaurant it boasts is actually a diner—the studio had some more . . . *luxurious* houses built for their stars. They're designed to be leased on a very temporary basis, meant mostly for those who don't like living out of their trailer or don't want to travel back to their real homes on the weekends and between shoots. The place I leased from them for six weeks is perfect for my purposes, mainly because Kurt, my younger brother, has certain living requirements that make trailer, hotel or apartment residences nearly impossible to navigate with his wheelchair.

I'm still surprised that he wanted to come down here with me. He doesn't like getting out of his element much and, as shitty as it sounds, I was sort of counting on that to keep him at home.

But it didn't.

Maybe he needed a break from home, too.

For Kurt, home is Texas. He's comfortable there, but I never will be. Once I left the town I was born in, I didn't plan to return. Ever. Too many bad memories. I thought my brother and I had both managed to escape when we enlisted in the military. I thought we'd both have a better life. Him not worrying about Dad, me not having to worry about either of them. But when Kurt got hurt, I was all he had. I gave up my career in the military, the family I'd made there, so I could come home and take care of him. I went back to fighting because other than Delta Five, my covert ops team, it was all I knew. It's what I had to do. Kind of like coming back to Texas to take care of my brother.

I had to put down roots for Kurt's sake, and Texas is where he wanted to be, so Texas it was. I ended up going all the way around the world only to end up back in the same shitty memories I had just barely managed to escape. Between that and Kurt's assholery and feeling trapped in a life not entirely of my making, I was sort of looking forward to this gig as a breather, even though I felt guilty as hell for looking at it that way. But that didn't work out as I'd hoped. Now it's just the same shit with different scenery. There's just no avoiding obligation sometimes.

I would feel a lot more thwarted by the whole setup if it weren't for the lovely and intriguing Katie. She is proving to be a very welcome, very effective distraction. She was the last thing I was expecting. I'm not complaining, though. Just the thought of her brings a smile to my face. In a world of one-dimensional (albeit gorgeous) robots, she's a breath of fresh air. And it's looking more and more like that's just what I needed.

"Where the hell have you been? I thought you were done shooting at six, *Keefie*," Kurt snaps from just inside the doorway, bringing my attention back to my current predicament—I'm late.

I take in his posture—spine straight, shoulders squared, arms crossed—and the fact that he called me Keefie—something my father used to do that he knows I hate—and I know he's furious. Ready to fight. I don't even need to look at the hard set of his jaw or the angry green eyes so like my own to see it. But I do. And I'm struck for about the millionth time by how sad it is to see such bitterness etched into such a handsome kid's face. I know I'm responsible for at least part of it. He was angry with me long before he lost the ability to walk.

I keep my reply calm and level. "I left you a voice mail. Didn't you check your messages when you got up?"

If anything, he gets even madder. "Why the hell would I? Is it too much to expect that my brother might keep his word and be home when he says he'll be home? Jesus! It's not enough that I lose my legs in Afghanistan, but now I have to hold your hand like a damn kid who can't remember to wipe his ass."

I scrub a hand over my face, suddenly exhausted. Not from activity. I can take a beating inside the ring and not feel this shitty. No, this is purely emotional. Spending very much time with Kurt just drains me.

"I'm sorry. There was nothing I could do about it. One of the producers wanted me to have drinks with some of the regular cast. Sort of an introduction. I couldn't really leave without looking like a shitheel."

"Boo hoo! What a pissy life you have, with your money and your fame and your legs. Tell that shit to somebody who gives a damn about your selfish ass."

With that, my brother grips one wheel, spins around and speeds off down the long hall that leads to his bedroom. I gave him the big master suite, which is on the main level, while I took one of the smaller bedrooms upstairs. I'd sleep on the roof if it put some distance between us. When he gets like this, he'll seek me out ten times before I go to bed just to fight. But only if he can get to me.

Another pang of guilt streaks through me. He's had a tough life and I feel like a bastard for getting frustrated with his attitude. Kurt isn't one of those guys who came back from Afghanistan wounded yet thankful to be alive. No, he came back with a chip on his shoulder the size of a Boeing 757. In the three years that he's been living with me, I've heard at least a thousand times how he can never catch a break and, honestly, I can see why he thinks that. He first had to deal with the world's biggest asshole for a father, who he escaped by enlisting, only to get wounded in a foreign land. I guess he has a few good reasons to be bitter. But damn! It sure is hard to listen to it day in and day out.

With a sigh, I make my way back to his bedroom. I can hear the sounds of *Call of Duty* peppering its gunfire through the crack in the not-quite-closed door.

I knock. No response. I knock louder. Still no response. I knock a third time, adding a very congenial, "Hey, man, can I come in?"

All noise ceases when he pauses the game. I know he heard me; he's just making me sweat. Kurt is never one to let an opportunity to punish me pass by. He pouts until he gets what he wants, which is essentially a nonspecific assurance that the entire world does, in fact, revolve around him.

He barks his acknowledgment of me a good minute and a half later. "What?"

"Look, bro, I should've called again instead of leaving a message. And if I couldn't get you, I should've just told them I had to get home to my brother." Another pang of guilt as I push the one button I *know* will get him off my back for a few minutes—his pride. He hates that he needs help, that he needs someone to take care of him.

Kurt spins around in his gaming chair, legs dangling limply in front of him, toes dragging lifelessly along the hardwoods. "Is that what gets you off, dickhole? Humiliating your poor crippled brother and using him as an excuse to get out of shit you're not man enough to get out of on your own?"

"So let me get this straight. Telling the truth makes me a dick-hole. *Not* blowing off the people who are paying me to be here makes me selfish. Damn, dude, what do you want me to do, then?"

His lean face is red with barely suppressed rage. I know the second I scored the winning point. His lips thin and his eyes narrow before he spins back around to face the television.

"Whatever, asshole. Just try to keep your word a few times before I'm dead."

I shake my head and back out of his room, closing the door behind me. That's as good as it's going to get for a while, so I'll leave that comment alone.

As I walk back down the hall, my gut burns, like my tactics were acid and I just swallowed a huge gulp. I knew I'd feel like shit about using his pride (which was just about the only thing left untouched by his ordeal) against him, but my brother really needs to take his head out of his ass every once in a while. Sometimes things can get ridiculous. I mean, all this over me being a couple hours late? When I left him a message to tell him so?

Seriously?

I grab a premium beer from the fully stocked premium fridge and stand in the kitchen as I down the first one. My phone rings before I can finish. It's Jasper, one of the men who feel more like my family than my own flesh and blood does sometimes.

"Missing me already?" I ask, hoping this is a social call, but pretty sure that it's not.

"You're not pretty enough for me. Now Tag on the other hand . . ."

I laugh. Tag is the lady-killer of the four of us.

Three, I remind myself. Reid, our fourth brother-in-arms, was killed not too long ago. Someone knew his location and led a mercenary right to him. Our commander, Colonel Denton Harper, is still trying to figure out why he was killed and by whom. It's very likely it had to do with one of the government covert operations we executed, but until the Colonel tracks down some answers, we are all in danger. For that reason alone, I suppose it's a good thing Kurt came with me to Enchantment. We couldn't be any better hidden if I'd handpicked a place for us to go. We're in the middle of nowhere in a town the size of my thumbnail. A stranger would stick out like a sore thumb here.

"I'll be sure to pass along your admiration when I see him." Tag works a vineyard on the side of a mountain not far from here. I'm sure we'll get together at some point.

"Just calling to say that I got a new lead. Turned it in to the Colonel. Hope it gets us something."

"Me, too, man. You heading back to the states?"

"Uhhh, not yet. It's not safe yet and there's . . . Well, I'll fill you in later. But no, I'm not coming back yet. Hopefully it won't be long before I do, though."

"Sounds good, J. Until then, watch your back."

"Watch *yours*," he warns.

"We'll get this bastard."

"Yes. We will."

I hear death in his voice. I've heard it before. We all have. We've all done things we'll probably never be able to talk about, but Jasper . . . he had demons that were riding him before we knew each other. I guess we all did, but his . . . Well, he's the most tortured of us. The deadliest, too. But he's my family and I'd trust him with my life. We all would. We all *are*. He's the one most actively searching for the person responsible for Reid and his mother's death. "Later, Ro."

"Later, man."

He hangs up with a click and I grab another beer before I head upstairs to go over tomorrow's script and then turn in. Jasper and the traitor are very much on my mind. To distract myself, I think of

Katie . . . maybe a bit too much. After an hour, I've looked at the same page a dozen times and retained exactly none of it. I have, however, managed to successfully recall every minute detail about the sexy-as-hell makeup artist. When I wake up just after three a.m., it's with my hard dick in my hand and an auburn-haired beauty on my mind. That's the first time I realize that I might damn well be in trouble.

NINE

Katie

I woke up feeling determined, determined to remain calmly unaffected by Kiefer Rogan. He's just a man, probably a total jerk when he's not trying so hard to be charming.

Total jerk, I say to myself over and over again as I make my way down the hall. I'm halfway to my door when I pull my mind back to the present enough to notice that my coworking cohort is missing from my walk. Mona gets in before I do and usually she is filling my ears with all manner of gossip, romantic elation or relationship heartbreak by now. Only this morning she's not.

And when I get to my "office" I see why.

There, leaning up against my makeup table, gawking at Kiefer Rogan, is Mona. I don't know which part of the scene shocks me more—Mona gawking or Rogan beating me to work. Again.

I pause in the doorway. "G-good morning," I offer the room at large.

Both Rogan and Mona turn to look at me. Mona is wearing the

biggest smile I've ever seen. I wonder if I should be concerned that her face might split right down the middle. "Kitty!" she screeches gleefully.

Rogan is wearing damp hair, a tight white shirt and a lopsided grin that makes my insides turn more somersaults than an Olympic gymnast. Holy monkeys, is he hot!

Total jerk, total jerk, total jerk, I remind myself to cool my bubbling insides.

I offer a politely unaffected smile to both occupants of the room, ignoring the fact that Mona is practically vibrating with excitement. I assume it's because of his close (and very handsome) proximity until I see her eyes continually dart to his hand.

That's when I start to get suspicious that something's up and that Mona's zeal might not be entirely due to Rogan's nearness.

I narrow my eyes on first Mona and then Rogan. Before I can ask any questions, however, Rogan stretches out his hand. In it is a coffee cup.

"Extra hot, extra cream," he says simply, his eyes shimmering with charm and his grin glistening with sincerity.

I feel the frown furrow my brow. "Thank you," I mutter, reaching for the coffee.

"Aren't you going to ask how he knew you liked it that way?"

I glance up at Mona. I don't think I've ever seen her quite this . . . animated. If a person can *look* like a squeal *sounds*, then that's what Mona looks like. "I assume he heard you announce it yesterday when you brought me some."

She looks a little crestfallen because I guessed it, but it does little to dull her enthusiasm.

"And he *remembered*," she adds.

"So he did," I reply, at a loss as to what else to say. It shouldn't be any big deal that the guy overheard something and was able to retain it overnight, right? I mean, why is Mona so excited?

As for me, I'm immediately suspicious. Why is Rogan being so nice to me? Why is he working so hard to hide "total jerk" from me? Because I know it's in there. It *has to be*, right? He *is* that guy, isn't he?

And what could he possibly gain by deceiving me? It's not like I'm some great prize or anything.

Rogan's gravelly drawl breaks into my introspection. "Impressed yet?"

My befuddlement overshadows his flirtatious question and I blurt what's on my mind, which I never do. "Why are you being so nice to me?"

Rogan doesn't answer right away. We just stare at each other as his smile dies, replaced by a puzzled expression of his own. "Honestly, I don't know. There's just something about you that . . . I don't know. Makes me want to see you smile, I guess."

Ruthlessly, I ignore the flutter in my stomach and push past it with rationale. Letting feelings get the better of me will only end in disaster.

"But why? Why me?"

Rogan's emerald eyes hold mine firmly, his brow now creased with a frown of his own. "I've been asking myself that since yesterday," he admits quietly.

"Well, at least you're honest," I mutter on a sigh, not intending to say the words aloud.

"I'm always honest."

Although his words are sincere, there's no reason for me to believe them. But, strangely, I do. I know I shouldn't, but I do.

For a moment, it seems Rogan and I are alone in the room,

immersed in a strange moment of truth and self-awareness. He nods to me, I nod to him and somewhere, deep down, I feel a small part of my inner hardness soften ever so slightly.

Coming to work the next day feels different. Nothing out of the ordinary has happened. In fact, my morning has gone like every other morning before it, almost down to the greeting I get from Ronnie, one of the set designers, as he enters the building a few seconds behind me.

"Looking sweet this morning, Katie," he calls out to me. I turn toward the familiar voice and the familiar redheaded thirtysomething guy, waving and smiling my reply, just like always.

But today *feels* different. I don't know why, but I suspect that it has something to do with my first client and the way my stomach is curled with anticipation. I *do* worry about that, but worrying doesn't seem to change it. Neither do all the reiterations of how bad a guy like Rogan could be for me. Nothing seems to be able to penetrate the dangerous spell he's so effortlessly weaving over me. I'm fighting it, but still I find myself looking forward to seeing him. And that's not a good place to be. Not for me, anyway.

Today, I'm not surprised when Mona doesn't greet me as she usually does. I have a feeling I know exactly where to find her.

Just before I turn the corner to walk into my "office," I smooth my hair into its neat wave that flows over my left shoulder, concealing the side of my neck. I straighten my shirt and pull a cat hair from my sleeve, and my hand stops dead as I let it drift from my fingertips into the subtle air current passing by.

I'm primping. Preening. And that's not like me either. I mean, I try to look nice and decent every day, but today . . . today I want to be attractive again. I didn't really realize it until *just now*. And that worries me.

It's that worry that I carry through the doorway and into my office. I'm wearing it like a shield, but still, it's unable to stop the arrow of attraction that strikes me when I see Rogan sitting in my makeup chair, chatting amicably with my friend.

How can he do this to me? And how can I let him?

Or do I even have a choice?

Before I can offer a greeting, Mona chirps from beside Rogan, "Good morning! Look who has your coffee. Again."

She's glowing. Again. I think she's getting a bigger kick out of this than I am. Of course, I'm making a concerted effort *not to*. It's not bad for Mona's health to enjoy Rogan, but I can't say the same for me.

"Impressed yet?" Rogan asks, standing and walking toward me to hand over the tall white cup. His wink says that he's teasing me. His grin says that he's pleased with himself. He's like a proud little boy, sporting his first blue ribbon.

I stare up at him, so handsome in his charm, and I wish I could look away. But I can't. "Impressed? You mean that you don't suffer from short-term memory loss after being punched in the head too many times?" I say, garnering my defenses, defenses that I worry are crumbling even as I speak.

"Hey, in my line of work, that's a distinct possibility."

I smile politely up at him, determined not to let him see that he affects me. "Well, it takes more than a cup of coffee to impress me."

He isn't the least bit put off. "Even *perfect* coffee?"

"Too easy."

"Too easy?" he asks in mock offense. I arch one brow at him and he gives in. "Maybe you're right, but I'm giving you fair warning," he declares, his voice dropping to a low, seductive timbre.

"Fair warning?" I ask.

He nods, all playfulness gone now. "Fair warning. I've got six weeks to impress you. And impress you I shall, Beautiful Katie."

As I look into those captivating eyes, I remember his words. *Makes me want to see you smile, I guess.* I can't help asking my one burning question again, only softly this time. "Why me?"

He doesn't hesitate with his answer. "Something tells me you're worth the effort."

Air stops moving in and out of my concrete lungs, and all I can do is gaze up into Rogan's incredibly handsome face as he reaches out to brush the pad of his thumb over my cheekbone. Through the fog of his considerable charisma, though, alarm bells start to ring inside my head.

"You're wasting your time," I manage to breathe out, trying desperately to hold on to my indifference.

"For the first time in a lot of years, I feel like I'm not."

We stand like that—nose to nose, the backs of Rogan's fingers against my cheek—staring at each other for who knows how long before I see a familiar smiling face peek over his shoulder. Only Mona, Amazon that she is, with the added help of her stilettos, could accomplish such a feat.

Her appearance and my subsequent blush break the spell. I glance back to Rogan, who is still watching me, paying Mona no attention whatsoever. "I guess I'd better drink some of this coffee before my client gets here. He's always late. Unruly. Mean as anything. Just an *impossible* bear of a guy," I tease lightly, anything to diffuse the tension that's suddenly vibrating between us.

"Maybe I could give you a few tips on how to turn him into a pussy cat."

"Oh, I don't think he has any problems with pussy," Mona murmurs snidely from behind Rogan.

My mouth drops open and it takes all my effort not to laugh, but when Rogan's emerald eyes crinkle at the corners and his smile returns, full blast, I can't seem to help myself.

"Mona!" I chastise around my chuckle and burning cheeks.

"What?" she asks. Her face is the picture of innocence as she rounds Rogan and stands beside us. "It's the truth."

Rogan clears his throat. "On that note, I think I'll go have a seat and wait for my makeup artist. This conversation isn't gonna do me any favors."

As he walks back to the chair in front of the mirrors, Mona and I have an entire conversation in absolute silence.

I widen my eyes at her. *Mona!* She raises her brows at me. *What?* I shake my head once. *Don't do that!* She gives me a little nod and a roll of her eyes. *Fine.* I take a deep breath. *Calm, calm, calm.* She reaches out and squeezes my hand. *You've got this.*

"Well, I guess I need to take myself upstairs and let you get to work. White won't know how to act when I walk in this early. I usually bring my best friend some coffee, but since someone else has taken over my duties . . ."

She grins again and I peek around her to the broad-shouldered god sitting in my makeup chair. He doesn't appear to be paying us any attention, but I know better than to assume that's the case. He's obviously much more observant than what I've given him credit for.

"Lunch?" I ask before Mona leaves.

"Lunch," she replies, giving my hand a final squeeze before she dances out of the room, calling over her shoulder, "See ya later, Rogue."

I grin when Rogan's head whips around toward the door. "Did she just call me 'Rogue'?"

"She did. She must've decided she likes you. She only gives nicknames to people she likes."

I take a sip of my coffee, letting it warm what little bit of my insides aren't already toasty, as I make my way to my station.

"And what do *you* do once you decide you like somebody?"

I turn to look at Rogan over my shoulder. He raises guilty eyes to mine, eyes that I caught staring at my butt. My prim reply dies on my lips and another bubbles up in response, a response that's reminiscent of the old me. Because, for some reason, for just a heartbeat, I feel like my old self again. The self who had confidence and hope for a bright future. The self who was able to hold her own with guys no matter what they looked like. The self who was worth so much more than what I've become.

"Wouldn't you like to know?" I taunt pluckily, letting a touch of a grin play with the corners of my mouth. It's both liberating and terrifying to get a glimpse of Kat, the old me, rising through the ash that people know as Katie.

"Hell yeah, I would," Rogan returns with unadulterated enthusiasm.

I turn away with my grin, but just as soon as my attention is back on my wide array of cosmetics, Kat disappears, leaving only Katie behind.

I feel the pinch of sadness grip my heart. My smile suffers a slow death when I realize that little glimpses are all I'll ever get of the old me. Kat is dead. She died in a fire a long time ago and she's never coming back.

TEN

Rogan

This woman . . . Holy shit!

What *was that*? I don't know how the hell I got lucky enough to see her drop her carefully maintained exterior for a few seconds, but I'm damn sure glad that I did! Seeing her come out of her shell for that one comment, for that one quick flash of flirtatious fun was so unexpected it was like hearing a wildcat roar come from a fluffy little kitten.

Katie . . . Jesus, she's fascinating! Even though I've only spent what amounts to probably a couple of hours with her, I'm dying to know everything there is to know about her, about why she hides such a wild and sexy woman behind that shy smile and those haunted eyes.

On the outside, she's like many of the other women I've dated—beautiful face, great body—only she doesn't have to *try* like they do. Not at all. She just *is* beautiful. But on the inside, I can already tell that she's more. She's obviously not superficial or stupid or easy, all of which are so common in this business. I'm getting all the *opposite* vibes from her. Just interacting with her the little that I have makes me think that I've never met anyone like her. I kinda like that she's a little shy and a little hot. It's a great mixture. It implies depth, and depth has been in short supply in my life. But now that I see it, that I *sense it*, I want it. I want it all. It's like seeing the ocean after only playing in puddles, or tasting rich cream after only ever having candy.

"What's your favorite kind of candy?" I ask out of the blue just as Katie starts to swirl a brush over my cheekbone. Her hand stills and her deep blue eyes fly to mine.

"Pardon?"

"Candy. What's your favorite kind?"

"Why?"

"I was just thinking about it and wondered."

"You were just thinking about candy?" she questions dubiously.

"Yep," I reply with a grin. She shakes her head and resumes her swirling. When she doesn't answer, I prompt, "Well?"

"Snickers," she admits after a long pause. "My favorite candy is Snickers."

"Snickers satisfies," I mutter, loving how blood pours into her cheeks, turning the porcelain of her skin to a pale pink. "But it's not candy."

She slides her gaze to mine again, her finely arched brows tucking together. "Of course it is."

"No, it's chocolate."

"Chocolate is candy."

"Chocolate is *not* candy."

"Then why is chocolate in the candy aisle at the store?"

"Because the world is deluded. I'm sorry to have to be the one to tell you that, but it's true."

She drops her hand and tips her head to the side, giving me a withering look that makes her even more adorable. I've never wanted to kiss someone so much in my whole damn life. "*You* are right and the rest of the *whole world* is wrong?"

"Precisely. You're one smart cookie, Beautiful Katie," I declare, adding, "Also not a candy, by the way."

Her lips twitch, but she refuses to smile. I have no idea why. Five minutes ago, she was playful, and now she's . . . guarded. Maybe that's what makes her so intriguing to me—the inconsistencies, the contrasts. They fill me with the desire to see how deep the ocean really goes, to taste how rich the cream actually is. I want to know what makes this woman tick and then I want to touch every cog, stroke every wheel. I want to be inside her head when I'm inside her body.

Christ Almighty! I really am *starting to sound like a woman!*

"Were you disappointed a lot as a child?" she asks.

"More than you know," I reply too honestly, immediately regretting it when her eyes get all puzzled. I recover quickly, though. Something else I've learned over the course of a life spent blocking fists. "But never about candy. I was an authority then and I'm an authority now."

"Is that right?" Her expression is comically doubtful. "Well do tell, Mr. Authority. What, in your infinite wisdom, qualifies as candy?"

"Anything that has an ingredient list consisting mainly of sugar and has an assortment of additives that I can't pronounce that are numbered or include the word 'lake.'"

"So anything that contains words you can't pronounce is considered candy?"

"Precisely," I repeat.

Her eyes go all wide and innocent, belying the sarcasm to come. "Wow! The dictionary must be the mother lode of candy."

Katie's expression doesn't change, her face straight and serious, which makes me want to kiss her again. Kiss her until all I see is a reflection of my desire for her. If she ever lets me get that far, I'll close the door and keep kissing her until I'm all she can see or think about or feel. All over. Inside and out.

"See? You learned something new today. Impressed yet?"

"You're certainly making *an* impression," she says dryly, still not giving in to her urge to smile.

"Since you are otherwise engaged today, how about lunch tomorrow? I feel like if I'm gonna impress you, I'm going to need more than a few minutes in the mornings."

"As . . . interesting as that sounds, I think I'll pass, but thank you."

"You leave me no choice then," I tell her vaguely.

"No choice but to what?"

I pause for effect and then let it drag on for a little longer, just to crank up her curiosity. "Wouldn't you like to know?" I ask, throwing her own words back at her.

I laugh when she narrows her eyes threateningly. I'm going to do much more than kiss her before this is over.

ELEVEN

Katie

On the fourth morning, I don't even expect to see Mona until I reach my office. I think she's as taken with Rogan as everyone else seems to be. I'm trying desperately not to fall into that trap, but it's getting a little harder each day. Especially when I walk in to find him sitting in my makeup chair, early as always, patiently holding a cup of coffee that I know will be mine.

I try to enter quietly so as not to interrupt whatever Rogan is telling Mona that has her complete, undivided attention. She looks mesmerized, like the cobra in front of the snake charmer. As I look at her, leaning sexily against the counter all tall and blond and beautiful in front of one of Hollywood's newest obsessions, I wonder why Rogan isn't bringing *her* coffee and torturing *her* with his knee-buckling grin.

I don't know the answer to that, I only know that when he turns to find me standing in the doorway and his eyes light up, I'm kinda glad that he's not. Not that I ever *wanted* to feel this way again—giddy, flushed, excited over a guy—but if I'm honest, I have to admit that I missed feeling this . . . *alive*.

There's a few seconds of silence, during which his sparkling green eyes just roam over me from head to toe. Then he stands to his full tall, lean height and carries my coffee and something else across the room to me. He holds me captive in his gaze, a hold that's getting harder and harder to break the more he does it. In my peripheral vision, I see Mona's blinding smile before she slips out the door, virtually unnoticed.

"Good morning, Beautiful Katie." He says this so softly that I *feel* the words as much as I hear them. They're like a warm breeze on my skin, a tender kiss on my lips. A velvety touch to my soul.

"Why do you call me that?" I ask, struggling to hang on to my resistance. Even to my ears, though, my question sounds weak. It wasn't supposed to be. It was supposed to be defiant, maybe a little aggravated. Instead, it sounds like a futile effort. And it might very well be. At this point, I can be sure of nothing.

"Because that's your name. And because it's true."

"I wish you wouldn't call me that." Some tiny voice inside me argues, *No! Never, ever* stop *calling me that!*

"Well, it's that or darlin'. You pick."

Hearing him call me darlin' in his rough-yet-soft Texas twang is enough to twist my stomach into a knot. I'm not sure which is worse.

I clear my throat and try to maintain my composure in the face of his assault. Because that's what it is. It's a full-on assault of my senses, of my better judgment, of the person that I've constructed to keep everyone away from the real me.

"Maybe you should let me pick something else."

"Nope. Those are your only choices."

I sigh. "Well, since both are inappropriate, I'll leave it up to you, then. I get the feeling it won't do me any good to argue with you anyway."

Half of his mouth quirks up into a grin. "You're a quick study. And now that we got that out of the way, I've got something for you."

"Let me guess. Coffee," I say with a wry grin, my insides secretly bubbling over his continued interest in me, in this game. I genuinely figured he'd tire of it within hours, especially after spending his days on set with all the beautiful people.

"You're half right," he admits, handing me my cup of coffee, no doubt exactly the way I like it. I take a sip and watch him over the rim of the pseudo-Styrofoam. "I brought you *fake* candy," he says, reaching into a box that I hadn't even seen to produce a cute bouquet of miniature Snickers made to look like a spray of flowers in a short, red vase.

"But I also brought you *real* candy," he continues, pulling a package of Skittles from inside the box, "and finally, smart-ass candy."

I have to laugh when he removes the last item from the box. It's a pocket-sized *Webster's Dictionary.*

"What an . . . interesting assortment of gifts," I say, my lips still curved. How is it possible that he's made candy and a dictionary feel like diamonds and roses?

Because you're stupid, my inner bitter girl snaps.

No, it's the thought that he put into these things that makes them special. It's no wonder women can't resist him.

"They're actually dessert. For after you have lunch with me today."

I glance back up at him, feeling my resolve weaken like the rest of me. But I can't let it go. I can't give up on it yet. The risk is too great.

"I really appreciate the offer. All of this," I say, indicating my armful of goodies, "but I'm just . . . You're not . . . I just don't think it's a good idea."

For the first time, I see his unflappable good humor flag. "What's it gonna take to win you over?" he asks. His tone is a vague mixture of irritation and exasperation.

"I'm not sure it can be done."

I hate the sadness in my voice. Somewhere deep down, there's still a girl in me who *wants* to love, who *wants* to trust, but she's afraid. She's afraid to risk it. But she's also afraid that no one will ever try hard enough to dig her out, to unearth her from the rubble and debris that have kept her buried for so long. Because if no one does, she'll die alone. Old and alone.

I thought I'd heard the last of that girl—her voice had gone so quiet—but Rogan has shown me that she's still very much alive. And that men like him are still a danger to her.

Rogan tips his head to one side to study me. I resist the urge to tug my hair over my shoulder more securely, terrified that he'll see too much, that he'll ask too much.

"I've never lost a fight," he says after so long that I almost startle when he speaks. "And I don't intend to start now."

With those words left hanging in the air between us, Rogan shakes off his seriousness, gives me that irresistible wink-and-grin combo, then turns to lope back to his chair.

When he's seated, he kicks his ankle up onto his knee and starts to whistle. That's when I realize that I might've found the one person who can outlast me.

I've never really loved *or* hated work. It's just . . . work. I liked it less when I had to prepare Victoria Musser and a couple of her really nasty co-stars my first year here, but even then, I didn't really hate it. Hate—or love for that matter—implies some active emotion, which requires being fully involved in one's life. I don't feel that I've been fully involved in my life since the accident. Maybe it's a side effect of having everything you've ever known, wanted and loved taken from you in a single night. Maybe it's depression when left untreated. Or maybe it's just a symptom of being . . . me. Weird, abnormal, slightly less-than-average *me*. Whatever the reason, I haven't experienced many strong emotions—positive *or* negative—in roughly five years.

Until today.

It's been almost three weeks since that first morning when I stumbled upon Kiefer Rogan sitting, big as life, in my makeup chair. I didn't have a clue at the time what a force to be reckoned with he could be.

But I do now.

Each day that I've seen him, he's battered away at whatever kind of emotional stone castle I've ensconced myself within. Now I feel weaknesses all around me. Part of me is alarmed by that, but it's been such a pleasant battering, I've barely noticed him doing it. All of a sudden, I'm just . . . different. Different than I was yesterday, even more different than I was the day before, and *even more* different than I was a week ago. I doubt anyone other than me notices, but I can feel it. And I know who's to blame.

Each morning, Rogan has presented me with some kooky gift that relates to whatever little tidbit he managed to glean about me the day before—a package of Fireballs (when he found out I love cinnamon), a stuffed teddy bear (when he found out that was my favorite childhood toy), a polka-dot umbrella (when he found out it was the one thing I asked for on my sixteenth birthday and never got). And those are just a few things. I have no idea how he comes across half this stuff in a town like Enchantment, but he does. Maybe he orders it, I don't know. But try as I might, it's getting harder and harder not to love his thoughtful determination.

I'm not sure what to expect from today. Yesterday, he asked me a wide range of questions, so it's hard to say what he might've focused on. I'm already smiling in anticipation, though. He always seems to surprise me. And very pleasantly so.

"There she is!" Mona exclaims boisterously when I walk through the door. "Looking mighty . . ." She pauses to flip to a random page of the pocket dictionary that now occupies a spot on my counter-top, courtesy of Rogan. Mona's new morning routine is to pick a word from its pages and use it as often as possible throughout the day. "Magnanimous." Her smile is proud and delighted.

I grin. "And just how does one *look* magnanimous?"

"Well," she begins, glancing back into the dictionary for the meaning of the word. She slaps it shut, straightens her snug button-up blouse and pulls at the very short hem of her black satin shorts. "It's your hair. It makes you look very . . . generous."

"My *hair* makes me look *generous*?"

"Yep. I've always told you that you have great hair. That's why. It makes you look magnanimous." She nods as if to say that explains it all.

I hear Rogan snort from behind her, drawing my attention to him. As usual, once my gaze is there, I can't pull it away until he chooses to let me. His eyes have a kind of magnetism, like a lush forest of higher gravity that draws me inexplicably toward it and then it refuses to let me go.

"I could say many things about her hair, about the way it shines like a dark penny in the light, or the way it frames her breathtaking face, but I have to say that it has *never once* brought to mind the word 'magnanimous,'" Rogan teases, his gaze still trained on me even though he's addressing Mona.

"Of course *you'd* say that. You're infatuated with her. I can view her more *objectively*," she says, winking at me as she uses yet another of her pocket dictionary treasures.

"*That* I am," Rogan confesses quietly, one corner of his sculpted mouth dipping in to reveal the dimple in his cheek that I haven't seen since that first day. It's enchanting, just like the rest of him. And he didn't need any more help.

Mona pats his shoulder. "Hang in there. You've got Mona on your side. You'll crack that nut before too long."

Her comment makes me wonder what all they discuss before my arrival each morning. Up to now, Rogan seems to be uncovering enough of me *without* her help. God help me if she gets involved.

I make a mental note to give Mona a good talking-to about Rogan and how he doesn't need her help to get under my skin. Damn the man, he seems to be doing just fine on his own.

"Well, I gotta go. White's got me making arrangements for some sort of . . . *thing* involving his boat and an island at the lake." With a deep sigh and a roll of her eyes, Mona breezes past me, brushing my cheek with her lips and swatting me on the butt as she goes. "See ya, Rogue."

"Lunch?" I ask before she disappears.

Mona turns, her eyes flickering to Rogan for a second before returning to mine. "Lunch."

When I turn around, Rogan has gotten up and moved in right behind me. His face is straight and serious, which is unusual for him.

"I won't bother with asking you to lunch today," he says, bringing a stab of disappointment to my gut. It's been a bit of a game between us—he asks me to lunch every day and every day I turn him down. I guess he's officially reached his limit. He gave up the fight. Even though he said he wouldn't.

"I brought you this," he says, handing me my coffee and today's special gift. "All I ask is that you take it with you wherever you go until you go to sleep tonight."

I take the delicate wineglass from his fingers, marveling at the exquisite cut of the crystal around its stem and the etching that bleeds from there up into the goblet. Although it's just an empty glass, my heart stutters. It seems like . . . more. Like a promise.

He asked me yesterday what my favorite kind of wine was. I told him I liked sweet reds. Maybe this means nothing. Or maybe it means he plans to show up at some point and pour something into it. It's hard to say knowing Rogan, but it still fills me with anticipation to think that he *might* have plans to show up in my life later. I should be stern. I should tell him right now that if that's his plan, he need not bother. But I can't. I can't because, with every day that passes, I *want* him to bother. I want him to show up somewhere else in my life. I want more of Rogan. As unhealthy and inadvisable as it is, I want more.

"Will you do that for me?"

His voice is low again, serious. I look up into his eyes and see more of the same. I wonder if he really is tiring of our little game. It would be a shame if he was.

A pang of loss shoots through me at the mere suggestion that I might not get to enjoy this every day. That I might not get to enjoy *him*.

"Yes, I'll do that for you." I can't even consider *not* doing it.

His smile is slow and more subtle than usual. He stands, towering over me, looking down at me, for longer than usual today, too. His eyes flicker over my face, stopping on my mouth. My lungs seize and I wonder if he's going to kiss me. Much to my surprise, I want him to. I *really* want him to. As stupid as it is, I want to feel his lips on mine, feel the warmth of his chest against mine, feel the strength of his arms around me.

"Don't do that," Rogan whispers hoarsely.

My eyes fly to his, puzzled. "Don't do what?"

"Don't stand there and think about me kissing you. It's hard enough as it is."

My mouth drops open a little. "I . . . I, uh . . . I wasn't . . ." I feel my face burn. How the hell did he know?

He smiles. A full smile that makes his eyes shimmer and my knees weak. "You're a terrible liar."

My insides feel twitchy, like I'm fighting the urge to laugh. "Better than a great one."

Rogan reaches up and brushes the back of one finger over my bottom lip. A bolt of electricity rockets straight through me, lighting up every nerve along the way. "That it is."

We stand like this for seconds. Minutes. Hours, it seems. And then, without another word, he turns to resume his seat in my makeup chair, leaving me alone in a bubble of my own mixed emotions.

TWELVE

Rogan

I've managed to avoid Victoria almost entirely for nearly a month. I knew my luck had come to an end when I saw her come through the door at the diner today. I was right. Damn it. She made a beeline for me, so now here I am, making nice with my ex, playing stupid as she throws every hint in the book about us getting back together.

I think I've done an admirable job of paying her just enough attention not to be rude. That lasts right up until Katie and Mona walk in. Even though this is pretty much the only place to eat in town (other than the deli at the grocery store and the pseudo-meat gas-station fare across the street), this is the first time I've run into Katie here. It didn't take me long to realize that she eats at different times, probably based on what kind of need there is to do retouches or specialty makeup.

My gut twists when I look at her. *God*, she's . . . Hell, I don't even know. Yeah, she's beautiful in a clean and wholesome way, and yeah she's sexy as hell on Sunday, but there's just something about her that gets to me. Maybe it's the shy way she keeps her chin down when she walks in, like if she doesn't look up no one will notice her. Or maybe it's the small smile that plays with her lips, like she wears this polite mask all the time. Or maybe it's the glimpses I've been getting at what she's *really* like, when the walls are down and she's not quite so guarded. Damned if I know, but this girl is under my skin. In a big way.

I sneak glances at her as she and her friend are seated. I watch her laugh, albeit quietly, and I watch her lips move as she orders. She hasn't seen me. She makes a point not to look around. God forbid someone notice her.

When her food comes, I find it even harder to pretend that I'm listening to Victoria. I'm not surprised when Katie orders *real* food in the form of a burger, fries and a milk shake. For some reason it fits. And watching her eat . . . Jesus H. Christ! She takes voracious bites, bites that make me want to strip her down, stretch her out up on the table, and enjoy eating her the way she's ravenously enjoying her meal. Right in front of everyone. I wouldn't care who was watching. She captivates me *that much*, dominates my thoughts to *that degree*.

And, evidently, it shows.

"What's so interesting?" Victoria asks, a little ice in her tone.

"Huh?"

"You're staring. What's so interesting that you can't even listen to what I'm saying?"

I resist the urge to roll my eyes. "Oh, nothing. I was just thinking about, uh, something I saw on television last night."

Lie. Big, fat lie, but I'm *not* getting into this with Victoria of all people. Katie doesn't deserve that kind of negative attention.

Her expression says she believes me Not. One. Bit.

But considering the level of her vanity, my distraction does absolutely nothing to dissuade her from continuing her one-sided conversation.

I try to pull myself back to the table a few times, but mostly I continue to watch the little witch across the room. I figure I'm about thirty percent successful until the waitress delivers a piece of pie to Katie's table. That's when I lose the battle.

Her eyes get wide and a real smile spreads across her face as the waitress sets it in front of her. She grabs her fork without even taking her eyes off the cream-covered triangle.

And then she digs in.

I can't take my eyes off her when she brings a heap of pale green custard to her mouth. She slides it onto her tongue and then closes her lips around the fork, pulling it slowly from between them. She doesn't chew for a few seconds; she just lets the pie sit in her mouth. Her eyes close in ecstasy and I can all but *hear* her moan of delight.

Blood rushes to my cock as that imaginary moan accompanies my previous thought of her lying naked beneath me.

Holy hell!

I've never thought food, or watching someone eat it for that matter, to be a particularly erotic activity, but I stand corrected.

I'm watching, waiting for Katie to take another bite, when I'm brought back to my own table by a loud, waspish, "Rogan!"

Irritated at the interruption, I bark at Victoria, "What?"

I manage to pull my eyes away from Katie long enough to focus on my ex's furious expression. "What the hell are you so interested in over there?" She turns in her seat and scans the diner before swiveling back to me. "What? Did you spot Elvis or something? I don't see what you find so fascinating."

Even though she had to have seen her, Victoria obviously doesn't find Katie a noteworthy sight and can't imagine that *I'd* find her noteworthy either. I guess Katie has become so adept at being a wall-

flower that she has others overlooking her, too. I don't see how. I don't
see how anyone can overlook her wavy auburn hair, her flawless skin,
her perfectly round tits, tucked away under a shirt that screams
TOUCH ME NOT and makes me want to touch so, so much.

Shiiit!

The strain of my hard-on against my zipper is a better wake-up
call than ten pissed-off Victorias. I'm in a public place, for God's
sake. With my vicious ex. Not *at all* the time to let lurid thoughts
of a hot-and-shy little makeup artist get to me. I can wait until
tonight. Maybe then I'll be able to taste what's been keeping me
awake at night.

Shaking my head, I clear my throat and nod toward Victoria's
half-eaten salad. "You done?"

I suppress my sneer. I'd much rather Victoria eat like an *actual*
person than like a starving bird. I'd much rather she eat like Katie.
But she's no Katie. Not by a long shot.

"Yes," Victoria replies in one petulant syllable.

I throw some bills onto the table. "Good. Let's get out of here."

I follow Victoria to the door, sparing one last glance in Katie's
direction. When I find her, her mouth is open and her fork is raised,
but she's not sliding the bite of pie onto her tongue. She's stopped
dead, mid-bite. Frozen. When I see her eyes, I don't have to ask why
she stopped. The wide, hurt orbs are burning right through me.

THIRTEEN

Katie

All afternoon I thought if I could just get home I'd feel better. I thought once I got away from work, away from where it seems I'm surrounded by thoughts and memories of Rogan, that I'd find a little peace. But I was wrong. Now that I'm here, I'm too restless to sit still.

So is that why he didn't invite me to lunch today? He gave up and decided to go back to more . . . fruitful orchards? Because I feel *sure* Victoria is as fruitful as they come.

What an asshole!

I pace the living room floor, Dozer's head moving back and forth with me, like he's watching a ping-pong tournament. "I knew better, Dozer. I knew better than to believe that he might actually like me. What was I thinking?"

He lets out a short purr at his name, his big yellow eyes riveted to mine.

"You wanna get out of here? How 'bout a walk? We haven't

been to the park in three days. That's a travesty!" Normally, I walk Dozer every evening if it's not raining.

Dozer jumps down off the arm of the couch and trots over to me, as though in answer to my question. It seems he's in favor of a trip to the park. No doubt he's missed it, too.

I get his leash and my purse and head for the door, hoping that maybe the distraction of a public place will help my poor brain find some rest.

I scoop up Dozer and turn to lock the knob. My eyes fall on the empty wineglass sitting on the table just inside the door. With a rebellious sniff, I slam the door shut, leaving it right where I left it when I got home. Rogan can kiss our little game and any promises I might've made him good-bye. He doesn't need the attentions of a simple girl like *me* when he's still getting *more than enough* from Victoria.

I both seethe and ache just thinking about seeing him at the diner with her. And then I feel just stupid. Stupid for believing that he could be interested in me. Stupid for letting him charm me out of my good sense. And to think that I was actually starting to feel *excited* about him, about going to work and getting to spend some time with him each morning.

What an idiot! I chastise, wishing that I hadn't let down my guard with him at all. I guess I just didn't give him enough credit. He's a more talented actor than I suspected. He almost had me convinced.

Ten minutes later, Dozer is hooked up to his leash, darting happily from bush to tree, eyes wide and ears alert for any dogs in the vicinity. I pay little attention to the odd looks that get thrown my way when people see me walking my *cat* on a leash. I'm used to them. I realize it's far from conventional to walk a cat in a dog park (or anywhere else for that matter), but I'd seen it done before, so I thought I'd try it. Turns out it's the perfect fix for a cat like Dozer, one who grew up indoors, but likes the outdoors.

Despite the much-needed break of the dog park, though, I can't seem to shake the grip of this . . . *funk* that's had a hold on me all afternoon. I'm trailing along behind my cat, my mind wandering everywhere but here, when a small terrier of some sort zooms past me. Dozer jumps up and whirls around, ears flat, teeth bared, hissing and ready to defend himself. I gasp, but just before the little dog can get a chunk of his nose clawed, he reaches the end of his leash. He comes to an unwilling stop with a strangled yelp. Heavy footsteps race up behind me, and I wonder briefly what kind of owner can't control a forty-pound terrier.

Then I hear a disturbingly familiar voice. It brings chills to the nape of my neck before I can remind myself that I'm *not* affected, that I'm done with him.

I maneuver myself in front of the now-stopped dog to sweep Dozer up into my arms, my hackles as prickly as his, and I spin to face Rogan.

"Whoa, darlin'!" he cautions amicably.

"Don't you 'darlin'' me. You need to keep your dog under control."

Rogan's lopsided grin appears. He's unflappable, as always.

"I was talkin' to the dog," he says with a wink.

With a small frown, I glance down at the terrier. It's standing on its hind legs, trying to get to my cat, proudly displaying its furry dog parts. It's furry *boy* dog parts.

"You call your *male* dog 'darlin'?"

There's venom in my voice and I hate it. Its presence just reaffirms what I already knew—I let Rogan upset me. I care when I *shouldn't*. It shouldn't matter with whom he spends his time. Yet it does. It matters so, so much.

Rogan, too, glances down at the hyper canine. His smile widens when his eyes return to my face. "Well, would you look at that!"

Oh my God! He doesn't even bother to know the sex of his dog? What a complete and total jerk! Just like I thought.

Before I can throw buckets of disdain his way and then excuse myself, leaving Rogan with no uncertainty about my feelings toward him, I catch him looking me over, even leaning to look around behind me. "What are you doing?" I snap.

"Looking for your wineglass. Did you bring it? Or are you the kind of girl who doesn't bother to keep her promises?"

"To someone like *you*? I won't lose any sleep over it." My tone is frigid.

Finally, Rogan starts to catch on that I'm not playing, and his smile begins to fade. His eyes narrow the slightest bit. "Is something wrong?"

I'm further infuriated that he has the audacity to stand here and pretend that everything is fine, like it shouldn't bother me one bit that he's flirting with me and still seeing Victoria.

"Of course not. I'm just a little surprised that you're here alone." It's my turn to lean around him, looking for something. Or some*one*. "Or did you leave Victoria in the car with the window cracked?"

Damn me and my sharp tongue! Damn Rogan for loosening me up and then going for the kill! Damn Calm Katie for abandoning me when I need her most!

After a few long, tense seconds during which I manage to make myself so angry that I'm huffing, Rogan's smile reappears, bigger than ever.

"Do you see a gun to my head?" he asks, confusing me.

"What?"

"Do you see a gun to my head?" Rogan makes a show of turning to look behind him. "Because that's the *only way in hell* I'm spending time with her away from work."

"I didn't see anyone brandishing a firearm at the diner today," I rebut.

"I was already eating when she came in and made herself comfortable. I figured the last thing I needed to do was make a scene at the only place I can get some decent food in this town. What if the cook is like the Soup Nazi and refuses to serve me if I make Victoria cry?" he asks dramatically.

The mere image of the Soup Nazi sternly turning Rogan away from the diner—No food for you!—is enough to make the corners of my mouth twitch. That and the incredible relief I feel that he didn't go to lunch with her willingly. On purpose. Like a date.

"Victoria cries?" is all I can think of in response.

Rogan snorts. "Only over bad head shots."

Before I can stop myself, I'm smiling a little. Rogan has spent almost a month convincing me that he's so much more, so much *better* than what I gave him credit for in the beginning and, even though I shouldn't care what he's like, the soft parts of my heart are elated that it seems I might still have been wrong about him. This is one instance in which I'd *love* to be mistaken.

"So . . . a cat," he says, visibly holding back a laugh as he eyes Dozer in his little cat harness, cuddled up in my arms.

The hard edge is gone from my voice when I ask, "So . . . a terrier." I have to admit that I wouldn't have pictured Rogan as the small-dog type of guy. A Rottweiler, sure. A Doberman, absolutely. But a terrier? Not so much.

"Nah. I gave fifty bucks to some lady sitting on a bench at the park entrance to let me borrow her dog for half an hour." Rogan's mischievous wink makes my stomach flutter.

"And she let you?"

He shrugs and grins. "I think she might've recognized me. Otherwise, she'd probably have told me to go to hell. I was willing to risk it, though. And to overlook the fact that I think she's discreetly following me through the park. Maybe she's thinking, 'That damn Kiefer Rogan has a sick dog fetish!'"

His laugh is an easy, sexy rumble that slips and slides along my skin. Yet still, all I can think is that he did this to see me. All this. For me.

"How did you know this is where I'd be?" I ask, assuming Mona is the guilty party.

"What makes you think I came here to see you? This is my thing—going around to parks and renting strange dogs for a few hours. I find it very relaxing," he explains. His face is so sincere, his words so matter-of-fact that I assume he's serious.

"Really?" I ask, not meaning to wrinkle my nose in disdain.

"No, not really," he confesses, rubbing his index finger down my curled-up nose. "I most definitely came here to see you."

My heart patters excitedly in my chest and I press my face into Dozer's fur to escape the appreciative look in Rogan's eye.

"Buuut, since you didn't bring your glass, you've ruined my whole plan. Fido here is very disappointed."

I glance down at the dog again. He's sitting in the grass, tail wagging furiously, ears perked, staring at Dozer. "Sorry, Fido," I whisper. "How can I make it up to you?"

The dog's tail wags even harder.

"Now you're on the right track," Rogan exclaims with a suggestive half-grin. "I think if you invite us over to your house for a glass of wine, he might find it in his heart to forgive you."

"Oh, is that what it'll take?"

"Jump if you want Katie to take me home with her, Fido," Rogan says, snapping his fingers. Fido's ears twitch and he leaps straight up into the air.

"Wow! You're great with rented dogs."

"Thank you, but the real question is: How am I with beautiful makeup artists who walk their cats in the park?"

I look up into twinkling eyes, now the color of moss, and I answer honestly before I can think twice. "Better than most, dog whisperer. Better than most."

I carry a still-shaken Dozer back to the park entrance, where Rogan drops off his rented dog. I can see the bedazzled look on Fido's owner's face when Rogan smiles his thanks. I know just how she feels. That smile is a showstopper for sure!

"So," he says, putting his hand on the small of my back as we resume our walk to the parking lot, "which one is you?"

"Right there, but I don't have any wine at my house," I admit as I point to my blue convertible.

"What?" he exclaims, his expression stricken. "It's a good thing I got here when I did. This could've ended badly. Luckily, I have just the thing. A sweet, aromatic red that will make your wineglass very happy."

I stop before I step off the curb, sliding my eyes up to Rogan's. He's so close I can see the flecks of silver around his pupils, spraying out into the deep green of his irises like spilled mercury. The sparkling orbs drop to my lips and stay there for several seconds, forcing me to lick their dry surface. Almost without meaning to, he mirrors my action, the tip of his tongue trailing just along his bottom lip.

"I'll follow you," he rumbles quietly. I nod, tucking my chin as I start off across the lot. "And yes, I'll be watching your ass as you walk away."

I neither turn nor comment, but my butt feels suddenly warm and I smile all the way to my car.

FOURTEEN

Rogan

I'm not the least bit surprised by the little house that Katie pulls up in front of. It suits her perfectly. It's cute and pretty in a quiet, understated way. It looks calm and soothing, a place I can easily picture Katie unwinding each night.

I pull to a stop behind her convertible. When she gets out, she casts an odd look my way. I know what she's thinking. It's about my form of transportation.

I grab the bottle of wine and extra glass that I brought and get out to follow her up the neat sidewalk, through a wrought-iron gate and onto an even neater walk that leads to her front door. I bet Katie pulls every weed that comes up within sight of her house. She strikes me as the type who likes things tidy and in order, but that's not what makes me smile. What makes me smile is the image of her in some tiny shorts and a tiny tank top, hair piled up on top of her head, pulling weeds.

Down on her hands and knees.

Mother of hell!

"What are you smiling at?" she asks as she shifts her cat to finagle her key into the lock.

I don't tell her exactly what I was thinking, of course. I go back a thought or two until I find something that *wouldn't* send her running like a frightened deer. "Just wondering if I was right about what you were thinking."

When she misses the hole the second time, I take her keys from her and let us in. She pauses in the doorway, blocking my entrance with her small body. "And just what do you *think* I was thinking?"

"That you wouldn't have pictured a guy like me driving a minivan."

She looks sheepish and I know I was right. "I guess I *am* a little surprised."

"I figured," I admit as she finally moves inside, allowing me to follow. The instant I close the door behind me, the cat jumps out of her arms, walks about ten steps into the living room, flops down on its side and goes straight to sleep.

"Damn, does the cat always do that?"

Katie catches my eye and follows it back to the cat. She grins. "Yep. That's how he got his name. I call him Dozer because he dozes off in four seconds or less."

My laugh is a short bark. "I love the way your mind works," I confess impulsively.

She turns her big blue eyes back to me, pink infusing the apples of her cheeks. I love that she gets all shy and flustered over something so simple. She tucks her chin, just like she does at work, like by doing so she can hide. I reach forward and hook my finger under it to lift her face back to mine.

"And I love that me telling you that embarrasses you."

"So you do that *on purpose*?" she asks, mildly accusing.

"Maybe. Those blushes *are* awfully addictive." She smiles, a hesitant spread of her lips, prompting me to add, "Almost as much as your smiles."

She gets all fidgety and nervous and adorable under my scrutiny, so I release her. Albeit reluctantly.

"So, a minivan," she says, dropping her eyes and clearing her throat. I love that I put her off balance. I doubt much gets under this girl's skin and I'm happy as hell that I appear to be making my way in, slowly but surely.

"A minivan," I confirm, raising the wine bottle and glass questioningly.

"Oh, sorry. Kitchen's through there." Katie points to the most obvious doorway and I head in that direction. She follows after a few seconds. When I stop at the small island, she breezes past me, setting down the glass that I brought her and keeping her face averted. Makes me think she might be blushing again. After she rummages through a drawer for another minute, she turns her composed self back to me, a corkscrew in one hand. "There *has to be* a story behind it."

"Behind what?" I ask, content to just watch her rather than talk. Or think.

Her grin is more pronounced this time. "Behind the minivan."

"Oh, right. The minivan. I have a brother who came with me. He's handicapped. I dropped him off at the gym on the way to the park."

Her expression softens. Visibly. "Y-you have a handicapped brother?"

"I do."

"And you . . . you take him places with you? You take care of him?"

I shrug. "Well, I don't know about that. I mean, he's grown, so . . ."

"Does he live with you?"

"For the most part."

"That's . . . that's . . ." Katie is looking at me like she's just now seeing me. *Really seeing me.* After several seconds, she glances down at the counter, at the glasses she's arranging in a straight line with the bottle of red. "That's very kind of you. I'm sure he appreciates it."

"I'm sure he does, but like most guys, he's got a piss-poor way of showing it."

"Just like a damn man," she says softly, glancing up at me from beneath her lashes, the hint of a playful smile still curving her lips.

"Bastards," I reply.

Her eyes sparkle up at me and it takes every ounce of willpower I have not to haul her into my arms and kiss her senseless. Which might take a while. She's got plenty of sense about her. Too much, maybe.

After a minute, when the temperature in the little kitchen is rising noticeably, Katie clears her throat again, pulling that swath of rich auburn hair over her shoulder like I've seen her do before. "So what is it that you drive when you're not carting your brother around?"

"Maybe if you're nice to me I'll show you one day."

She grunts indignantly, her lips parting yet still curved. "I'm always nice to you."

"But you could be nicer," I tell her with a half-grin.

She raises one dark brow, the sexiest damn thing I think I've ever seen on a woman. Besides her licking the corner of her mouth when she's concentrating or nervous, that is. "And just how . . . *nice* are you expecting me to be?"

"Not *that* nice," I answer. "Unless you just *want to be* that nice. I would never argue if you wanted to be extra, extra, extra nice to me."

I give her my widest, most innocent smile. She laughs outright, an action that fills the kitchen with a delicate tinkle and turns her face from beautiful to breathtaking. A display like this from her is pretty rare, so pulling it out of her makes me feel like I've won the lottery.

"Do that again," I request quietly, so drawn to her that I can't stop myself from moving closer, from reaching out, from touching.

"Do what again?" she asks. When I cup her silky cheek in my palm, she straightens, but she doesn't back away. A good sign.

"Laugh."

"I can't laugh on command," she explains, her eyes flickering up to mine and away, up to mine and away.

"I swear to God, I think I'd do just about anything to hear that again, to see your face light up like that."

My thumb blindly stroking the crest of her high cheekbone, I catch and hold her eyes this time. They're like melted sapphires, a fathomless liquid that I could easily let myself drown in.

Katie's lips open and close a couple of times, like she's trying to find words where there are none. But the time for talk is over. I feel like I've waited patiently for an eternity to taste, and now it's time for my reward.

Slowly, I bend my face toward hers, hoping she won't move away, praying that she won't stop me. "You've been on my mind since the first day I saw you, Beautiful Katie. It's time you give me the answer to a question that's been haunting me for weeks."

I can feel the sweet, shallow puffs of her breath fanning my lips as I get closer. "W-what's that?"

"Do your lips taste like cotton candy?"

"How would I know?" she asks a bit dazedly.

"Give me five minutes and I'll tell you."

I bring my other hand up to hold her face still as I brush my mouth over hers. When she doesn't move away, doesn't push *me* away, I sink into her lips like I might sink into a bed made of marsh-mallows. Sweet, plump, light-as-air marshmallows. And, God help me, Katie sinks right back.

Maybe she's been wondering about me, too. Maybe she's as curious about *me* as I am about *her*. Maybe, just maybe, she *wants me* as much as I want her. Whatever the reason, I'm delighted when she parts her lips and tilts her head, a silent plea for me to deepen the kiss.

And deepen it I do.

The first touch of my tongue to hers is mouthwatering. She tastes sweet, sweeter than the marshmallows, sweeter than the wine I brought, even though she's not had a drop of it yet. I step closer to her, bringing my lower body in light contact with hers. She leans into me, and my groan floods her mouth. Almost in answer to my involuntary reaction, she gasps, drinking in my breath, taking part of me into her body. The thought, so simple and innocent, nearly snaps the thin thread of my control.

When Katie drags her tongue along the side of mine, the warm silk of her pushes me a little too far. I weave my fingers into her hair and I dive into her mouth, into her kiss.

And I'm met with a brick wall. Katie stiffens in my arms, her hands coming to my chest to push me away. Surprised, I release her instantly. I open confused eyes to her frantic ones as she scrambles away from me, tugging her hair back over her shoulder like a security blanket.

"Did I hurt you?" I ask, clueless as to what I did to cause the sudden change.

"No, no," she responds, smoothing her hands over her hair, over and over and over as she takes deep, calming breaths. "Sorry, I just . . . It's just been a long time since someone has kissed me that way."

"I would say I'm sorry, but I'm not. I'm only sorry that I made you uncomfortable."

She flicks her eyes toward mine in a sideways glance that says she's far from fine. She won't even face me.

"It's fine. Really. I think I'm just . . . I'm just tired. It's been a long day." I can hear the excuse coming before the next word leaves her lips. "Can we just call it a night?"

I swallow my sigh. *Shit!* "Of course. We can do this another time."

She gives me a fake smile that barely curves her lips and never reaches her eyes. "Maybe."

She glances away again, hugging her arms around her middle. I would say she's freezing me out, but she's not. She's not being cold or bitchy; she acts almost . . . *wounded*. Like the frightened deer I was worried about seeing. But what the hell did I do? I only kissed her. And she kissed me back.

I figure now's not the time to ask. The best thing I can do is leave; leave her in peace and hope I can pick up the pieces tomorrow.

FIFTEEN

Katie

Whereas I've been so excited to come to work these last weeks since Rogan's been here, today, for the first time, I'm actively dreading it. *God!* Rogan must think I'm some sort of weirdo freak.

And he wouldn't be wrong.

I never really wanted him to find out, though. I don't know how, exactly, I planned to avoid it, but I had been living in some sort of fantasyland where it was entirely possible that he wouldn't.

Maybe I just thought that this whole thing could play out in my head without ever really getting . . . *real*. Or physical. Even though I'll admit to being curious about his kiss. I've thought about it more times than I've probably thought about *anything* else. And the reality of it . . . Sweet Mary! I couldn't be any more thrilled with that.

Even as I think back on it, I shiver. I can't ever remember someone's kiss making me feel like my insides are on fire. But Rogan's did. It's probably a good thing he ran his hands into my hair, snapping me back to reality. I was enjoying that far too much. I was lost to everything but him and what he was making me feel.

And that could never end well.

Despite my dread and upset, even now, my stomach feels warm and my legs feel tingly at the mere thought of his lips and tongue. What kind of a kiss makes a person's legs tingle? A damn good one, I guess. And the sad thing is that it was *just a kiss*. He wasn't touching anything below my collarbone and it was . . . was . . . *oh God!*

I stop just outside my "office" door and take a few deep breaths. I wait until my heartbeat is a little calmer and I can breathe like I didn't just run a fifty-mile marathon before showing myself.

When I feel a bit more collected, I turn the corner into my space, fully expecting the same scene that has greeted me for weeks now. To say that I'm disappointed at what I find is a tragic understatement.

My area is empty. There's no flirty Rogan in my chair. There's no mischievous Mona talking his ear off. It's just . . . empty. Just me and my space. And no one else. I'm surrounded by the quiet and the solitude that I've craved for years now. It's always made me feel *alone*, but never *lonely*.

Until today.

I go about my usual early-morning duties in slow motion, chastising myself the whole time for being ridiculous. I mean, why get so upset over something so silly? And how stupid was it of me to expect *anything* from a guy like Rogan? He was bound to disappoint me one day. Might as well be today.

I'm lost in thought, opening a pack of new brushes, when a familiar deep voice suddenly breaks into my tailspin. My movements still as I listen to Rogan laugh from out in the hall somewhere, a sound that's accompanied by Mona's excited giggle. I hear them drawing closer to my room and I resume my activity, anything to keep my now-trembling hands busy.

Just before they enter, I hear Mona and Rogan quiet. I listen closely, but hear no sound at all. Afraid to turn around, I place brush after brush in a straight line in the neat and orderly drawer that contains other similar brushes, until the task is complete. I crumple the plastic in my hand and close the drawer quietly before I'm forced to turn around.

I nearly head butt Rogan's chest. Somehow, he managed to creep up behind me without me hearing a single sound.

A surprised squeak-gasp combo squeezes past my lips. "You scared me!" I admit breathlessly.

"I'm sorry!" he replies. Then, with his sincere eyes locked on mine, he adds, "I didn't mean to scare you. I promise."

I know he's referring to more than just this morning. He's probably apologizing for what happened last night. Immediately, I'm off-kilter. But that's what Rogan does—he throws me off balance. With no conscious effort on his part, it seems. I doubt he realizes that he's practically turning my fickle emotions inside out.

"It's fine," I say, taking a step back. I feel the counter brush the backs of my legs. I can retreat no farther, which only frazzles me even more.

His eyes, brilliantly green this morning, search mine for several tense seconds before Rogan raises his hand between us. "I brought coffee."

Thankful to have something, *anything* else to focus on, I look at the cup. It's shorter and fatter, and boasts the label *Main Street Diner* on the side. I take it from him, frowning as I sniff.

"The coffeemaker here is broken so I went across to the diner to get some. Extra hot, extra cream, although I'm not sure how the extra hot held up during the commute."

"It's fine, I'm sure." To prove my point, I take a sip. It's plenty warm, but it doesn't threaten to scald my lips off, which is the way I like it. "You didn't have to go to all this trouble just to bring me coffee."

"You're no trouble at all," he rejoins softly.

God, don't let him be sweet! Let him just be a jerk so I can stop thinking about him, stop wanting things I shouldn't want. Things that I don't want to want!

"You don't know me well enough to say that for sure."

One side of his mouth lifts in a ghost of a grin. "I'm willing to risk it."

There's a quiet moment, colored only with the deep green of Rogan's eyes as he stares down at me, when I think he might try to kiss me again. Or, worse, touch me. I feel his internal battle like static in the air. But, thank God, he refrains. This time, anyway.

I didn't imagine that he'd give up so easily. But I had hoped.

Well, some part of me did, anyway. Some other part . . . didn't.

"You two are so cute together," Mona croons from the doorway. Rogan's grin becomes more pronounced as the click of heels brings my friend farther into the room. We stand facing each other as she passes by, heading for the counter, on which she perches one hip as she flips through the dictionary. "You should date."

"*I'm* not the one who needs convincing," Rogan mutters.

"Oh you don't need to tell me that. Katie's stubborn to a fault and blind to her own beauty. She's . . . *erudite*, but sometimes she can be a little dumb." Rogan frowns and I wrinkle my nose, both of us holding back a laugh. After a few seconds, Mona notices. "What? Did I use it wrong?"

"No, but it's freakin' me out," Rogan says with a chuckle.

"Why? I'm smart. I can learn new words. I can be *erudite*."

"Of course you can," I say, covertly nudging Rogan with my elbow. I don't want his teasing to hurt Mona's feelings.

"Well," she says, standing and dusting her hands off like her job here is done, "I suppose I'd best let you two get to it. You've got a lot more body to make up today."

More body to make up? I was so ready to leave yesterday, I didn't check the notes for today, and this morning my mind was elsewhere.

Is he doing a shirtless scene? Or, God forbid, is he doing a nude scene?

My pulse speeds up at the mere thought.

With a smile that says she *knew* that I had no idea, Mona flounces out of the room, pausing only to kiss one of my cheeks and smack Rogan on the butt. "Lunch?" she says from just the other side of the door.

"Lunch," I reply, watching the tips of her blond hair disappear from view.

Tension rushes in to fill the room, crowding in on me like a vibrating cloud. I take a step back from Rogan, tugging at my hair as I nod toward the drawer where I keep my script notes from Kelly.

"I guess I'd better check to see what I'm doing for you today." I turn, resisting the urge to run and grab the papers. I'm proud that my walk is slow and that my knees are steady.

"No need. I can tell you," he says from behind me. I pay him no attention as I rifle through the other papers in search of my instructions. When I have them in hand, I swing back around to face Rogan. The pages slip silently from my fingers to swoosh across the floor.

Standing not two feet away is a half-naked Rogan.

Before I can collect myself, I take him in. Savor him like rich chocolate or decadent cake. I thought he looked amazing in clothes, but . . . dear God! The man is positively heart-stopping without them.

He looks ten feet tall and bulletproof. His shoulders must be a mile wide and perfectly formed, collarbones straight, deltoids flaring.

The overhead lights, though soft, highlight the rounded domes of his pecs and the stair-step ridges of his abs. They clench with each slow breath he takes. And covering all that glory is lightly tanned skin and a smattering of hair that reaches from nipple to nipple and then narrows to a trail that disappears into the waistband of his jeans. I dare not look beyond that. I don't think my heart can take it.

I'm enjoying the journey back up when his voice cuts into my thrall.

"Ya know?" he asks, as though not for the first time. Evidently, while I was raping him with my eyes, he must've been saying something.

My eyes fly to his face. "I-I'm sorry. What were you saying?"

His face breaks into the most satisfied grin I think I've ever seen. All proud peacock. He knows what I was doing. He knows I was mesmerized. And he's loving it.

My face stings with embarrassment at being so blatant. And getting caught.

"I was just saying that I think it's weird that they'd put makeup on my body just to show me working out, ya know?"

"Yeah," I say dazedly.

"Where do you want me?" he asks, one brown brow shooting up suggestively.

My stomach churns hotly. Why, oh why does *he* have to be the *one guy* on the planet who can break through my thick layer of ice and scar tissue? Why, why, *why*?

I bend to gather my notes from the floor, and I study them closely as I straighten. Not because I need to see what they say, of course, but because I need a reason to look at something else for a minute.

"Looks like the closest shots will be of your back and shoulders as you're doing some pull-ups. They want the tattoos left intact, but any other imperfections covered, so I'll do your face and then let you lie down for the rest."

My heart is thumping so hard, I worry that Rogan will hear it when he sits down in the chair. I set about applying the same products I've used on him most other days, going a little heavier on blush to give him a slightly flushed look. That's all my role entails. They'll spritz him to make him look sweaty right before the filming starts.

I try not to think of Rogan sweaty. Smooth skin glistening, muscular chest huffing, flat stomach gleaming. No, I need not go there. It's just . . . it's just not a good idea.

He's uncharacteristically quiet as I brush and swirl and dab, but not once do his eyes leave my face. Even if, in my peripheral vision, I couldn't see them following my movements, I'd still know he was watching me. I can feel it all the way down to my nerves. His gaze, his scrutiny strums them like strings on a harp.

When I'm finished with what little I can do to make his face even more gorgeous, I lean back, giving him a tight, nervous smile. "Okay, you can go lie down on your stomach. I'll do your back first and then when you sit up, I'll work on your chest a little."

Rogan nods, rising to head over to the long, padded table that's used for bodywork and more extensive specialty applications. I grab a few pods of makeup that match his skin tone, some cream and a few different-sized brushes, taking my time and inhaling huge, calming gulps of air as I gather. When I turn to face Rogan, he's lying on his stomach with his arms folded under his head, his face turned toward me. His emerald eyes, trained on me, glint in the light, but his expression is unusually serious. I want to ask if something's wrong, but I'm afraid. I'm afraid of what he'll say, what I'll learn about him. I don't dare let him get under my skin any more than he already has.

I clear my throat and pull a small rolling table closer to me,

setting my supplies on it. Applying the makeup is something I
could do in my sleep. That's not what I feel I must ready myself for.
Putting my hands on Rogan's skin, touching him all over his body
this way . . . *That's* what I need to prepare for.

I notice that my hand is shaking when I squirt a dollop of cream
into my palm. I rub my hands together to warm it before I lean
forward to smooth the lightly shimmering lotion onto his back. I
feel the muscles twitch and flex under my fingertips, and I try to
ignore the way my belly reacts. "Th-this is just to give your skin a
bit of a glisten, like you've been exercising. You have enough color
that I don't need to add any tint to it," I explain in a voice that
sounds breathless even to *my* ears. *Oh God!*

Rogan says nothing, makes no comment, which is something else
I find odd. Normally, he doesn't miss a chance to tease or taunt me.

Touching him feels good. It feels *too good.* Right, even. At least
touching him this way means I don't have to worry about him
touching me in return. I don't have to concern myself with keeping
hidden things that I don't want him to see. With that in mind, I
let myself go, just enough that I can really enjoy having my hands
on him.

His skin is so smooth and warm. Supple. I can feel the reaction
in every muscle I touch. It incites a corresponding squeeze in my
stomach.

I'm so caught up in these sensations, in this moment, that I find
myself asking about his tattoo in order to prolong the pleasure of
the skin-against-skin contact.

"What does it mean?" I ask, tracing the angry-looking letters that
span the top of his back from shoulder to shoulder. At first glance, I
thought it was just some sort of tribal tattoo. It looked a little like a
twist of teeth or claws. But on closer inspection, I can see that there
are letters intricately woven into the wicked-looking spikes.

"It's Latin. *Pugnare superesse. Vivere pugna.* Fight to survive. Fight to live."

Makes sense for a fighter, I suppose. It doesn't register that the words might have a deeper meaning until I more closely examine his skin.

When the cream is rubbed in thoroughly, I make myself pull my hands away. Holding back a sigh, I reach for a dish of makeup, swirl a small brush through it and lean in to attack a scar that runs around his shoulder blade in a semicircle. It's an odd shape, but I don't ask any questions. For all I know, he had some sort of surgery that he doesn't want to talk about. It's as I'm applying coverage to the pale pink line that I begin to notice other things that I was too distracted to notice before, when I was rubbing my hands over Rogan's flesh and asking about his tattoo.

There are three long white gashes that run down his back. Not like claws, but at different places, like something scratched or cut him in separate lashes. On his lower back are five small dots in an orderly pattern that's a little bigger than the size of my palm. And on his right side, just below his ribs, are two perfectly round scars about the size of a pencil eraser. I can't imagine what the other marks are, but these two look suspiciously like cigarette burns. Old ones.

Fight to survive. Fight to live.

What has he had to survive? What has he had to fight for?

As I'm working, my mind is running a mile a minute. Unfortunately, my hands are nowhere near keeping up. In fact, I'm rubbing my index finger over the tiny dots when Rogan speaks, causing me to jump guiltily.

"I bet you weren't expecting to have to work this hard for your money today, were you?" I glance up at his profile. One side of his mouth is quirked, but there's no humor anywhere else on his face.

He's covering up. I know that for a fact. I recognize it because I've been doing it for years.

"I would expect nothing less from a man who fights for a living," I reply softly, letting him off the hook. I would want someone to do the same for me if the situation were reversed. Some scars can't be talked about for fear of opening the old wound and bleeding to death. I know *that* for a fact, too.

A grunt is the only reply I get from him. As I set about camouflaging more quickly rather than so rudely examining this enigmatic man's body, I can't curb the sense of sadness that fills me. *Or* the sense of connection.

For all his cute winks and sexy grins, for all his charisma and devil-may-care comments, this man has a past. A violent past. And something tells me that it has nothing to do with fighting for money and *everything* to do with fighting for his life. Despite the attraction that I feel toward him, Rogan just became more dangerous to me than ever before. Now I can relate to him on a deeper level, a purely emotional level. I can relate to a violent past. And the desire to escape it. Now we share something important. Now it will be *even harder* to fight him.

When I'm finished patching up his back, making it so that the world doesn't see what's been done to him, I tell him quietly, "You can sit up now."

I back up as Rogan swings his long legs around and pushes himself into a sitting position, muscles flexing everywhere as he moves. As always, I'm aware of his beauty, but now, as perverse as it sounds, he's even more appealing to me. He seems real and fallible and maybe a little bit broken. He hides it well, of course, but now I know. And I can't *un*know.

I avoid his eyes as I treat his chest to the same consideration that I gave his back, only with slightly less attention to detail since the camera shots will be focused mainly on his back. I'm fully aware of his mossy gaze on me as I squirt more cream into my hand and rub my palms together. He watches me as I reach for his pecs. He watches me as I let my fingers trail up to his collarbones, across his shoulders, over his bulging deltoids. I make my way back to his midline and then down his abdomen. It's when the ridges of muscle tense under my hands as I near his waistband that my own stomach begins to react. Warmth blossoms in my core, turning my insides to hot, twitchy mush.

"Careful," he whispers, drawing my eyes away from his torso.

His pupils are wide and there's heat in his gaze, but it's subdued this time. Vulnerable almost.

Ignoring his warning, I respond as though I didn't hear him. "I—I won't have to highlight your abs. They're already defined well enough for the camera," I say, clinging to thoughts of work to diffuse the tension. Not that it's effective.

Rogan's eyes narrow on me just before fire of a different kind appears inside the luminous emerald of his irises. So fast I gasp in surprise, his fingers flick out and snap around my wrists like iron cuffs, stilling my movements. "Don't feel sorry for me."

I'm stunned. "Wh-what?"

"I don't want your pity," he growls.

Although he shocked me with his quick movement, I calm immediately, understanding his reaction. Being pitied is an awful sensation. "I don't pity you. I—I just . . ." I don't know how to tell him that I feel closer to him *now* than I did last night when he was kissing me. And even if I could, I wouldn't. He doesn't need to know that. He *never* needs to know that. "I get it."

His eyes search mine. For what, I don't know. But he must find it because his expression relaxes back into the subdued mask he was wearing earlier.

"Aren't you going to ask me about them?"

I don't have to inquire what "them" he means. He's referring to the scars. "No."

"Most people don't notice, but those who *have* assume they're the result of my fights. Like you did at first." He pauses, scrutinizing me like he can see right into my soul. "But you don't now, do you?"

Reluctantly, I shake my head.

Before he can say anything more, a shadow darkens the door behind him. I glance up just as one of the techs announces that she's here for Rogan. "Stage Four is ready."

"Just a sec," I reply, avoiding Rogan's eyes as I quickly dab some makeup on two more round places that dot his ribs just under his left pectoral. Except for the one around his shoulder blade, these scars, just like all the others, are so pale they're barely noticeable. And I'm sure Rogan likes it that way. And I envy his body's ability to naturally conceal things that might otherwise cause him discomfort. My body saw no such need to help me out. What's wrong with me is impossible to miss if I don't take measures to hide it.

When I finish, I steal a glance back up at Rogan's face. He's watching me again, only this time with an odd expression marring his otherwise perfect visage. When he leans close to me, he does it quickly as he stands so that I have little chance to move away. His lips graze the shell of my ear as he speaks. "Whatever I did last night, I'm sorry."

And with that, he swipes up his shirt and follows the tech right out my door.

SIXTEEN

Rogan

"Cut! Let's try this again. Right from 'You wanted it.'"

I grit my teeth. Why the hell can't I get this right?

The answer to that question is a word. A single word. Or rather a name.

Katie. Sweet, beautiful, intriguing Katie. Katie with a dash of fire that she keeps as close as the hair around her neck. Katie with lips that taste like the wine we never got to drink. Katie with the eyes that push me away and then beg me to stay. *That Katie.*

I push her out of my mind and smile at the tall redhead across from me, the one with whom my onscreen relationship is heating up. She watches me with her appreciative gray eyes, pulling her bottom lip between her teeth as she stares up at me. She's made her interest in me known. I've been polite in my *disinterest.* She's all but ignored it. Obviously, she's not the type to give up.

Her attention doesn't bother me. Her titillating teases don't faze me. I'm not tempted. I'm just . . . distracted.

I just keep smiling, unaffected, as I run the lines through my head again. When I can recite them perfectly in the silence, I nod back at the director. My mind is clear and focused. I'm ready.

I roll my head on my shoulders, trying to regain my usual level of concentration. That's when I see her. She draws my eye like a bright flash of light, only there's no flash, no light. Just her.

I've never seen her come out to watch filming before. And wouldn't you know that today, of all days, she'd show up. Normally I wouldn't mind, but I'm having enough trouble keeping my head in the game as it is. She certainly isn't going to help that.

"Rogan?" Rayelle, the redhead, leans left, putting her face in my line of sight, making it a nonissue for me to look away from Katie.

I grit my teeth again, something I've done all day, something that has given me one helluva headache, and I nod once more.

"Take fourteen. Action!"

The instant Tony, the director, says 'action,' the words just leave me. Again. My eyes flicker to Katie. On her face is a blank mask. She's neither excited nor blasé, neither interested nor disinterested. She's simply here. Watching. I'm beginning to know her well enough to guess that something is going on just beneath the surface, though. It didn't take me long to figure out that her still waters run very deep.

"Cut!" Tony barks again. "Rogan, what the hell? Is your head in your ass or what?"

I curl my fingers into fists. This isn't like me. I never bring less than my A-game to anything that I do. I'm an all-or-nothing kind of guy.

"Sorry, Tony. I don't . . . I don't know what's wrong, man." The aggravated disappointment on his face makes me feel like shit. He's been singing my praises since the first day I got here and I hate to let him down.

He gets out of his chair and walks over to me, reaching up to drape his arm around my shoulder. It's an awkward position for him considering the height disparity, but he does it anyway so that he can lead me off set. "Are you running your lines? Putting in the time?"

"I read over my lines every night. I just . . ." I feel like punching something. I need some time in the ring to get rid of a little aggression.

"Maybe get Rayelle to help you out a couple times a week." His wink says he thinks she can help me with more than just my lines. I'm sure she'd be more than willing, but *she* can't fix what ails me. Only one woman can, and I've hit a brick wall with her.

Then it occurs to me. "I think I might know just the person to, uh, help me out."

"Fine, fine. I don't give a damn who it is, just make it work."

"I'll be right as rain by Monday," I pledge, my mind already on the weekend and how I can convince Katie to spend it with me.

Tony grins and slaps me on the back. "That's my boy!"

With that, he turns back to the set. "Get Groenig in here. We'll shoot the mansion scene this afternoon instead."

My enthusiasm spikes to a more normal level and I swivel my head back to where Katie was standing. The spot is empty now.

Why come if you were planning to leave so soon?

I don't understand her at all, which is probably part of the appeal. She's such a contradictory female I don't know what to make of her. She doesn't react to me like most women do.

I think back to the way she looked at me when she saw my scars. They affected her. Why, I don't know. She didn't appear to be disgusted, so I don't think it was that. Regardless, I'm more determined than ever to get inside that beautiful head of hers.

I'm smart enough to know she damn sure ain't gonna spill her guts for me. But if *she* has come to know *me* at all, then she ought to know that I don't give up. I'm no quitter. I *will* know her. And I'll know her *well*.

Ignoring all the chaos surrounding me, I tug my shirt over my head and make my way to Katie's brightly lit cosmetic cove. I stop just inside the doorway, catching and holding my breath so that she won't hear me. Her back is to me, her rich hair spilling between her shoulder blades like a coppery waterfall. She's doing something with her hands, something I can't see, but she's also humming. She's swaying the tiniest bit to the music inside her head and, at this moment, she looks more peaceful than I've seen her so far.

The scene makes me ache to touch her, but the song she's humming makes me smile through the discomfort. "Ten Feet Tall." It's funny because something about her, something about the way she tries not to care but can't seem to help herself, makes me feel that way—ten feet tall. Like I'm somehow an exception to her rules, whether she wants me to be or not. I don't think anyone has gotten close to her in a long time.

Maybe until me.

Suddenly, she turns to throw something at the trashcan. I don't have time to warn her of my presence and she gasps in alarm, her big sapphire eyes getting bigger as she stumbles backward. The makeup chair clips her behind the knees and I see her start to go down. Her arms shoot out and her mouth rounds into an O, as in *oh shit!* I rush forward, reaching out to wind my fingers around her thin wrists and pull her toward me. The shift in momentum causes her to overcorrect and she falls against my chest.

"Oh!" she chirps, stunned. "Thank you. You startled me."

"You're welcome, and I didn't mean to. I was enjoying the show."

Color pours into her cheeks and she tucks her head. "How embarrassing."

"Why?"

"Because. It just is. I mean . . . I don't know."

"I love that song, by the way."

"You knew what I was humming?" She seems surprised.

"Of course I did. Now if it were *me*, it would be anybody's guess. I can't carry a tune in a bucket."

Shyly, she glances up at me, a wry twist to her lips. "For some reason I doubt that. I bet you've never sucked at anything in your whole life."

"I suck at things all the time," I reply, hoping to keep the conversation going so that she doesn't become too aware of the fact that I'm still holding her. Because I like holding her. I love the way she feels against me, all tiny and warm and curvy. And if she thinks too much about it, she'll pull away.

"Like what?"

"Like origami. Like crocheting. Like ballet. Like—"

She grins up at me. "Have you actually *tried* any of those things?"

"I have."

"Dare I ask why?"

"No, you dare not."

"Secrets. A man after my own heart." She says it in jest, but I know she's only partially kidding. I don't doubt that she has a lot of secrets. And I want to know them all.

"I'll tell you anything you want to know." I inject every bit of sincerity into my voice that I can muster. I don't know why I would even offer. There are several things I couldn't ever tell her. *Wouldn't* ever tell her. But something tells me she'd never take me up on such an offer. That's not who she is. I'd say she respects a person's privacy. And asks them to do the same of hers.

Her eyes are locked on mine so I see the very second that awareness sinks in. Her expression starts to shut down before she physically backs away.

"Everyone is entitled to their secrets. I'll be nice and let you keep some of yours," she says, trying to be light and playful about it.

Even though I knew it wouldn't be her style to want all the details, some part of me wants her to know all the ugly, all the unacceptable, all the things that no one else *really* knows. I want her to know about them and *still* give me the time of day. *Despite* them. "What if I want you to know them? What if I want to share them with you?"

"You don't."

"And why don't I?"

"You don't want to get involved with someone like me. I'm not the . . . I'm just not . . ."

I reach out to take her chin between my thumb and forefinger, capturing her before she can completely escape. "What do I have to do to convince you that I *do* want to be involved with you? Not someone *like you*, but *you*."

That was too much. I can see it in the way she shrinks away from me.

I'm about to lose control of this opportunity and, knowing Katie, I might not get another one any time soon.

I plaster on a big damn smile even though I'm frustrated as hell.

"Luckily, I didn't come here to discuss your worth as a human being. I came here to collect."

"Collect?" she repeats with a frown.

"Yep. You totally derailed me on set today and Tony chewed my ass for not knowing my lines. Made me promise to rehearse them this weekend. And guess who got volunteered?"

I paraphrased, of course. She didn't get volunteered, except *by me*. But paraphrasing isn't lying. Is it?

"Who, *me*? Why me?"

"Well, I volunteered you. Mainly because you were the source of my . . . distraction to begin with. I figure it's only right that you make it up to me. To *this show*." I throw the last in for good measure, just in case my argument wasn't convincing enough on its own.

She starts to make excuses. Just like I imagined that she would. "I'd love to help, but—" She stops abruptly, tilting her head to the side the slightest bit. As she considers me, I think back to the moment when she looked up at me after having examined my back. That same soft look is back in her eyes now. She pulls those big blues away from me for a heartbeat, but then she brings them right back. "Okay. I'll do it. I'll help you." She squares her chin, like she's bolstering herself, but bolstering what? Her courage? Her resistance? Her determination?

I must admit to being pleasantly surprised. I know I can be hella convincing when I want to be, but I was beginning to wonder if Katie is in possession of some sort of Rogan Immunity Charm that I'm not aware of. But now, I'm thinking that maybe inadvertently revealing something about myself, about my past, has made her see that I'm not such a cocky, obnoxious sleazeball after all.

Damn, this woman . . . She's making me crazy!

But still, I consider this a victory, so my smile reflects as much. It's genuine. And it's big. "You will?"

Why the hell did I just give her an out?

She smiles in return. A small one, but a smile nonetheless.

"I will. But *just* to rehearse lines," she adds sternly.

I laugh, giving her a sloppy salute. "Ma'am, yes, ma'am! I'll pick you up at seven. We can eat and work and then maybe take a swim."

It only takes about ten seconds for it to register. Panic. That's what shows up on her face, in her eyes. Panic, pure and simple.

"No, I, uh, I can't stay out too late. I've got some, um, things to do in the morning. But thank you. Just the lines."

"And dinner. You have to eat *some time*." She reaches for the hair that is ever-present at her shoulder and smoothes it around like a comforting blanket. Her nervous tick. "My brother doesn't get out much and he could *realllly* use the company."

"He has you," she argues.

I give her a withering look. "Yeah, but I'm . . . me. Have you met me?"

The corners of her mouth twitch and I'm immediately gratified. "As a matter of fact, I think I have."

"See what I mean?"

"Well, you *are* pretty disagreeable," she jokes.

"A real bear of a guy, I hear."

She exhales. "Okay. Just dinner and lines, but then I have to get home."

"Fair enough," I announce, backing away. I feel good that I'm making some headway, but I don't want to push my luck. "Seven o'clock."

She nods, her eyes shining. Right this minute, she doesn't look worried or hesitant or guarded like she so often is. She just looks . . . beautiful.

I decide that this is the way I like her best. And that I'll do everything I can to make sure I see it more often than not.

SEVENTEEN

Katie

What would I call my mood? I ponder this as I sit on the couch in the living room, wiggling my foot and waiting for the clock to strike seven.

Dozer is lying about three feet away, eyeing me suspiciously. Evidently my excess energy and increasing anxiety are pronounced enough to keep *even him* awake, which is really saying something. He's practically narcoleptic.

How would I define it? Nervously wary? Or maybe anxiously skeptical? I don't exactly know what kind of label my inner turmoil deserves. For all I know, it warrants a unique name all its own.

I hear a racy rumble come roaring down my street, getting louder as it approaches. My heart thunders along at a somewhat similar cadence, like the noise alone triggered my internal throttle. No, I don't know that to be Rogan on his way to pick me up, but then again, yes, I absolutely do. Somehow it *sounds* like him. I'm already getting a mental picture, even though I'm still sitting on my couch.

He told me he might show me what he *chooses* to drive. Something tells me he's about to.

When the throbbing engine reaches its peak and then dies right outside, I leap up from my seat and run to the window. My insides twist and slither like a clutch of snakes when I see what's parked outside. A black-and-silver machine, reading *Ducati* along the shiny gas tank, rests along the curb. And on its back is Rogan.

Even with his head covered by a matching helmet, I recognize him. I recognize his body and his body language. I recognize the way I respond to him. Even when I don't want to.

He's wearing a snug white T-shirt and ratty blue jeans. Nothing that would identify him. It's *the way* he wears his clothes, the way the fabrics hug his lithe form, even the way he sits on the bike, like he is one with a wild, untamable animal, that is uniquely Rogan.

When he pulls off his helmet, I'm aware of two things. One, that his hair sticks up all over his head in blond spikes that make my fingers itch to touch. And two, that his eyes are on mine. All the way across the yard and through the sheer curtains that cover the glass of the window, they're trained on mine. I can feel it. It's like he knows I'm looking at him, like he can feel it, too. And that he honed in on it, on *me*. Instinctively. It sounds completely insane, but I don't doubt it. This isn't the first time I've felt him watching me. And it only gets more and more disconcerting.

For a few seconds, he just stares at me. He's not smiling; he's just straddling his bike, holding his helmet between his big, strong hands. The intensity of his gaze burns along my nerve ends, causing me to feel both terrified and excited all at once. It also makes me wonder why I agreed to this. I'm not entirely sure I can be trusted around him. He makes me forget. And that's dangerous.

Finally, his face breaks into a breathtaking smile and I jump away from the window. I keep backing away until I'm safely ensconced in the shadows on the opposite side of the room. I pull in several gulps of air, fanning my flaming face with my nervous hands. I wait impatiently for the moment when he'll knock and I'll be face-to-face with what could end up being a nightmare for me.

But he could end up being a dream for you, too, my inner optimist chimes. I don't hear from her much, but it seems she's more vocal of late.

Three firm knocks on my front door have my insides snapping with the electricity of attraction. Probably not the best way to start an evening where I need to maintain a cool head so that I can keep a charming, gorgeous man at arm's length.

"You can do this, you can do this, you can do this," I mutter under my breath. The thing is, I don't know for sure that I can. I haven't been this attracted to anyone in a long time. Actually, I don't think I've *ever* been *this* attracted to someone. Period. Not even my ex, who basically ruined my entire life. He's part of my aversion to Rogan. Him and the horrific memories that he and he alone is responsible for. The other part consists of the things about me that would surely run Rogan off, things I would never let him see.

Those sobering thoughts are like a bucket of ice water right in the face. My breathing levels and my face cools, so that it's with my usual calm that I open the door and greet him.

"Hi," I offer with a mild smile.

"Hi, yourself, darlin'," he drawls, leaning against the doorjamb and running his jewel-tone eyes over me. "Not only do you look beautiful, but you're dressed perfectly."

I glance down at my low-rise jeans and simple pink tee that reads *Fat Lewey's* across the chest. "I am?"

"You are. I didn't have to bring the van tonight." He nods toward the curb, where his glossy motorcycle awaits.

I glance behind him at the gleaming yet intimidating machine.

It looks dangerous, much like its driver, which is something that I've made a point to avoid in my life.

Until Rogan.

"I see that. You must have a death wish," I comment wryly.

"Not tonight," he murmurs in a voice that moves over my skin like rich, dark molasses. He straightens with a crooked smile and holds out his hand. "Come on."

For the space of five or six heartbeats, I wonder what I'm agreeing to, what this night will mean in the grand scheme of my life. Before I can come to any conclusion, he's reaching forward to curl his fingers around mine, sending a shiver up my arm and a thrill down my spine.

I follow him out onto the stoop, turning to close the door behind me. "Sleep tight, Dozer," Rogan calls to my cat where he sits on the back of a chair near the door. As I'm pulling the door closed, I see Dozer wink one yellow eye and then promptly fall asleep.

Rogan pulls me down the sidewalk behind him, his grasp firm and warm. He stops beside his bike to unstrap another helmet from behind the tiny perch that qualifies as a backseat. "This is for you," he says, gently sliding the smaller version of his helmet onto my head. I reach up to keep my hair in place as he buckles a strap under my chin. "Shit!" he says in irritation.

"What?" I ask, mildly alarmed.

"How the hell can you look hot in a helmet?" he asks, slapping my face shield down.

He can't see my smile as he turns to ready himself, throwing one leg over the motorcycle. He rights it from its reclining position before he raises his hand to assist me. He says nothing and neither do I as I slide my fingers across his palm and climb onto the Death Machine (which is how it will forever register in my head).

I sit clumsily on the little perch, not knowing what to do with my hands or my legs. Rogan fires up the engine, revving it a few times before he twists to reach back and put my feet on the two little chrome stubs sticking out on either side. The action brings my knees up higher and forces me to lean forward slightly. A little yip escapes because I feel like I might fall off. Rogan grabs my hands and pulls them around his stomach, bringing my chest to his back.

"Just lean into me and hold on," he says, his voice coming through loud and clear into my helmet. So clear, in fact, that I can hear the smile he's wearing even though I can't see it.

I like this, this bike, this anonymity. I can enjoy touching him, being wrapped around him without having to explain myself or worry about his all-seeing eyes. Maybe a motorcycle isn't such a bad thing after all.

That's what I'm thinking right up until he darts away from the curb and accelerates so fast that I fear the front wheel will come off the ground. After that, my only thought is survival.

I squeal, surprised and excited and a little afraid, to which Rogan's only response is a throaty chuckle. It vibrates along the surface of my skin much like the motorcycle vibrates beneath my butt.

As we zip along the streets of the outskirts of Enchantment, I concentrate less on the landscape that's speeding by and more on the intriguing man that I hold in my arms. He's obviously had some bad things happen to him in his life. He's obviously fought to overcome them. Only now, rather than hiding away from life and danger and risk, he embraces it. He hunts it down and conquers it. I can see it in the way he masters the curves of the road, in the way he tips his chin up to the world, grinning as if to say *Bring it on!* rather than tucking it in submission. In fear. Therein lies the difference between us. What happened to me crippled me. I became a victim, forever changed by my past. Rogan rose above, became a victor, and refused to let his past change his future.

We both fought to survive. But only one of us fought to *live*. Really live. And he won. He's *still* winning.

Like sunshine creeping into the skies at dawn, I feel a ray of light break through the darkness that I've been drowning in for so long. It's inspiration. It's motivation. It's the sight of someone rising up and overcoming.

It's Rogan.

Feeling eases back into places that went numb a long time ago, places I thought were all but dead. The things that Rogan has made me feel, most of them against my will, are like thin wires feeding electricity into my nerves, my muscles, my heart. They tether me to him and pull me inexorably closer. This common ground between us, this way in which we could understand each other like most people never will, might just be the strongest one so far.

Rogan turns off the road on which we've been traveling for several minutes. I knew we were heading toward the foot of Brasstown Bald, which is the mountain that sits behind Enchantment, because I know that's where the luxurious homes were built for the elite of the studio's employees (i.e., the actors). I assumed that's where Rogan would be staying.

When we reach a small brick guard shack to the left of an enormous wrought-iron gate, Rogan slows to wave at the guard. He jumps to his feet, smiles politely and triggers the mechanism to let us through. Rogan waits patiently, easily balancing our combined weight on his bike. It seems effortless, and I understand why when I glance down at the long muscles of his thighs. I can see them standing out, bulging inside the denim of his jeans.

As soon as the gate is open enough for us to squeeze through, Rogan sharply twists his wrist, sending us hurtling between the slowly opening halves. He cuts it so close I can almost feel the cool metal of the gate brush the skin of my arm. Almost.

Less than two minutes later, he pulls to a stop in the circular driveway of a sprawling contemporary home. It looks like little more than a sea of glass amid a field of sharp angles. He raises his hand, which I take to use for balance as I dismount. I work on unfastening the buckle beneath my chin as Rogan settles the motorcycle on its kickstand and kills the engine. My fingers work clumsily and slowly in my distraction. I can't seem to take my eyes off the man as he tugs off his helmet, runs his fingers through his hair and drags his lean body off the machine.

He casually hooks his helmet on one handlebar and turns to face me. One side of his mouth quirks. "Need some help?"

"No," I reply, fumbling with the strap.

Rogan watches me with an amused look on his face for a few seconds before he leans in and takes over. "Here, let me do it. You'll never get it undone with those shaky hands."

I glance down at my trembling fingers. "You didn't scare me. I don't know why I'm shaking." Even though I think I really do.

"Adrenaline. You can't help but feel it on that bike."

I say nothing, more than happy to go with *that* explanation.

When Rogan finally frees me of the helmet and hangs it on the opposite handlebar, he reaches for my hand again. He's very matter-of-fact as he curls his slightly rough fingers around my unsteady ones.

"Do you like stir-fry?" he asks as we walk side by side up the path made up of geometric concrete shapes that dot the grass.

"I do."

"Good. I was trying to think of something that wouldn't ruin by the time we got here, so I just cut up all the ingredients and left them in the fridge. It won't take long to cook them."

I pull up short, my shocked eyes turned to Rogan. "You *literally* cooked for me?"

"Well, not yet. I literally *cut and chopped* for you, though."

"Wow. I'm impressed."

Startling me yet again, Rogan throws both hands up into the air and shouts, "Finally! Thank *God*!"

"Finally what?" I ask, confused.

"Finally! I managed to impress you."

I suppress a grin. "Like you ever had doubts."

"I was beginning to wonder. It was startin' to look like God had given you the gift of anti-Rogan blood."

"Is there such a thing?"

"I didn't think so, but you had me scared there for a minute."

His grin is so cocky, yet so charming and cute that the only thing I can do is smile and roll my eyes.

"Well, there's no reason to worry. You've accomplished your mission. Now you can stop trying."

"Where's the fun in that?" he asks with a wink just before he reaches around me to open the big white front door.

He motions for me to precede him, which I do, looking around the spacious foyer-slash-great-room combo as he closes the door behind us. When I make it full circle to once again face Rogan, I stumble back a step. I wasn't expecting for a man in a wheelchair to have somehow silently rolled up and stopped less than a foot from where I stand.

The guy reaches out to grab my wrist just as Rogan's arm comes around my waist to steady me.

"Sorry," he says in a low, gruff voice. "Didn't mean to scare you."

"You must be Rogan's brother," I say kindly, trying not to feel put off by his frown. If it weren't for that, he'd look a lot like Rogan with his blond hair and green eyes. He even has the same strong jaw and slightly crooked nose. But where Rogan appears happy and charismatic, his brother just seems . . . cold.

"Yep. I'm the cripple," he remarks snidely, casting an angry glare at Rogan.

"He didn't mention that part," I lie in an effort to diffuse the palpable tension. Well, it's not *technically* a lie. Rogan didn't say he was crippled; he said he was handicapped. Semantics, yes, but still . . . "Thank you for having me to dinner."

"Like I had much choice." Another fuming look thrown at Rogan.

"If I'm imposing, I can come back another time. I don't want to put you out."

Finally, the brother looks at me as though he's seeing *me* for the first time and not some tool Rogan is using to infuriate him. "No, you're fine."

For some reason, I feel sorry for this man. I know it would kill him to know this, but I can't seem to help it. It's not for his handicap that I pity him, though; it's for his anger. I know from past experience that anger and bitterness can eat you alive and steal away what life you have left if you let it. It's best to just let go and move on whenever possible.

It's with this sense of sorrow that I feel for him that I stick out my hand and put on my biggest smile. "Great, then. I'm Katie. It's nice to meet you, Rogan's brother."

He watches me silently for several long seconds before he looks down at my outstretched hand and then back up to my face.

"Kurt. It's nice to meet you, Katie," he replies, a very small smile curving his lips.

I feel gratified to get civility from him. "So I hear we're having stir-fry. Your idea or his?" I tip my head to indicate Rogan, who is standing quietly at my side, watching our interaction. When I glance over at him, I see that it's now *his* brow that's creased with a frown. I smile at him and the wrinkles deepen. What is it with these men?

"Mine," Kurt replies, shooting Rogan a quick grin as he wheels his chair one-hundred-eighty degrees and takes off toward the kitchen, which is separated only by a raised bar in this open floor plan.

"He's full of shit. I'm the brains in this operation."

"No, you're the legs. I'm perfectly capable of doing *everything* else," Kurt calls from in front of the refrigerator. When he turns back around, he's holding two covered bowls in his lap and boasting a cocky grin that's one hundred percent Rogan. "My legs are the *only things* that don't work right."

I smile again, sliding my eyes over to *my* Rogan. "He's *definitely* your brother."

I don't know what happened to make him frown back there at the door, but his wink assures me that all is right with the world again.

By order of Rogan, I am confined to a chair during dinner preparations. "How can I impress you with my extensive culinary expertise if you help?" he asks.

"You won't have to worry about that. She'll be too dazzled by me to give you a second thought," Kurt says.

"You haven't dazzled anybody since Regina Lawson in the second grade."

"You wouldn't know dazzling if it exploded right beside your head."

"I'm the *definition* of dazzling."

And so the banter goes until the table is set, the wine is poured and dinner is served. Time passes so pleasantly, so humorously, so *effortlessly* that I can't quite remember how the conversation turned to *Star Wars*. I only know that the guys are hilarious as they debate who would've made a better Han Solo.

"I have better reflexes, which would make me the better pilot of the *Millennium Falcon*," Rogan declares.

"But I'm a better kisser, and where would Han be without Leia?" Kurt argues.

"How the hell could you possibly know that you're a better kisser?"

"Amy Steadman told me."

"Amy Steadman? The only reason she kissed you is because you were gettin' all girly and emotional and shit over that sophomore who broke your heart. What was her name again?"

"You're a damn liar! Amy kissed me because she was tired of putting up with your cheatin' ass."

"I didn't cheat on her. We weren't seeing each other when all that happened. Which brings me to my next point. I'd make the best Han Solo because I'm taller. You'd get stuck being Luke."

"You're only taller because your legs work. I'm taller sitting down."

"Bullshit! I'm an inch and three quarters taller than you. Have been since you peaked the year you graduated. Not my fault you stopped growing too early."

"This is getting us nowhere. Let's ask our own Leia," Kurt suggests, turning his slightly less dazzling green eyes to me. "Be honest, who would make the best Han Solo? Kief or me?" Kurt gives me his most winsome smile, winking and nodding and gesturing for me to choose him, all of which makes me laugh.

"You can't ask me that! You'd both make great Hans."

"Well, you know the only way to know for sure, don't you?" Rogan's brother asks.

Something about his wide grin makes me instantly suspicious. "I'm not sure I *want to* know."

"You'll have to kiss us both."

"*What?*"

Kurt shrugs. "Sorry. I don't make the rules."

Open-mouthed, I turn to look at Rogan. "Are you hearing this?"

His face is relaxed and his lips are curved, but there's a hardness to his eyes that gives me pause. "I'm hearing it. The only thing that's keeping me from kicking his ass is sympathy. I know how it feels to want to kiss a beautiful makeup artist."

"I don't want to kiss just any beautiful makeup artist. I want to kiss *this one*."

My face flames under the heat of so much attention. I glance shyly from Kurt to Rogan. Something about his expression tells me that he's no longer having fun. I wonder if the cause is his brother's overtly flirtatious commentary. That seems to be the only thing that has changed, and as much as I shouldn't care whether Rogan is jealous, the prospect that he *might be* sends a little thrill through me.

"Well, unfortunately, you're both out of luck. I'm a terrible kisser, so it would hardly be fair for me to judge."

"That's highly unlikely," Kurt declares.

When I glance at Rogan, his eyes are a dark emerald sparkle in the handsomely tanned landscape of his face. "Liar," he says softly.

Clearing my throat, I stand and grab my plate to take it into the kitchen, but Kurt stops me. "Leave it!" he barks. I freeze, mid-motion, glancing across the table at him questioningly. His face breaks into a boyish grin. "You're a guest. You shouldn't have to clean up."

"But I—"

"Ah ah ah," he clucks, shaking his head and wheeling around to my side of the table. "No arguments."

Kurt takes my plate from my fingers and places it in his lap before he wheels around to collect the rest of the plates from the table. With one aggressive fling of his powerful arms, he sends his chair careening across the hardwood and into the kitchen.

When I can only see the top of Kurt's head in front of the sink,

I turn to Rogan. His expression is unfathomable and his eyes are heavy-lidded as they watch me. I try not to fidget under his curious scrutiny and my voice is a hoarse croak when I speak. "Thank you for dinner."

"Thank you for coming."

"A-are you okay?" I ask.

"Why wouldn't I be?"

I give him a one-shouldered shrug. "I don't know. You just seem . . . off."

Rogan grins, an action that transforms his face into the one I'm most familiar with, making my belly do a little flip. The brooding version was like a stranger. "Does that mean you prefer me when I'm *on*?"

His eyes twinkle as he comes to stand before me, less than six inches separating us as he stares down into my face.

"I didn't say that," I reply, a bit more breathless than I'd like to be.

Rogan reaches up and drags the back of his index finger under the edge of my lower lip. "You didn't have to." For a few seconds, I tense, wondering if he's going to try to kiss me, but then he winks, reaching for my hand and tipping his head toward the other side of the room. "Since Kurt volunteered for cleanup, let's go out onto the patio and get started, 'kay?"

I nod, shivering at the heat that pours from his palm into mine. It flows up my arm as Rogan leads me through the living room to a wall of windows. Two of them are giant sliding panels that open onto a softly lit travertine patio. Directly in front of me lies a lagoon-style pool, the water inside it a deep blue. Overflow spills from the attached spa, creating a soothing backdrop. It gives the backyard a Zen garden feel.

An area rug to one side holds a grouping of wicker furniture that sits beneath a pergola. A dozen creamy lanterns hang overhead. They shed their warm, romantic light on the intimate setting like twelve tiny moons.

Rogan moves to the sofa and releases my hand, gesturing for me to have a seat. "We can go over the lines a couple of times and then try it a few times without cheat sheets," he says with a grin, referring to two sets of script pages that seem to have appeared in his other hand like magic.

I nod again. "That's fine." I take the proffered pages from his extended hand and sit stiffly on the edge of a cushion.

A stab of nostalgia slices through my heart as I look over the two pages of dialogue and notes. There was a time when something like this would've energized and motivated me, a time when my place was in front of the camera rather than in the shadows behind it. But that time is past. Now, I just feel . . . empty. If I'd only known how much my dreams would cost me . . .

"Have you ever read through a script before? Do you want me to—"

"Yes, I'm familiar with them," I answer soberly.

Rogan gives me several minutes to read silently through the pages before he asks, "Ready?"

Again, I nod. "I think so."

"I'll start from where shooting will resume." Rogan clears his throat.

Back and forth, we read our lines. The first time, it's more perfunctory. The second round has a little more emotion to it as I get used to the scene. The third time seems much more relaxed and real.

When he finishes with the last line, Rogan glances up at me. His brow wrinkles slightly. "You're not reading from the script?"

"No. I think I've got it down pretty good."

Rogan's eyebrows shoot up. He's impressed. That pleases me,

even though it shouldn't. I just hope he doesn't start asking questions.

"Do you want to try them standing up, then? The scene calls for us to be standing in the office of my character's club."

"Sure."

Rogan stands and I quickly follow suit, wiping my damp palms on my jeans. The scene somehow plays a little too close to reality for me and I wonder if Rogan will try to finish it completely. With a kiss. My stomach feels all squirmy just thinking about it.

Rogan walks to the edge of the pool where the lantern light is mostly faded. We are minimally illuminated by the blue glow of the water. For the most part, we are in a dark bubble all by ourselves.

The first line drifts through the night, bridging the small distance between us like a velvet cord, drawing me into Rogan's world.

"You wanted it. You wanted the truth."

"Not like this. Not this way. I thought you were different. I thought—"

"Bullshit!" he explodes, startling me even though I knew what he was going to say. *"You knew exactly what you were getting in to, what kind of man I am."*

"But I've never . . ."

It's easy to be timid, to play the role of this confused, cowed girl trying to resist that which she wants so badly. That which she knows will destroy her. In some ways, she's not a far stretch for me.

"You've never what? Had someone want you because of how it feels instead of what you can give them?"

Rogan's voice is low as he takes a step toward me. I can feel the shivering of my nerves, just as this character probably feels the shivering of hers.

"You know who my father is. Some people will do anything to get close to him."

"Well, I'm not one of those people. I don't give a damn about your father. And neither should you. This is about us. This is about what I'm going to do to you the second you stop pretending you don't feel this, too."

I lick my lips. Not because I'm pretending to be someone else, but because right now, with Rogan so close that I can smell his soap, I'm *not*.

"I can't . . . This isn't something that I . . ."

The arguments are the same stilted ones I would use if this were the real Rogan talking to the real me, trying to convince me to let go of my hang-ups.

"Liar. You can. And this is something that you—"

"If they ever find out . . . If anyone ever knows . . ."

"It's too late for that, sweetheart. You're already mine."

"I'm not yours yet. *There's still time."*

"No, there's not. I'm going to kiss you. Kiss you like you need to be kissed. Like you've always wanted to be kissed. And in a week's time, I'll be back. On that night, you'll have a decision to make."

My heartbeat is a tap dance, a clickity-clack against my ribs. My pulse is a song that plays its quickened rhythm just for Rogan. It doesn't seem to matter that these are just lines from a show. From a single scene. It doesn't seem to matter that they're someone else's words about other people's lives. Even though I'm not Becca and he's not Drago, even though they're not even real, my insides are trembling like loose leaves in the autumn breeze.

"Can I finish?" Rogan's words are his own, soft whispers carried to me on breath that teases my cheek.

"Finish what?" I ask, equally softly.

"Finish the scene."

Here in the dark, pretending to be someone I'm not, I can be brave. I can keep hidden that which taunts me every time I look in the mirror. I can taste fearlessly, behave recklessly. Just this once. Only in the dark.

Fight to survive. Fight to live.

Just this once, maybe I can live again.

"Yes," I breathe.

The syllable has barely left my lips when his mouth drops to cover mine. It dies in the darkness, consumed instantly by the fire of what's between us. There's no tentativeness, no hesitation. No wading in slowly after what happened before. There is only heat and want.

His lips move over mine in a moist, hot dance that's meant to do one thing—incite. And it's working. Already, my chest is tight with my heaving breath and my body wants to lean into his.

When Rogan tilts his head to one side, deepening the kiss, I wind my arms around his neck and dive in with him, letting go with an abandon that I haven't felt in years. I part my lips and he enters my mouth with one long lick and a groan that vibrates along my tongue.

With one big hand cupping the back of my head, he slides the other down my back to curl around my waist and hold me to him. I feel every sharp ridge and every hard plane of his body, pressing against mine from nipple to knee, and something inside me melts.

I ease my restless fingers into Rogan's short, spiky hair. It's soft and silky, yet prickly enough to tease my palms. When I run my tongue along the side of his, Rogan moves both hands up to cup my face, pulling his mouth away from mine and staring down into my eyes for long, toe-curling seconds.

"God, how you make me *want*," he growls, tipping my chin up with his thumbs, holding me still for his delicious torture. "To taste," he says, licking and sucking at my lips. "To feel." His fingers thread into my hair, pushing it over my shoulders and moving it away from my neck. I tip my head slightly to the left, exposing only the right side. He strokes the pads of his fingers down my throat, stopping at the edge of my shirt to dip them just inside. Chills radiate from his touch like flame, scorching the skin of my chest and making my breasts throb. "I want to know all your secrets. To strip you down. Lay you bare. Just for me." His lips trail from the corner of my mouth, across my cheek to my ear. "Would you like that?" he whispers, his hot breath teasing the shell.

His words . . . *God!* They're so tempting. *He's* so tempting. I'd give anything to be able to just let go and be with him. No worries, no insecurities, just wet kisses and sweaty skin. But he has no idea what he'd be exposing, what he'd be baring if I let him strip me. Because if he did, he wouldn't want me at all.

"You don't want to do that," I mumble, wishing I didn't have to think or fear or *know*.

"Darlin', if you could see inside my head, you wouldn't doubt it. You'd see. You'd see just how much I *do* want to do that."

"Not everyone is Hollywood perfect."

At that, Rogan stills. With his lips pressed to my pulse and his palm pressed to the swell of my breast, he stops for a second and then raises his head. "There's no such thing as perfect. Everyone has flaws."

I'm glad he can't see the sad smile I offer. "Some worse than others."

Rogan brings his hands back to my face, his thumbs drawing soothing arcs over my cheekbones. "Show me your worst. It won't matter. I'll want you anyway."

Lies. He can't possibly know that. Because he can't possibly know *me*.

Reality rushes in and the spell is broken. All too soon, I'm reminded that this was just one moment in time. Perfect yet fleeting, which is all it can ever be for someone like me. In the harsh light of actuality, nothing has changed. Not from today or yesterday or two weeks ago. Rogan is still a star and I'm still a ruin.

I take a step back, lowering my face and pulling my hair back around to its customary place, hiding behind the thick wave like I've done for so long. "Well, I guess I'd better get going. I think you've got this scene mastered."

Although he lets me go, Rogan is still too close for my peace of mind. When he speaks, I can smell his sweet breath, a mixture of wine and something that's just Rogan. "I'll let you go. For tonight. I think I could still use a little more help, though. I can't screw it up again Monday. One more night oughta do it. Two at the most." Even in the dark, I can see the white glint of his teeth between his spread lips.

Holy crap, that smile! It starts back to work immediately, weakening my resolve.

"What if I have plans?"

"Do you?"

I hedge. I'm always hedging with him, it seems. "I'm not sure yet. But I'll let you know." It's getting harder and harder to say no to him, so I stall until I can. Until I've been away from him long enough for my brain to clear. Until I can think past the fog of his closeness.

"Just give me a call. Or come by. I'll be here. Waiting."

My lips want to smile. My blood wants to sing. My heart wants to soar. But there, in the background, is dread. And sadness. That's why I can't let him see how I feel. No one else can know that, least of all Rogan.

I give him a nod and take another step back, hiding. I'm always hiding.

"Now, for the return ride on the Death Machine," I say, hoping to put things on a more casual level.

Rogan laughs. "It's better you think of it that way."

"Why?" I ask. I'd rather talk than focus on the way it feels when he takes my hand to lead me inside, like it's the most natural thing in the world.

"Because you'd blush a thousand shades of red if you knew how *I* see it. With you on the back. Those legs of yours wrapped around my waist . . . I call it something else."

Heat rushes to my core. His words, the sexy lilt to his voice, the picture that he paints . . . I can fill in the blanks. All too clearly.

"Maybe you should've picked me up in the minivan, then."

"You don't even want to know what I've thought of doing to you in that back of *that* thing."

I feel my mouth twitch in amusement. "Is that all you think about?"

"No." He stops to look down at me, his sparkling green eyes luring me in again. "I think about the way your eyes start to look haunted when you think no one is watching. I think about the way you try not to smile when someone *is* watching. I think about the way you lick the corner of your mouth when you concentrate and how you lose yourself in your work."

"What?" Knowing that he watches me that closely makes me nervous, but it also makes me feel like laughing. And singing. And twirling.

"You think I don't see you, don't you? But I do. I see you. I could watch you and *see you* all day and never get tired of it."

"You'd be bored in no time." I laugh. It bubbles out before I can stop it. It warms me all the way to my toes to know that he pays such close attention to my mannerisms, to my habits. To *me*. "What else?"

"I think about the way you try to disappear. And how much I don't want you to."

As if giving credence to his words, I duck my chin and reach for my hair, teasing the edges, drawing solace from its presence like a reassuring talisman.

Rogan's sigh is so slight I almost don't hear it. But I feel it, like the empty space in a dark room. You can't *see* that it's there, but you can somehow feel it. "Will you ever let me in?"

As though he knows what my response will be, Rogan shakes his head and pulls me forward again, tugging me through the glass doors into the living room, walking me silently back out to his motorcycle.

EIGHTEEN

Rogan

I've got a rip-roaring case of blue balls. I took a shower after I dropped Katie off. Got all hot and soapy, thought about that lush little body of hers and how she pressed her tits to my chest when I kissed her. Thought I'd remove the poisons from the building, if you know what I mean. No dice. I get the feeling only one thing's gonna take care of my . . . problem. And I'm far from cracking that nut.

Shit.

I hit the pulse button on the blender, gritting my teeth as if *I'm* actually pulverizing the fruits, vegetables and whey. When the mixture is nothing more than a foul-looking goop, I pour it into a glass and start chugging.

"Did you save any for me, asshole?"

Kurt.

I'm not in the mood for his attitude this morning.

"There's a little left," I reply mildly, wiping my mouth with the back of my hand. "Help yourself." I can't bring myself to baby his belligerent ass this morning.

"You don't have to be a dick," he snips, grazing my hand with his shoulder as he wheels by me.

"I wasn't being a dick. That's your thing, not mine."

Rather than jerking around toward me, ready to fight, Kurt turns a smug look my way. "Katie didn't seem to mind."

"What the hell *was that*, by the way?"

I'm glad he brought it up so I didn't have to.

"What do you mean? Does it bother you that she flirted with your crippled younger brother?"

"She didn't flirt with you, dude. She was just being nice. That's the way she is."

Although I'm nonchalant about his claim, a stab of jealousy rockets through me. Katie *did* seem more natural, more relaxed, even smiled more when she interacted with Kurt. That shouldn't piss me off. I mean, he *is* my crippled brother. I should be happy for him if he could find someone to love and to love *him*.

Just not Katie.

Evidently I'm not that good of a person. At least not where she's concerned.

"Keep telling yourself that, man." Kurt clucks, smacking the side of the blender to get out the last of the smoothie. I could help him. But I don't. Because, like all Rogan men, sometimes I *can* be an asshole.

I take a swim after my workout, pushing myself harder than usual. There's a bug up my ass and I'm determined to drown it in endorphins. Unfortunately, they're not even strong enough to do the trick. After a shower and lunch, I'm still antsy. I've glanced at the clock a hundred times. The minutes aren't passing swiftly enough. What I really want is to see Katie. Only she hasn't called.

I thought of surprising her this morning. I considered it again this afternoon, but I know I can't push her. She's obviously had some kind of bad experience, likely with a guy, that's made her gun-shy, and the worst possible thing I could do is press her too hard, too fast. But it's frustrating as shit to go so slow when I find myself thinking about her all the time, wondering what she's thinking and what I could do or say to make her smile.

I've never met someone who I had to work for. Hell, I've never wanted to.

Until now.

Until Katie.

There's just something about her. As vague and stupid as that sounds, there *is*. Of course I want to kiss her and peel her prim clothes off to see every inch of her satin skin. Who wouldn't? But I find myself in the unusual place of wanting to get inside her head, too. To find out what scares her and to protect her from it, to do everything I can to take away that wary, distrustful look she carries around so often.

But to do that, I'll have to go at her pace, which is slower than any snail in the history of time.

I glance at my watch again. Maybe she'll show up at my door in another hour or so to rehearse again tonight. I left the invitation open. And if she doesn't, then I'm going to find her. Slow is one thing, but I have to see her tonight. I have to.

Frustrated and full of restless energy, I head back to the pool for more swimming. I have to stay busy or else I'll be on my bike, heading across town, and I damn well know it.

I'm not sure how much time has passed when I'm sitting on the edge of the pool letting my shorts dry. That's when I hear the doorbell.

My smile is immediate. She came.

I leap up and head back through the house, calling out to Kurt in case he heard it, too. "I got it!"

No answer. He's probably wearing his headset, gaming with someone online. Even better. He can stay the hell in there all night. That would suit me just fine. I want Katie all to myself.

I yank open the door without even looking through the glass on either side of the big double wooden panel. I'm not at all pleasantly surprised when I find Rayelle standing in front of me, looking hot in a tank dress that reveals a crazy amount of cleavage and barely covers her ass at the bottom. Yeah, she looks good, but I much prefer Katie's natural, relaxed beauty to this.

My smile is bland. "Rayelle. What are you doing here?"

Her lips curve in a gesture a hungry lioness would be proud of. "I came to help you with your lines. Tony wanted you to rehearse, and who better to help with that than me?"

Likely story. I don't have to ask what she's *really* doing here. I know. I can see it in the eyes that are eating up my mostly naked form.

She came for me. Plain and simple.

I grin at her. "That's awfully nice of you, but I've got plans for tonight. In fact, someone is coming over to read lines with me, but thanks for the offer."

Obviously not one with whom subtlety is effective, Rayelle takes a step toward me, leans in to smash her tits up against my chest and plants her mouth onto mine. Her tongue is working its way between my lips at the same time that her hands are skimming their way down my bare stomach to the waistband of my shorts. I don't push her away. I wait until she breaks the kiss. This is going to be awkward enough as it is.

I look down into her smoky eyes as she reaches inside my shorts. That's when I take her wrist to stop her hand.

"I'm pretty sure that's not in the script," I tell her lightly.

"Not yet. But you know it's coming. Why not get a little practice in? You know, for the love of the craft. Make it as convincing as possible." Her smile is sexy and feline as hell. She's all but purring and rubbing herself on me like a damn cat. "I promise you'll enjoy it."

"As, uh, *tempting* as that sounds, it's just not a good time."

The heat in her eyes fades just enough that I know she's finally getting the hint. "Is this about Victoria? Are you two back together?" She steps away. No one wants to be on the receiving end of Victoria's claws.

"No, it's not Victoria."

Now she just looks confused. I'm sure a girl like this can't fathom any other explanation for being turned down. I doubt rejection is something she even considered when she was driving over here.

Her eyes narrow and then widen, like she just thought of the *only possible reason* I might not want a no-strings-attached bang. "Are you gay?"

I would laugh if it weren't so pathetic. She'd rather chalk it up to me being gay than just not being interested. "Hell no, I'm not gay."

"Then, what?"

"I've got other plans tonight. With someone else," I say gently, trying my best to protect her ego. I don't need any more claws pointed in my direction. *Damn, these divas are complicated!*

That only makes me appreciate Katie that much more. Only Katie's not here. And my guess is that she's not coming.

I'm relieved when my phone rings, interrupting what is becoming an increasingly uncomfortable situation. It gives me an excuse to get rid of Rayelle, which I do immediately.

"Thanks for coming, Rayelle, but I need to get this." Without further explanation, I close the door in her shocked face and tap the ANSWER button. I don't really give a shit who it is, but I want to thank the caller with an expensive bottle of scotch.

Until I hear the voice. And then I want to thank her with a long, hot kiss and three hours of worshipping her body.

It's Katie. I put my number in her phone last night. I'd hoped she'd use it. Or better yet just show up. At least she's doing one.

"Rogan?" she asks, uncertain.

"Damn, am I glad to hear your voice," I tell her honestly.

Her laugh is light and pleased. "Why is that?"

"Besides the fact that it sounds like warm honey in my ear, you just saved me from getting devoured."

"Oh?"

"Yeah. Surprise visit from Rayelle. Unexpected and not at all welcome."

"Poor you. What a chore it must be to fend off the advances of beautiful women."

"It is when there's only one beautiful woman that I'm interested in. Are you coming over?"

Shit, bro, could you be any more anxious?

"No, that's why I'm calling. Mona needs me to run some errands for her. It's important. I'm sorry, but I won't be able to make it."

"You can come after. Sunset over the pool would look amazing on your skin."

"Uhhh, thank you, but I'd better not."

"I assume there's nothing I can say to change your mind."

I'm disappointed. Very disappointed. I wanted to see her again. Hell, right now it feels like I *needed* to see her again.

"No, I'm afraid not."

I don't push Katie and I certainly don't tell her my plan, but I *will* be seeing her tonight. I just need to get ahold of Mona to find out where she'll be.

NINETEEN

Katie

I'd already been nervous about agreeing to see Rogan again today, so when my phone rang, I was relieved that it was Mona. I wasn't really looking for an excuse to back out of my date tonight, but when my friend practically handed me one, gift-wrapped, I jumped on it.

"White had me arrange a party for some of the cast on his boat. He wanted to spend the day out here and then take them all to that little private island for the rest of the night. The problem is, the liquor for the bar hasn't arrived. Ronnie is on the island now, setting up sound and some of the other stuff White wanted. He said the bar is still empty, though, and I'm freakin'! I mean, what's a Hollywood party without alcohol?" she'd explained. There was panic in her voice, which is the biggest reason I agreed immediately.

"Okay, just calm down. What is it that you need me to do?"

"Could you go to the liquor store and pick up the things on the list I just texted you and bring it to the island? Please, please, please, please, please!"

"Mona, I don't have a boat. How am I supposed to get it there?"

"It's not a *real* island. They just call it that because it sticks out into the lake like an island. There's a gated drive that leads to it from Downton Drive. Do you know where that is?"

"I know where it is. Give me an hour to get it and have it there for you. Will Ronnie still be there to help me unload it?"

"I'll tell him to wait for you. You're a lifesaver, Katie! Have I ever told you that?"

I smiled. "I think you might've mentioned it a time or two."

"Don't leave until I get there, okay?"

"Okay. I'll wait for you."

That was over an hour ago. I called Rogan and then left right away.

The guy at the liquor store was more than happy to help me cram my vehicle with boxes of assorted liters of alcohol. I wondered if my little car would even be able to move when I drove out of the parking lot. Heaven forbid I break down or get into a wreck. It would surely look like I have an enormous drinking problem. It seems to be doing fine, though, as I carefully take each curve on the way to the lake.

I slow down as I search for the gated drive that will lead me to the "island." Even though I'm watching for it, I cruise right by the entrance. I drive farther down the road, searching for a place to turn around. It seems there's just a big bunch of nothing past the very private entrance to the island. Finally, I just stop, check my rearview for oncoming traffic, of which there is none since this isn't exactly a well-traveled street, then I steer the car into a wide arc and perform about a six-point turn right in the middle of the road. I'm relieved when I don't get caught or hit. On my return, I watch

more carefully for the gate. From this angle, I see that it's slightly
ajar. Probably Ronnie, making it easier for me to get in.

I smile as I think of him. The friendly redhead has been very
very nice to me from day one at the studio. I see him almost every
morning and he's always kind and sweet.

The trees on either side of the road part farther, forming a clearing that boasts an amazing view of the lake. Six cheerfully-striped
canvas cabanas housing intimate seating groups are set up in a
semi-circle. They face a central tent in white canvas that covers
several tables. Each is draped in linen and set with all kinds of
food. Sitting along the back "wall" is a tiki bar.

I look around for signs of life. I don't see Ronnie anywhere, but
at least I know where I'm supposed to take all this liquor.

I park sideways. I'm blocking the road, but I don't really care.
It'll be easier to unload my car this way.

I lug the first of the boxes out of the trunk. I carry it toward the
lake, between two cabanas and under the main tent to the bar at the
back where I set it down on the ground. Dusting off my hands, I go
to turn around. I yelp when I find Ronnie standing right behind me.

"Wow!" he exclaims, his eyes raking me appreciatively from
head to toe. "And I thought you looked amazing in work clothes."

I didn't think to change clothes before I left. Not that I would
have. I mean, the jeans and scoop-necked tee I'm wearing are hardly
indecent. They're just a bit more . . . fitted than the clothes I normally wear to work, which consist of either loose cotton dresses or
dress pants and blouses. Nothing fancy, nothing with much personality. It's been years since I've dressed to impress anyone.

Until Rogan.

Damn it.

"Thanks," I reply casually. "Wanna help me unload some boxes?"

"Anything for you," he declares with his easy smile.

A dozen boxes and enough liquor to rot a small town's liver later, we are finished setting up the bar.

Ronnie is standing with his hands in his pockets, grinning at me. "What do you say we open up one of those bottles of vodka and break it in?"

I put on my politely removed face. "I'd love to, but I can't."

"You sure?" he asks, walking to the bar and pulling out a clear liter. He disappears for a second and when his head pops back up, he's holding two martini glasses, a shallow dish of something and a lemon. "I make a kick-ass lemon drop."

I'm just about to reiterate my refusal when my phone rings. It's Mona again.

"Did you get the liquor? Did you find the place? Was Ronnie still there?"

"Yes, yes and yes. Now breathe."

So she does. She exhales so loudly I can hear it *whoosh*ing in my ear. "You are an angel. An absolute angel!"

Even though she can't see me, I shrug. "It was no problem."

"I appreciate it more than you'll ever know. White would've . . . Ugh! Yeah. You know how that would've gone."

"I know. Not pretty." White is anal, which is probably why he makes such a good producer. He's a details man.

"We should be there shortly. Will you stay for a few minutes after I get there?" Her tone is hopeful.

"Meh. I'm really not in the mood to—"

"Katiiie!" I can almost hear Mona stomp her foot. "You're never in the mood. Can't you stay? Just for a little while? For me? Pleeease!"

I frown. This isn't like Mona. Normally all she ever needs is White and she's happy as a clam. Unless things aren't going well. "Is something wrong?"

The long pause and her short response say it all. "It's White."

Her voice is small and wounded, and I can hear the resignation in it.

I don't have to ask what he's done. It's the only thing he ever does to hurt Mona. Unfortunately, he does it with disgusting regularity. "Who is it?"

"Peony," she answers miserably, bringing to mind the mental image of a trashy, raven-haired beauty. She plays the resident freak on the show and she's very convincing. Mainly, we suspect, because she's such a freak in real life. Dark, brooding, daring. Admits to loving sadomasochism. Observes some pretty scary "personal pleasure rituals." Thinks the devil talks to her. That kind of thing.

"Peony? Ewww. Why?"

"I know, right? White doesn't even like brunettes. And she's named after a stinky old flower. I just don't . . . I can't . . ." I hear the tremor in her voice and I know she's about to lose it. Now is definitely not the time to tell her that peonies don't stink. They actually smell quite good.

I hold back my sigh. My friend needs me. "Of course I'll wait for you."

Like a ray of sunshine breaking through thick, ominous clouds, I hear the pleasure and relief in her voice. She needs to be with someone who won't hurt her. Someone like me. "Really? You will?"

"Really. I will."

"Promise?"

"I promise."

"You're the best, Kitty."

When we hang up I turn back to Ronnie, who is just slurping the last sip from his martini glass and preparing to make another. "Why don't you make that two?"

Ronnie smiles and whoops enthusiastically. I feel an answering smile curve my own mouth.

An hour later, I'm two drinks in, Ronnie is starting to slur and Mona still hasn't arrived. I check my phone to make sure I haven't missed a call.

Nope. Nothing.

"Excuse me for just a second," I tell Ronnie when he pauses in his rambling long enough for me to get a word in.

I get up and walk toward shore, scanning the dark lake horizon for the lights of an approaching yacht. I see nothing except the reflection of the dozens of flaming tiki torches that are burning to illuminate the island setting.

I turn back and slip into one of the cabanas for a little privacy as I tap Mona's number into my phone. The way she answers, I can picture her with one finger stuffed in her other ear so she can hear me on the phone. "Don't leave!" she says without preamble, practically screaming. "We'll be there in just a few minutes."

"It's getting late. I need to get home."

"It's nowhere near late, Katie! Don't you dare leave yet. I'm coming. I swear."

"I'll wait as long as I can, but if you're not here in another thirty minutes, I'll have to go."

She huffs. "Fine. But give me thirty minutes. We aren't that far away. We'll be there shortly."

"That's what you said an hour ago."

"Well, that's what I thought an hour ago. Nautical . . . *stuff* isn't exactly my area of expertise."

"Okay, okay," I say in frustration. "Thirty minutes."

"See you soon." And then the line goes dead.

I inhale deeply and turn to find my way back to Ronnie. And run right into him. He's standing behind me in the cabana. I grab my chest to still my runaway heart. "Ronnie! God, you scared me."

"Sorry," he slurs softly. "I just wanted to make sure you're okay."

"I'm fine," I say, taking a step back, away from his crowding closeness.

Ronnie takes a step forward. "You look so beautiful tonight. I just can't get over the way your ass looks in jeans."

What a crude thing to say, especially from Ronnie, who's always fairly mild in his appreciation.

A little thread of unease weaves its way down my spine. "Thanks. I think. Let's go back out to the tent. Mona said they'll be here in a couple of minutes."

I start to walk around him, but he winds his fingers around my upper arm to stop me, pulling me against his side. "Sit and talk with me then. Just for a couple of minutes."

Still gripping my arm, Ronnie pivots slowly, backing toward the day bed–type structure that's piled with pillows. There's one in each cabana. As inviting as it looks, I don't want to sit on it and talk to a drunk Ronnie.

I plant my feet, resisting his guidance.

"I don't think that's a good idea. You've had a lot to drink, Ronnie."

He laughs, giving me a sharp tug that unbalances me. I careen forward, right into his arms, which he folds around me as we fall together back onto the makeshift bed.

I make a strangled squeaking sound, surprised by the sudden movement. Alarm flashes through me. I go from uneasy to distinctly uncomfortable with Ronnie's insistence. I push against his chest in an attempt to find my feet, but rather than letting me go, he laughs and rolls until I'm trapped beneath his weight. Considering how short I am and what a big guy Ronnie is, he holds me down with little effort. I'd say he's easily twice as heavy as me.

"I think we've flirted around this attraction long enough, Katie, don't you?" he says, his voice gruff with intoxicated passion.

Before I can set him straight, Ronnie smashes his mouth against mine. I clamp my lips together, my body going stiff as a board beneath him. That does nothing to deter him, however. He runs his overly wet tongue over my cheek and down to my neck, his hands multiplying by the second. They're everywhere—massaging my breast, rubbing my side, gripping my butt, tugging my legs apart.

My alarm increases tenfold when he wedges his hips between mine and starts to grind against me. He's moaning against my throat, licking and kissing and crushing me with his weight. I feel breathless, but not in a good way. It's as though the pressure of his thick chest is collapsing my lungs.

"Ronnie, stop," I manage in a pant.

"I know you want this as much as I do. You don't have to pretend. I heard you on the phone. They won't be here for a while. We've got enough time, sweet thing."

As I struggle to bring up my chin and pull in gulps of fresh air, Ronnie's fingers curl into the neckline of my shirt, dragging it down and pressing slobbery kisses to my chest. Panic begins to well within me when I hear the seam crackle.

"You feel so good, Katie. I can't wait one more minute."

Ronnie leans up as if to start taking off my clothes and I use the moment of freedom from his suffocating torso to twist my upper body out from under him. I try to wriggle away, but my movements seem only to further inflame him. "That's right. Show me some fight. If you like it rough, I'm down with that."

As if to prove his point, Ronnie runs a determined hand between our bodies, pressing his palm to the apex of my thighs and rubbing hard with the heel of his hand. I buck my hips against him, trying to unseat him, but he holds me down effortlessly.

"God, I can't wait to be inside you," he mumbles as he rubs.

I don't stop fighting. I can't.

When I've managed to wiggle us toward the foot of the bed, a little closer to a possible escape, Ronnie seems to sense the direction I'm thinking and he runs a hand beneath me to push us up farther onto the bed. This time he stretches out full-length on top of me, trapping my legs between his as he rolls his top half away. For a second, his face is illuminated by the flickering torches and I see a mad desire in his eyes. That's when true fear blazes through me. In my gut, I realize that he's not going to take no for an answer.

"Ronnie, I mean it. Get off me *right now*," I hiss.

"If only your body agreed with what that filthy little mouth is saying," he says with a growling laugh, taking both of my wrists and jerking my arms above my head. His hands are so big, he subdues them both in one of his, leaving the other free to roam over my torso and follow along with his mouth.

My shirt has ridden up my abdomen, leaving my midriff bare. He rubs his palm over the skin and then shoves it up under my shirt, easily pushing my bra up with it. I feel him turn his hand and, with a yank, snap the front closure open, exposing me to the cool night air.

I catch and hold my breath, the reality of my situation momentarily paralyzing me. He finds my right breast immediately, kneading and pinching painfully. It's the way that he attacks my naked flesh, like a ravenous dog, that puts me into motion.

Jerking, kicking and twisting every muscle in my body at the same time, I fight Ronnie with all the fight that I can find. I unearth a panicked scream somewhere from the bottom of my burning lungs just before he grabs a handful of my shirt and rips it from me in one sharp wrench.

I don't even try to cover myself with my hands. I flutter them around, trying to keep them from being recaptured. When I find his face, I sink my fingernails into Ronnie's temples. I dig in and pull, raking my nails down and tearing his skin as I go. Ronnie howls in pain and, even in the dark, I see the streaks of blood appear on either side of his face.

"You bitch! That's *too* rough!"

Ronnie dips his head and bites my chest. I push at his shoulders and cry out in panic, tears of pain and fear streaming from the corners of my eyes to wet the hair at my temples.

Ronnie leans back, clamping his thighs around mine as he works the button and zipper of my jeans, opening them despite my thrashing. When he stills, so do I. I don't know why he suddenly stopped, but I'm prepared to fight like a hellcat when he moves off my legs.

"Damn, what happened to you?" he asks, the sneer of disgust plainly visible on his shadowed face. The swift change takes me by surprise, but only for a second. Then it registers. I don't have to ask what he means; I already know. My scars. "Lucky for you, you're still hot enough to make this worth my while."

I feel the grip of his thighs lessen ever so slightly. This is my chance. My muscles are tight with readiness. I'm going to kick out with all my might, aiming right for his balls, the instant I can get my legs free.

They loosen a bit more, and then suddenly I'm free. Aiming for his crotch, I squeeze my eyes shut and lash out with my feet as hard as I can. Strangely, they meet nothing but air.

Although I'm confused, I don't waste valuable time wondering what happened or looking around for Ronnie. I roll quickly to one side and scramble to my feet, running wildly in the opposite direction of the cabana. I have no intention of stopping, maybe ever, until I hear a voice. A familiar voice. A voice that's not Ronnie's.

"What the hell do you think you're doing, you piece of shit?"

I whip my head back around, my wide, terrified pupils immediately focusing on Rogan's tall, hulking form hovering over a curled body. It's Ronnie, lying in the fetal position on the ground at Rogan's feet. He's holding his stomach.

Rogan bends, taking a handful of Ronnie's thatch of red hair and holding his head still while he brings his fist down. I hear the sickening crunch of bone just as blood spurts from Ronnie's nose. Rogan releases his head, letting it bounce against the sparse field of grass beneath him.

"Make him stop, Katie. Tell him to stop," Ronnie pleads in a pained, desperate voice muffled by the hands he's holding up to his face.

I don't tell him that I have no intention of doing any such thing. But I don't need to. At the mention of my name, Rogan whirls to face me, his eyes taking me in. He rushes toward me, bending slightly to put his face in line with mine. "Are you okay?" he asks, tenderly palming my cheeks. His expression is wild and worried.

The surreal quality of the moment is only intensified by the sound of hysterical hiccupping and sniffling that I soon realize is my own. "Ye-ye-yeah."

Rogan folds his arms around me, pulling me against his chest and stroking my hair with a soothing hand. "I'm here now, darlin'. You're safe. You're safe. I won't let anything happen to you."

And for some reason, I believe him.

TWENTY

Rogan

I'm torn. I want to go back and beat the ever-lovin' shit out of the asshat who put his hands on Katie, but having her in my arms . . . knowing how vulnerable she is right now . . . how much she needs safety and security and strength . . . Well, nothing could take me away from that. Away from *her*. Not even the lust for blood.

I'm so glad that I managed to track Katie down. It took some finagling, but I finally managed to get Mona's number once I was able to get hold of White. It pays to be an actor working on his show.

Mona told me where Katie was and that she was waiting for the boat to arrive. I hauled ass out here to find her. Passed the damn entrance twice. It was hard as hell to spot in the dark. And then when I did finally manage to get here, this is what I find.

I grit my teeth, holding Katie close and bending my head to whisper in her ear. "Let me get you out of here. I'll keep you safe."

She doesn't argue, just continues to cry softly into my neck as I sweep her up in my arms and carry her toward my bike. It's as I'm nearing it that I remember she's practically naked from the waist up. That image—the one of her standing at the edge of the light, chest heaving, perfectly rounded breasts swaying, eyes wild—will be burned into my memory for the rest of my days, I suspect. *Holy shit!* So will this rush of desire. I've never felt anything like it. It might be intensified by the rage that I'm experiencing, too. I thought I'd left that kind of emotion behind me, but tonight . . . *Mother of God!* Even growing up with a father like mine or during my time in the Army, I don't think I've ever wanted to hurt another person so much, so *violently*. I know that'll be another picture I won't soon forget—that asshole holding her down, touching her, trying to force himself on her.

My blood boils just thinking about it. With the iron will that I honed early on in my life, I make myself calm down, focusing on the wounded creature in my arms and how she doesn't need anything but tenderness now. My fury can wait. Katie comes first.

"Are your keys in the car?" I ask, pressing my lips to the crown of her head. Her hair smells like flowers and that hint of musk that seems to be unique to this woman.

She doesn't speak, only nods. Relieved, I change trajectory, going to her car rather than back to my bike. I open the passenger side door and place her gently in the seat. Her arms are crossed protectively over her chest. Despite the fact that her modesty is mostly preserved by them, I tuck the tattered remains of her shirt around her.

As I straighten away, Katie's glistening eyes meet mine. They look tortured. Ashamed even, which I find a little bizarre considering what almost happened to her. Maybe it's normal for the victim to feel shame. What the hell do I know?

She turns her face away, tucking her chin against her shoulder.

"Thank you," she murmurs. And then she starts to cry again, a delicate, heartbroken sound that claws at my heart.

"You don't need to thank me. I would never let anyone hurt you. Never," I tell her as earnestly as I know how.

That just seems to make her cry harder, so I close the door and round to the driver's side, scooting the seat back and sliding in behind the wheel.

With only the occasional muted sound of Katie's sobs to break the silence, I make the trip back across town to her house. After I park, I take the keys out of the ignition and go unlock her door before returning to scoop her out of the low seat and carry her inside.

I place her gently on the couch and turn to go close the door, but Katie's words stop me. "Please don't leave me," she whispers brokenly.

I take three long steps toward the door, just enough to get me close enough to kick it shut before I return to the sofa. I lean down to draw her into my arms one more time, settling her on my lap with her head on my shoulder. Then I answer her. "I'm not going anywhere."

With Katie cradled against me, we sit in silence, the only noise coming from the cat, who's purring loudly from his perch on the back of the couch. My arm falls asleep long before Katie stops crying. I don't know if it happens suddenly or if it just *feels* like it happens suddenly. Either way, it's like one minute she's shaking and the next minute she's looking up at me from beneath her lashes.

I'm surprised by what I see when I look down at her. There's fire in her eyes. Something like a rebellious anger maybe. I don't ask questions, even though I want to. I just wait for her to speak. I let her set the pace.

Finally, she levers herself away from me, sliding her legs between mine until her feet touch the floor. I miss holding her the instant I no longer feel her warmth against me. I liked being close to someone who's impossible to get close to. But I don't tell her that. I just hold my tongue and wait.

Katie stands to her feet, clutching the shreds of her shirt around her as she backs slowly away from me. She stops when there's about two feet separating us and she straightens. She looks like she's bolstering herself. I can see her spine stiffen and her chin ratchet up a few notches. The difference is subtle, but it feels profound. Fierce. And I'm instantly curious about it. Gone is the timid girl who hides away behind downcast eyes and a swath of comforting hair. She's been replaced by this bold, kind of ferocious woman standing in front of me.

Surprising the shit out of me, Katie lets the pieces of her shirt fall away. Bra, too. They dangle at her sides for a few seconds before she tears them off, almost viciously. She tosses them onto the floor with jerky movements. My mouth drops open as I take in the sight of her. Blue eyes flash hotly, lush lips thin into a determined line, chest swells beneath mouthwatering tits as she inhales deeply. She's fiery. And beautiful. And I've never wanted anything more in my whole miserable life. I'll never forget this either. I know that tonight is already full of images that will probably haunt me for a long time to come.

I can't stop myself from looking at the rest of her, so proudly on display. Her breasts are creamy and bigger than I imagined, capped with delicately pink nipples that pucker toward the sky. Her stomach is flat, dipping in at the sides to give her a perfect hourglass shape that flares into her slim hips.

God, she's amazing!

As I eat her up with my gaze, she shifts slightly, causing the light to glint off some less-than-smooth skin. My eyes focus on the pebbly texture that stretches from the left side of her neck down, grazing her shoulder and then disappearing until it picks up again below her ribs on the left side of her torso.

When she speaks, her voice is too hard for someone so breath-taking. "This is what I hide. This is what Ronnie discovered. This is what disgusted him." Her face is full of anger and bitterness.

"But, Katie, I—"

"This is why you don't want me. Not really. This is why I'll never be the girl for you. You just didn't know it." With her pause, she sticks out her chest in defiance. "But *now* you do."

It's obvious she's trying to push me away. I just don't understand why. I'm frowning when my eyes drift back up to hers, which are spitting fire. "You couldn't be more wrong," I tell her softly. She's more wrong than she could ever know. This doesn't make her any less perfect. It just makes her more fragile. If anything, I'm drawn to her in a totally different way. Something fiercely protective rises up inside me, something that rivals the way I felt at the lake a little while ago.

I have to know what happened to her. I have to know about her past. I have to know how she was hurt so badly.

I rise slowly to my feet and step closer to her, brushing over the bumpy skin with the tips of my fingers. I know it doesn't hurt her anymore. Scars don't have feeling. They're numb, thankfully. But I also know that some hurts run so deep they never heal. And I have a feeling this is one that goes all the way to her soul. "What happened? Who did this to you?"

Despite the way her eyes are flashing at me, I see her chin tremble. This is hard for her. *Very hard*, evidently. Maybe it's the memories. Maybe it's the fact that scars are often a thousand times uglier to the person wearing them. Or maybe it's some other ghost I know nothing about.

"I had a different life before this one. And it involved a man a lot like you. He used his fists instead of words and he prized beauty above all else. He thought I was beautiful. Too beautiful. He was always jealous of something or someone else in my life. When I left him, he couldn't take it. So he found me. And he set my car on fire. With me in it." Her chin trembles and her voice cracks. "And then I wasn't beautiful anymore."

My stomach clenches. Like I'm doing crunches, but it's involuntary. There are few people I've ever felt really connected to, people I've wanted to shield or defend. My brother. The men on Delta Five, my team in the Army. But with them it was different. It was like a brotherhood. Loyalty. Solidarity. Never have I felt anything like *this* before. Never.

Until I met her.

Until I met Katie.

My gut churns. Fury. Sadness. Determination. Defensiveness. Tenderness. And a thousand feelings I don't have names for.

All I can think of, though, is that she didn't deserve this. She didn't deserve what it has done to her life.

As these thoughts run through my head, I'm staggered by the desire to take away her pain, to guard her from the shitty curveballs life has thrown her way. And from any more that could hurt her.

"He was an asshole and a fool if he thought *anything* could make you less desirable. Now you're *even more* what I want."

If I hadn't been watching her so closely over the last few weeks, I'd never have seen the slight softening of her features. It's practically undetectable. But not entirely.

"But *why*? Why *me*? Can't you understand how ridiculous that sounds? Look at me! I'm scarred. Ugly. Men like you don't do ugly."

I move slowly, cautiously. I uncurl fingers I wasn't even aware of drawing into fists, and I reach for her again. I brush away the hair that wants to fall back over her shoulder, like she's trained it to cover her. I bend to press my lips to the curve of her neck, to the scars that have haunted her for so long. "This doesn't make you less," I tell her softly. "It makes you *more*. More beautiful, more desirable. It makes you a survivor. A winner. Someone worth having." I drop my voice into a whisper. "Someone worth loving."

I move to nuzzle the soft space beneath her ear, gratified by the subtle change in her breathing. It turns from a heave to a sigh as she leans into me just a few centimeters. But a few centimeters is enough. It's enough to assure me that I'm reading her right. Despite what has happened, despite the turmoil of the day, she wants me. Like I want her. She cares what I think. She might not want to, but she does. And that's good. Because I care, too. Maybe more than I should, especially for a girl who wants nothing except to push people away.

"Can't you just trust me? Just a little? Can't you let me love you?"

The pause before her answer is so long I think she might not answer.

But then she does.

"I–I'm afraid," comes her barely audible response.

"Don't be. I've got you. I won't let anything hurt you. Including me."

She's silent for a long time as I press tiny kisses along her jaw and cheek, stroking the smooth parts of her skin to put her at ease.

"Please don't disappoint me."

Her request is like a punch in the gut. The pain, the raw plea in her voice cuts through me like a knife.

"I'd rather take a beating than disappoint you."

She raises tentative hands to curl her fingers around my biceps. I feel them tremble. I feel her fight as clearly as if it were my own. But I also feel her give in.

"Then love me."

She doesn't have to tell me twice.

TWENTY-ONE

Katie

For the first time since I woke up from a medically induced coma in the hospital five years ago, I'm letting go. I'm trusting. I'm throwing all my caution, all my insecurity, all my reasons out the window and I'm letting someone in. All the way in.

For the first time, I'm trying to live.

Rogan has seen me. All of me. All the ugly, all the fear, and he still wants me. I might never experience this again, so for just this one moment in time, I'm giving in.

I don't protest when he slides one arm behind my back and the other beneath my knees to sweep me off my feet. In the bedroom, he sets me at the foot of the bed, but he doesn't back away. Instead, he stands so close I can feel the heat radiating from his chest, from his stomach, from his thighs, warming me through and through.

He lowers his mouth to mine in a kiss that sears me—my flesh, my heart, my soul. It says he accepts me. It says he wants me. It says that, for now, he won't hurt me. He'll only make me feel beautiful and special and loved. Not like a freak show.

With every soft brush of his lips, he rubs away Ronnie's touch. He rubs away Calvin, my ex's, fists. He replaces the flames of my past with a new kind of fire, the kind that kindles low in my belly and spreads through my limbs in a slow blaze.

"You taste so good," he mutters as he licks along the crease of my lips. "I bet you're delicious *everywhere*."

My knees go all soft at his words. It's been so long . . . So, so long . . .

Rogan spreads kisses across my collarbone and down the center of my chest. His hands come up to palm my breasts. He grazes my nipples with his thumbs and I let my head drop back on my shoulders, the sensation tingling all the way down my arms to my fingertips.

"So beautiful," he says as his lips travel to cover one nipple. The first touch of his tongue, hotter than any real fire, causes me to gasp. "Do you like that?" he asks, swirling wet heat around the sensitive peak. I don't respond. I simply thread my fingers into his hair and hold him to me. He laughs, a deep throaty chuckle that vibrates through my breast. "Mmmm, that's what I thought."

When he sucks my turgid flesh into his mouth, I arch my back, pressing into him. I feel as much as hear his groan. His response is immediate. He pulls and tugs and nibbles at my nipple as his fingers twist and tweak the other one. My stomach clenches and moisture floods my panties.

Switching from hand to mouth at my other breast, Rogan treats it to the same pleasure as he moves his palm down my stomach to the closure of my jeans. With a flick, he releases the button and slides the zipper down, running his fingers just under the elastic of my panties to cup my hipbone.

He releases my nipple and drags his lips down to my bellybutton, where he swirls his tongue inside, his hand coming around to cup my butt and push my jeans a little farther down.

"Seems like I've wanted this forever," he murmurs against me, kissing lower. "And it's even better than I imagined."

I steel myself against the urge to flinch when Rogan tugs the denim of my pants down my legs, his fingers grazing more scarred flesh. The burns splatter my hip and leg, running all the way to my knee. He doesn't seem to care, though, which relaxes me. He only presses his lips to each expanse of battered skin, as if he's telling the universe that it's okay for me to look this way. "So beautiful," he whispers, nothing but sincerity in his voice.

When he reaches my feet, he slips off my shoes and then my jeans, leaving me standing before him in nothing but my panties. I glance down, my skin burning up under his gaze as it travels slowly up my body to meet mine. What I see in his smoky green eyes makes me feel elated and excited and . . . happy. Happier than I've been in a long time.

"You're amazing," he claims sincerely. Reaching up, he runs his hands from my ribs all the way down my sides, his fingers skating over both healthy and scarred skin to curl into the edges of my panties. He pulls them off as he explores my legs. When I step out of them, I watch his face, eating up the pure lust I see there. I never thought anyone would look at me that way again. Not when they could *really* see me. But it's there. Plain as the nose on my face. More incredible than the sun in the sky.

His eyes don't meet mine as I watch him. He seems oblivious to my scrutiny, in fact. His attention is focused on the small triangle between my legs.

I throb when he licks his lips, my muscles clenching as though his tongue touched *me*.

I hold my breath as he leans forward to press a single kiss to the space between my navel and the top of my aching folds. My mouth drops open on a silent moan when his tongue sneaks out to flick and tease me all the way down to my crease. Air leaves my lungs in a hot rush when he dips it inside, laving my clit with the pointed tip of his tongue.

"Unh." I can't help the sound that escapes. I can't hold it in for one more second.

As he massages me, Rogan runs his palms up the insides of my thighs, urging me to spread them for him. So I do, opening me up to more of his fiery mouth. He licks me in long strokes, nearing my entrance, but not giving me the satisfaction of feeling him there.

Just when I'm beginning to feel frustrated, with his tongue still licking at my clit, Rogan eases a single, long finger into me, nearly causing my knees to buckle. He pulls out slowly then slides back in with two fingers this time. My lids drift closed as he thrusts into me, in and out, each stroke a little harder and a little deeper than the one before. Faster and higher he pushes me until I'm riding the edge of climax.

And then he stops.

I'm panting, my body tense and achy, as Rogan stands to his feet in front of me. "Not yet, baby. Not yet."

With my wanting eyes glued to him, Rogan pulls his own T-shirt over his head. In the low light pouring through the door from the living room, his muscles flex like malleable bronze. My fingers tingle with the need to touch the satin skin covering them.

His biceps twitch and the ropy muscles of his forearms glide as he works the numerous buttons on his jeans. I can't take my eyes away. As he bends to push them down his legs, I see his abs contract. And when he stands, straight and tall and naked before me, they relax and I see what lies south of them. He takes my breath away. Literally.

I feel lightheaded as I look over Rogan. I've never seen anything more perfect. I've seen a few bits and pieces, but the whole package . . . displayed all at once . . . just for me . . . it's overwhelming.

With curious, reverent hands, I reach out to test the smooth skin of his broad chest, to cup his rounded pecs, to palm his rigid stomach. When I reach his hips, I drop down to my knees in front of him, amazed by the sheer beauty and size of him. His erection is as long and thick and strong as the rest of him. Straight and perfect.

Without thinking, I wind my fingers around his satiny length, reveling at the way it expands inside my grip. I see a drop of fluid appear on the crown and I lean forward to capture it with the tip of my tongue, wanting to taste him like he tasted me. When I hear the hiss of his breath, I look up in question.

"Maybe you should save that for later. This has been a long time coming." His grin is crooked and charming and . . . *Rogan*. All Rogan.

Rogan moves so fast that he startles me, so I yip when he bends to scoop me up and throw me onto the bed. A laugh bubbles up in my throat and I set it free.

Rogan puts a knee on the end of the bed and crawls slowly up the mattress toward me. Like a predator. A beautiful, heart-stopping predator.

His lips are curved in a smile that makes my insides quiver. When he reaches me where I'm half-lying with my legs curled up toward me, he grabs my ankles and yanks gently, pulling me to him and spreading my thighs wide at the same time. I suppress the excited squeal and lie back to see what he does next.

His eyes are dark with passion. I'd never know they were green, they're so smoky with what's between us. "Now, where was I?" he asks me, his gaze boring hotly into mine before he bends his head to bury it between my legs.

With pressure from his hands, Rogan bends my knees and pushes them apart, exposing me fully to his ravenous mouth. He licks and strokes me with his tongue. He kisses and thrills me with his lips.

He brings one hand up, spreading me wide with his fingers so he can suck my clit into his mouth. I cry out in some feral sound that I've never made before. I can't help myself. It's a sensation like nothing I've ever *felt* before.

With my flesh in his mouth, Rogan flicks his tongue over it until my hips move against his face. I spiral upward, mindless and completely out of control.

As though he can sense how close I am to orgasm, he eases back just enough to make me want to scream. "God, you've got the most amazing pussy. I could drink come from you like wine. Sweet, creamy wine. But not this time. This time," he explains, his voice gruff and sexy, "I wanna feel you squeezin' my cock when you come."

He gently rubs his soft lips back and forth over me as he rustles a wrapper. Somehow he manages to keep me poised right at the edge, but not quite able to reach it. It's almost tantric in its torture.

When he's sheathed with a condom, Rogan increases his pace, making quick Zs with his tongue until I feel like I might explode. Just before I do, he stops. Quickly, he kisses his way up my body until he's covering me with his own. With his eyes on mine, he reaches down and hooks one arm under my knee, simultaneously tipping my hips up and widening my legs.

I can feel his engorged head hovering at my entrance, my body clutching at it. He remains still, green eyes melting into my blue. "You're beautiful. Every inch of you. Do you hear me, Katie?" he asks insistently. "You're more beautiful than anything I've ever seen."

I don't answer. I'm not sure I even *can*. But he wants me to.

"Tell me you hear me. Say it." He's panting now, his muscles trembling with his restraint.

"Yes. I hear you."

"Good. Uhhh." His fierce groan, forced through his gritted teeth, echoes the explosion of my heart as Rogan plunges into me.

My back arches in the pleasure-pain of his size as he stretches me in every direction. He pauses just long enough for me to relax around him and then he withdraws to thrust into me again, going all the way this time, so deep I gasp.

He grinds his hips into mine, his body hitting mine with the most delicious friction. I want to hold on. I want to enjoy this as long as I can. Forever. But it's too late. It feels too good. I can't wait one second longer, so it's with his third thrust that I come apart.

All the buildup of the last several minutes hits me like a tsunami. Waves of intense bliss roll through me, *all* through me. It tingles in my legs, throbs in my belly, squeezes in my core. Blood and pleasure rush through me in a hot release, like the bursting of a dam.

As my body contracts around his, Rogan growls, dropping his face into the curve of my neck. "*Holy mother of God* you feel so fucccc— Uhhh!" He sounds savage. Out of control. And I love it.

He pulls out of me, returning quickly to thrust sharply into me. Hard. Deep. He tilts his hips, reinvigorating my body's response to him. I wrap myself around him. I've never felt such powerful, consuming pleasure. My ears even ring with what's happening inside me.

After a few seconds of more intense spasms, Rogan pushes back onto his haunches, ready to chase his own peak. He presses my legs up and out, leans back and pounds into me. It isn't until he reaches between us and circles his fingers around the base of his cock that my eyes follow his. He's touching both of us at the same time, his long, thick erection disappearing into me like a jackhammer. It's shiny with my juices, the noises decadent and intimate.

When his eyes rise back to mine, I see in them what I'm feeling. Something hot and wild, something that makes me want to bite and lick and savor. I don't know how, but I find myself climbing as we watch each other, our bodies still colliding with a nearly brutal force that's the most delicious thing in the world.

Then I see his body tense, the muscles in his neck, in his chest, in his abdomen straining as he stiffens. His breath comes in several harsh gushes that sound like an animal getting ready to attack. Seconds later, he flexes against me and I feel the first pulse of his body inside mine. It's as though he's massaging me from within and without and it's more than I can bear.

My second orgasm washes over me in a series of unexpected ripples. I milk him and he presses against my walls and we drag each other deeper.

Finally, Rogan collapses onto me, both of us drained and boneless. As my heartbeat quiets and the ringing in my ears subsides, I hear him whispering against the side of my neck. "Incredible. So incredible."

Over and over and over, he vocalizes the feeling that roams on a circuit through my head.

"Don't ever forget this," he says. "Don't ever forget how beautiful you are."

I won't tell him, but he need not worry about that. I will never forget this moment, this night.

Or this man.

I feel like myself, yet not at all like myself. Not at all like the woman I've come to know. I'm not the child born as Kathryn. I'm not the old Katie, known to her friends as Kat. I'm not even the Katie I've been for the last five years. Right at this moment, I feel like a new creature, like a melding of all the lives I've lived—so separate, so different, yet ones that have come together to make me whole for the first time since I was a girl. I feel like I'm finally at peace with who and what I am.

Rogan is asleep behind me, his front pressed to my back in the best kind of spoon. His warm breath is tickling the scarred side of my neck. It's not as sensitive as the skin around it, but because I normally have the area covered with my long hair, it's not stimulated very often either. For that reason, the sensation of having someone's breath touch it is distinct. And liberating. And enough to keep me awake to enjoy it.

"What are you smiling about?" comes a rough yet soft voice from behind me. My smile grows.

"How do you know I'm smiling? You're supposed to be asleep."

"I am? You should've told me," he teases, nuzzling me with his scratchy chin. I shrug my shoulder automatically because it tickles. "Please don't hide from me like that." His voice is audibly pained, like my action was a grave insult to him.

I turn to look back at him, reaching up to stroke his cheek, noting the worry in his eyes. The curve on my lips turns tender. "I'm ticklish. That's all."

"Oh. My bad." His face relaxes into the lopsided grin that I love so much and he pulls me in closer, hugging me tighter with his strong arm. "I just don't want you to think that they bother me or that they're all I see when I look at you or touch you. I've felt that way before and it sucks balls."

I settle back in against him, cradling my head on my folded hands as Rogan's fingers rub soothing circles on my stomach.

"Felt what way?" I ask.

"Like my scars are worse than what they are."

"Your scars aren't that bad, though."

"To me they are. I just learned a long time ago that I couldn't let them, or that part of my life, ruin everything for me. I had to fight to survive, yes. But I also had to fight to live. To have some kind of happiness in life."

His tattoo. *Fight to survive. Fight to live.* Not just a tattoo. A credo. *His* credo.

I pause, debating the wisdom of asking the questions that are burning to be voiced. I mean, I *did* just share a huge piece of myself with him. And not only the physical; I shared the hardest part. But that doesn't mean that he's at a place where *he* will feel comfortable sharing with *me*. In a way, my hand was forced. His is not.

Before I can talk myself into or out of asking, Rogan starts to talk again. So I let him.

"I wasn't always comfortable with violence. I wasn't always a fighter. The first few years, when Kurt was just a baby, things were pretty good, pretty normal. It was after Mom died that it all went to shit."

"What happened to her?"

"Cancer. We didn't have much money and she always put her needs last. Eventually it cost her her life." I'm quiet while Rogan is quiet. I don't know if he needs time to collect himself, but I'm giving it to him anyway. I feel the storm of his story brewing, like an uncomfortable static in the air. "He didn't start drinking or anything. That's what the social workers always thought—that he was a mean drunk. But he wasn't. He was just a mean son of a bitch, *period*. He didn't need anything to bring it out. Life did. Just life. When Mom died, she took the only good in him with her.

"I was ten the first time he hit me. He was mad because I'd left my basketball outside. He found it when he came home from work. I was watching cartoons with Kurt and he walked in the door and threw the ball at me. Hit me right in middle of the face. Smashed the shit out of my nose. I started crying and he walked over, jerked me up by the arm and punched me in the stomach. Told me to stop acting like a little pussy bitch. Told me I wasn't tough enough, but that he'd make me tough. Tough like a man."

My hand is pressed to my mouth and my eyes are squeezed shut. Too easily I can picture a young Rogan, abused and grieving, struggling to make it from one day to the next.

"It only got worse after that. The older and bigger I got, the more creative he was. He'd burn me with lit cigarettes if I didn't wake up on time, he'd whip me with my football cleats if I missed a catch, he'd slice at me with a box cutter if I ran from him when he was mad. And there was nothing I could do. He told me if I told anyone about what happened, he'd kill Kurt. I believed him. And I think he would've done it. But I knew as long as I was around, he'd never lay a hand on him."

My stomach sloshes with nausea at the pain, at the heartache. At the betrayal and the loneliness he must've felt. I have to wait a few seconds, swallow a few times so that my voice doesn't reflect my inner turmoil.

"You mentioned social workers . . ."

"Yeah, I had a couple of concerned teachers over the years. I always made excuses, though. I knew if Dad ever found out, he'd hurt us. Hurt Kurt. And I couldn't risk that. And if they *were* able to help get us away from him, Kurt and I might've been separated in foster care. I guess to a kid like me, there were too many unknowns, too many risks. Besides, Dad was careful. He never broke bones and he was a star employee at work. But still, I heard them whisper. All my teachers thought he was a mean drunk that no one could catch." His laugh is bitter. "Anyway, he started working nightshift for the extra money when I was sixteen. I thought that might put an end to it, but it didn't. That's when I knew I had to find another way to protect us, so when I got my license, I started taking his car while he slept. I'd drive down to this dojo on the other end of town and I'd watch the boys in there as they trained. I practiced in my room after school, just waiting for the day when I could fight back.

"The old man who owned the studio caught me watching one day. I thought for sure he'd tell me I could never come back, but he surprised me by being cool about it. Not too many people were nice to me for a lot of years, but he was one who was. He offered to teach me how to defend myself.

"He didn't show me just one style, and none of the pretty stuff that they like to do at exhibitions. He taught me a little of everything—Muay Thai, Taekwondo, Krav Maga. He showed me how to take a man twice my size down to the ground. He didn't instruct me like he did his students—that violence was a last resort. No, he taught me how to fight so that I could survive. He knew that, for me, to survive *was to* fight. And so I did. I fought to survive."

As his story goes on, I feel the surge of satisfaction to come. Like watching a movie, knowing the climax is coming, I find myself anxious for Rogan to get to the part where he stands up to his dad, to get to the part where he finally gains his freedom.

But that's not how his story goes.

"My time eventually came. I'd been looking forward to it for so long. I was practically swimming in satisfaction the first time I ever hit Dad back. He just looked at me and then turned around and walked off. I felt pretty damn good about it until the next day when he beat the shit out of Kurt with a phone book. My poor brother was bruised from head to toe. Bloody lip, busted nose, black eye, blue splotches all over his chest and stomach and back. Even his legs. Dad came into his room when Kurt was curled up on his bed and I was looking him over. He just stood in the doorway, staring at me. That's when I knew. I knew I'd caused it. I'd caused him to hurt my little brother. That's when I realized that I was stuck. That

I'd have to suck it up and take it until I could find a way out. Or until Kurt could. And then we'd both be free."

Behind my hand, I bite my lip. I don't want to make a sound as the tears slip between my lashes and roll down my cheek to soak the pillowcase. I hurt for Rogan, for the little boy who lost so much, who had to endure so much. Within a few months, his entire life fell apart, yet here he is today—healthy and whole. And charming as the day is long. It's obvious that his strength is much more than just physical. This man is a survivor. Down to his soul, he's a survivor. And a winner.

"I'm so sorry, Rogan," I offer in as steady a voice as I'm capable of, but even to my own ears it sounds watery and weak. I feel him stiffen behind me, so I roll my shoulders back and turn to meet his eyes. They're dark in the low light and the set of his jaw is like steel. "What is it?"

"I told you I don't want your pity." I can hear that his teeth are gritted.

"I know you did. And you're not getting pity. My heart hurts for the little boy who lost so much, but I feel nothing but admiration for the *man*, Rogan. The man you've become is . . . he's amazing. I only wish I was as tough as you were. As you *are*."

His expression softens and he leans forward to kiss the tip of my nose. When he relaxes behind me again, I melt into him, something I'm finding is surprisingly easy to do.

It's nearly a full minute later when Rogan rises over me, his lips descending to cover mine. And when they do, I know the sad memories are over. He's put them back where they need to be, where they can't hurt him anymore.

Despite the heartbreaking conversation of moments before, a fire is kindled within seconds of his large palm skating down my stomach. He finds me unerringly. His fingers know the way to my core just like his words do. He touches me. Always he touches me, it seems.

I reach behind me to drive my fingers into Rogan's hair, fisting them when his tongue slides between my lips. Gently, he tugs my top thigh up onto his legs and guides his tip to my entrance from behind. He hovers there, his mouth devouring mine, his fingertip back to tease between my folds. When he stills and lifts his head, I open my eyes to find him staring at me. We stay like this for endless seconds until, with his gaze locked onto mine, he eases into me, slow and deep.

He covers my mouth again, my gasp perfectly timed with the breath he exhales. I breathe him in, take as much of him as I can into my body. And it's in these sweet, quiet moments that I realize I've never felt more myself than when Rogan is inside me.

TWENTY-TWO

Rogan

I don't know what I expected when I woke up, but to be in bed alone at nearly noon wasn't it. I can't believe it's so late! I haven't slept that well in years. Maybe ever.

I roll over to face the sun streaming in around the shutters that cover the windows. The other side of the bed is cold. I guess Katie has been up for some time.

For several minutes, I stare at the dent in her pillow, considering the woman who made it. I'm not surprised that once I unraveled the mystery of the shy girl with the haunted eyes that I'm *still* interested. Something told me right from the start that this one was special. And I wasn't wrong. She's different and special in the best possible way.

I finally drag my pathetic ass out of bed and find the bathroom directly across the hall. I pause in the doorway to listen. All I hear are sounds of battle coming from the living room. I smile to myself, shaking my head as I walk naked to the toilet. It's hard to tell what other surprises this woman might hold.

I borrow Katie's toothbrush and brush my teeth. I figure since we've licked each other from head to toe, she surely won't mind if I use it. In the mirror, I catch sight of my stiff dick, so I go back to the bedroom for last night's clothes. I figure it might be prudent to wear *something* other than a hard-on when I go out to greet her this morning. I'm ready for some more of the untamed Katie from last night, of course, but it's hard to tell where she might be in the bright light of day. Women and their mood swings!

When I'm dressed, I run my fingers through my hair and head for the living room. I smile when I see her. Like I do most of the time.

Katie is curled up on the sofa, covered with a blanket, munching from an enormous bowl of popcorn, watching what looks like *The Walking Dead*.

"Popcorn for breakfast?" I ask from the doorway so as not to startle her by walking up behind her and kissing her, which is actually what I *want* to do.

She cranes her neck to look back at me, eyes bright, lips curved. "Yep."

"And *The Walking Dead* before noon?"

"Yep."

"Another layer to your awesomeness? Jesus, woman! You're killing me!"

"I'm pretty sure you uncovered all my layers last night. And if all that sex didn't kill you, I think you're good."

Thank God! She's not all moody and shit.

She just gets more perfect by the day, and my cock twitches like it's in total agreement.

Down, boy!

I walk around the back of the couch to Katie's end, scooping her up as I pass and then turning to sit down with her in my lap, much like I did last night. "You fit like you were made to sit here, did you know that?" I ask, taking in her fresh skin, her pink cheeks and the little smile that's gracing her luscious mouth.

She gets all shy, laying her head on my shoulder and playing with some of her popcorn. It's not the painfully . . . *pained* shy look that I'm used to, though. The one that she usually wears. This one is different. In a good way.

"Well, you've got all sorts of nice places for me to sit," she finally mutters.

Through with pretending I'm not dying to kiss her, I tip her chin up and take her lips. Gently, even though I'd much rather ravage her. But I'm not stupid. I know there's still a chance I could scare her away, so I have to take it slow.

Slow. Damn it.

It'll be worth it, though. God forbid I screw it up now.

I rub my nose against hers. "Your nose is cold."

"It's chilly in here," she states, burrowing under her blanket.

I tuck the edges around her more securely, reaching under one end to grab her foot. Her toes are freezing. I rub them until they warm, treating her right side to the same as she returns her attention to the television.

"This is my favorite show," she says by way of explanation, not taking her eyes off the flat screen. "They're having a marathon today and tomorrow."

"Well, don't let me interrupt," I warn, moving my massaging hand up her bare leg.

I watch Katie watch the show. Her eyes are wide and fixed on the screen. She tosses a few kernels of popcorn into her mouth every few seconds and chews slowly, like she's trying to keep the noise down. I swallow a laugh. *God, this is the most adorable thing I've ever seen.*

Every now and again, she reaches back to blindly offer me a few pieces. I take them from her fingers, resisting the urge to suck salt from the tips.

As the minutes tick by, I work my way up to her knee, concentrating on her other leg, heating her flesh as I go. She pays me zero attention, so focused is she on her show. It *is* a great show, but I want to be more distracting than a bunch of zombies.

I ease my fingers up onto her thigh, taking turns gently squeezing her supple muscles and softly stroking her silky skin. Still, she doesn't take her eyes off the TV.

It's when I reach her hip that I realize something that has my cock filling with blood again, pressing up toward Katie's plump ass. She's not wearing any panties. Hell, she may not be wearing any clothes *at all* under that blanket. The thought has me gritting my teeth and mentally kicking myself for only having two condoms on me.

I rub my palm in circles over her hip and then back down her leg, making a wide path that travels from the outside of her hip to her knee and then back up the inside of her thigh, stopping just short of my goal. With each pass, I draw closer and closer to her center. I'm watching her closely, but she doesn't seem to even notice. So I go bold.

Starting at her knee, I run my fingertips up her leg, not stopping this time. I feel the narrow patch of short hair tickle my knuckles as I push my hand down between her thighs. They fall open just enough to give me access. I slide a finger into her crease, only to find that her pussy is hot and wet. Like *really* wet. *ShitDamnHell*.

I pause, closing my eyes and letting my head drop back as I find the satiny bump of her moist clit. Every kind of curse is running through my head on a string, followed closely by reprimands for not bringing a damn *box* of condoms.

I straighten and open my eyes to look at Katie. She's still facing the television, but her fingers, full of popcorn, are poised right in front of her mouth, which is partially open. I can see the rapid rise and fall of her chest, much faster than it was a minute ago. She might not be watching me, but she's sure as hell paying attention.

Her eyes slide to mine when I start to move my finger, so I stop. "Don't mind me. Just watch your show."

I clamp my lips together to keep from grinning as I watch her try to eat those few kernels of popcorn as though nothing is happening inside her body. She chews and then pauses, chews and then pauses. Finally, she gives up the act of eating, her hand falling limply into the big bowl. Her lips are still parted and I can see that her brow is wrinkled.

I move my finger a little faster, periodically sliding it down to tease her entrance and then back up again to resume my torture. Katie's other hand is fisted in the material of the blanket, her knuckles white as she tries to act casual.

I feel the subtle movement of her hips as she starts to gyrate against my hand. I don't increase my pace. I just continue to wind her up, fascinated by the play of emotions she's trying to hide.

She glances my way again and I nod toward the television. "Better watch. It's almost time for a commercial."

Reluctantly, she turns her head away from me again, little mewling sounds beginning to rumble in her throat. I don't even try to hold back my smile this time. I've never had so much fun watching zombies.

I tease and rub, pinch and flick until Katie is stiff as a board on my lap. I hold her right at the edge until the moment the next commercial comes on. The instant that it does, I whisper in her ear, "I'm gonna make you come in my mouth."

Before she can respond, I fling Katie's blanket off, spin her around to face me and then urge her to her feet. I palm one knee and set it

on the back of the couch by my ear, spreading her wide. Then I lean
in and bury my mouth against her slick folds.

She moans so loud and the taste of her is so sweet I think for a
second that I might lose my shit right inside my jeans, like some horny
teenage boy. Every little sound, every harsh pant is like a cattle prod
to my balls, spurring me on. She threads her fingers into my hair for
support and I dig my fingers into her ass, holding her pussy right
against my face.

With determination, I lick and suck her all the way over the edge.
She rides my face, my lips, my tongue like my cock is deep inside her.
And when she comes, I have to support her ass so she doesn't fall
backward.

She pours into my mouth and I lap it up. Honey. Pure, sweet
honey. And when she's done, I hold her tight and thrust my tongue
as far as I can into her, greedy for more. "God, your body . . ." I
mutter, my lips moving over hers until she goes completely limp in
my arms and slithers back down into my lap like a limp noodle.

Her head hits my shoulder with an audible thump and I cuddle
her close, covering with the discarded blanket what I see now is her
totally naked body. When she regains her breath, she tips her beautiful face up to mine, big blue eyes pulling me in like a life preserver
to a drowning man.

I expect her to say something, something . . . profound maybe.
What I get is not profound. It's even better.

"That's the best episode I think I've ever seen." I throw my head
back and laugh. "Even though I have no idea what happened after
you came into the living room."

Her grin is sheepish. My ego is happy. This time, I don't even
try to resist the urge to kiss her.

This might be the best morning I've had so far.

TWENTY-THREE

Katie

Rogan suggested a picnic in the park with Dozer. He said I had promised to help him with his lines and he was holding me to it. As he spreads out a plaid wool blanket, I smile thinking of it, stroking Dozer's head as I watch Rogan's lithe body move this way and that until the little oasis in the shade is perfectly smooth.

When he straightens and brushes grass off his hands, he grins up at me. "How's this for a place to rehearse?"

I sigh loudly. "I guess it'll do. I mean, if I have to rough it," I add, sniffing theatrically.

"Well, if this isn't to your liking, I feel sure I can think of something more . . . comfortable for you to sit on later."

I feel heat sting my cheeks and all the play drains right out of me, flushed away by the surge of desire.

"What, no smart-ass retort?" he teases, stretching out on his side and patting the blanket next to him.

"I'm sure I'd have one if I could *think*," I reply honestly.

Rogan laughs, a sound that I'm quickly falling in love with. It's a rich rumble that seems to come from his soul. It always makes me want to smile, like I can't help enjoying what *he's* enjoying. "I like your style, Ms. Rydale."

I know he doesn't mean *that* kind of style, but his comment brings to mind my wardrobe, which in turn brings to mind the concealing blouse I chose and the comforting swath of hair that resides where it does every day—covering my scars.

I kneel on the spread and set Dozer down. He walks all of four feet, to the edge of the blanket, and flops down, falling almost immediately to sleep. Rogan, watching him, shakes his head in amazement.

"A narcoleptic cat. Who knew?"

I giggle as I slide in beside Rogan, pulling my feet up under me. "So, what feast did you bring us?" I ask, inclining my head toward the huge basket resting behind Dozer.

"Ah-ah-ah. Work first, play later."

I'm surprised. "We're *really* going to run lines?" I thought it was just his way of teasing me.

"Yep. Sure are. I want to get this right the first time tomorrow."

"I'm sure you will. You're quite good."

Rogan looks genuinely pleased. "Thank you. I noticed that you've got mad skills at all this. Have you ever acted? Or considered acting?"

I feel myself tense. I know Rogan's question was innocent enough, but it still stirs memories that I never like reflecting upon.

I could hedge. Make up something to put him off, but since he's been so honest with me, told me such painful things, I feel that I owe him the truth.

I take a deep breath, gathering my courage. "Actually, that's what I originally went to school for."

"What? Acting?" Now he seems surprised.

"Yes."

"Why the hell didn't you pursue it? Is it because of your burns? Because—"

"No, no. Not really," I interrupt, not wanting to discuss them again. I would still much rather pretend that they aren't there, or that he can't see them. "Since I was a little girl, I always dreamed about being an actress. I tried out for every school play that I could, watched as many movies as I was allowed, studied the greats. You know how kids are. But my parents were very, very strict. They didn't want me in the spotlight like that. They wouldn't even consider letting me attend The Julliard. But I applied anyway and was accepted with a full scholarship."

Rogan sits up from where he was resting back on his elbow. "You got a scholarship to The Julliard?"

I smile, but it's no longer a proud smile. It's just sad. "I did. But they still refused to let me pursue it. They wanted me to be a pharmacist."

"Well, it's not too late, you know," he says, his expression rife with resentful determination. "You should chase your dreams, damn it."

I wave him off. "No, I actually did that. Only it didn't work out so well." I clear my throat, twirling a stray piece of grass between my fingers, anything to give my hands something to do and my eyes something to focus on other than Rogan. "It was what I wanted, and even though my parents were against it and very upset with me for applying anyway, I packed up and left. I did what I wanted to do. At the time it didn't matter what they wanted."

"But it didn't work out?" Rogan asks, his warm palm covering my bare foot nearest him.

"Not in the end. At first it was great. I accepted the scholarship and moved to New York. Within a couple of months of being at The Julliard, I was getting a lot of attention. Instructors, directors, local theater. They keep an eye on all the productions put on at the arts center and I guess for a while, I was the apple of their eye. The up-and-comer to watch." My laugh is bitter. I can't help it. It wells within me when I think back on my life, on my decisions. On fate. "I was in the paper a few times the summer after my freshman year. It was surreal. And *that* got me the notice of a guy."

I take a deep breath, girding myself for what's to come. Talking about it almost feels like reliving it. And I'd never want to do that. "He was charming and handsome, wealthy and accomplished. His father was influential. He was all that a girl with stars in her eyes needed to complete the picture. I dove right in, despite the fact that I didn't *really* know him. Not really. For a while, it was perfect."

When my pause drags on too long, Rogan prompts me. "But that didn't work out either?"

I sigh softly, like the sound leaked right out of the never-quite-healed gash in my heart, along with a trickle of blood. Still too fresh. Always too fresh. "No. We moved in together before I found out that he had a temper. And that he wasn't afraid of what a girl from nowhere might tell others. He knew no one would believe me."

Rogan's voice is steel when he asks, "He put his hands on you?"

I know he doesn't mean sexually; he means physically. Abusively.

I don't answer. I don't need to. And he knows that my silence is answer enough.

"It was worse when he was jealous, which he often was. He didn't want me to have friends, he hated everyone that I had class with, he didn't want me acting on Broadway, which I'd had an offer to do. Unfortunately, he expressed all this with few words and a lot of flying fists. And palms. And the occasional kick with his boot or whipping with the mean end of an extension cord." I don't glance up at Rogan. I can tell by his posture from the corner of my eye that he is rigid with anger. "When I finally got up enough nerve to leave him, he followed me. I should have known he would. He found me at a friend's apartment. I'd gone there to stay until I could figure out something else. He waited for me to leave for my night class. Waited until I got in and rolled down my window, like I always used to do. Then he walked right up and threw alcohol at me. Bourbon, I think it was. It hit my left side and splattered down the door and onto the floorboard. I remember looking up at him, wondering what the hell he was doing. I started fumbling, trying to get my window rolled up, but I wasn't fast enough. I saw him strike the match. His face was almost sad. Almost."

I can still feel the fear. I can still smell the alcohol. I can still hear the *whoosh* of flames erupting all around me.

"He threw the match through my window before I could roll it up completely. It landed right in my lap. Everything around me went up in flames. It melted most of the hair on my left side. Gave me third-degree burns on my neck and the top of my shoulder. Second-degree burns down my side and on my leg. All the places you saw. That was the end of my acting career." Even thinking back to that time of my life produces a crushing weight in my chest. "I guess my parents were right after all. And that's not even the worst part."

"How can it be worse?" he asks, his voice a coarse, husky croak.

"My parents were notified. They'd been on their way home from church that Wednesday night. They didn't even go home. They drove straight up to New York." I stop to meet Rogan's eyes for the first time, but I can't stand what I see there—a reflection of my own pain—so I look away before I finish. "They were both killed in a car accident on the way. I never even got to tell them I was sorry."

My throat is tight with controlled emotion. I haven't talked to anyone about this in years. It was easier than I thought it would be, but still not *easy* by any far stretch of the imagination. I lost everything that night, everything that ever meant something to me.

Rogan says nothing. And that's good because there's really nothing *to* say. I've heard all the platitudes from my friends and friends of the family. Yet another reason I moved to the middle of nowhere. I needed to be someone *no one* knew. I needed to be someone other than this poor girl who'd had such a tragic life. I *had to be* someone other than the girl who everyone pitied. But I also needed to get away from Calvin. Permanently.

After a length of silence, I glance up at Rogan, trying my best to smile. "I was in a medically induced coma for three days and in the hospital for twenty-four more. I had surgeries following that. Skin grafts for some of the worst places. But as you can see, there's no covering something like that except with clothes."

"Katie, I'm so—"

"Please don't," I plead. I can't take his sympathy right now. It would crush me.

He waits a few seconds before he asks, "What happened to the guy?"

"Since I was in such bad shape right after, the police ruled it an accident. Found a broken liquor bottle on the floorboard and two full bottles in the passenger seat. Calvin planned it well, made it look like I was heading out to a party or something. The friend that I was staying with had no idea what happened, of course. Turns out the police were going to charge *me*. I couldn't believe it. Until I found out why they hadn't. When I met with the cop who investigated it, he mentioned that my boyfriend's father had cleared things up for me and that I'd better be thankful that I 'had connections, young lady,'" I mimic, using my best deep, cop voice. "The whole thing was ridiculous. I knew *right then* that there would be no point in trying to tell them what really happened. Calvin was protected.

When your father is a wealthy, influential politician . . . Well, you know how that goes. I just got tangled up with the wrong guy all the way around."

"So that's it? No justice? That bastard just got off scot-free?" His tone has a hard edge.

I shrug. The ending to my story is far from perfect, far from even satisfactory, but I came to terms with the unfairness of life a long time ago.

"Some people have a get-out-of-jail-free card."

There's a pause during which I can hear Rogan's controlled breathing. I know he has something to say and I appreciate that he's not saying it. It won't help anything to be angry. It didn't help me at all.

"At least now I understand," Rogan finally says, his voice quiet as he sits up and reaches forward to stroke my cheek with his fingertips.

"Understand what?"

"Understand why you push people away."

"Most people don't. They don't get it. But it doesn't matter. This keeps me safe. Keeps me from getting hurt."

"I hope you know that I would never hurt you."

My grin is lopsided and humorless. "That's what they all say."

"Only *I* mean it."

"I think Calvin did, too. In his own twisted way. He just wanted something of his own, something no one could take away from him. And that thing was me."

"I don't care what he wanted. There's never a good enough reason for a man to hurt a woman like that. Never."

"I had to stop thinking that way a long time ago," I say, pulling Rogan's hand away from my face. I can't lean on him right now. I can't accept his strength. I need to be able to relive this and be at peace with it on my own. "I carried a combination of fear and anger and horrible grief with me for two years afterward. My family was dead, my dreams were dead. My present, my future, my hope— everything was gone. I had nothing. Thankfully one of my professors came to visit me at the hospital. She thought maybe one day I'd change my mind about acting. She thought I should at least keep my foot in the door, so she gave me the number of Sebastian, a man she knew in the makeup business. I'm glad she came, because without her and Sebastian, I'd have had no future.

"So, almost a year after the fire, after rehab and all the surgeries, when I felt and looked almost human again, I called Sebastian. He said my professor had talked me up and that he'd take me on as his apprentice, but only if I could show promise. He flew me out to California for what amounted to an audition. Turns out I had a knack for making ugly things pretty and beautiful things more so. I worked with him for a year and a half before I got the job here with the studio. I moved to Enchantment right away and haven't looked back since. Until now."

"I don't even know what to say," Rogan confesses. I see all sorts of tightly controlled emotions on his face, but there's only one I'm searching for. It's why I understood him that day in the makeup room when I first saw his scars.

"You see why I didn't pity you when I saw your scars? I knew how you felt. I knew that pity is like acid for people like us. It eats away at what little there is left of our soul. I'd rather someone hate me or think I'm backward and shy and weird than pity me."

"I don't pity you. But I do pity that asshole ex of yours if I ever run into him."

I shake my head. "He's not worth it. He's not worth another second of my misery. I gave him too much already."

"Sometimes we don't give it. Sometimes people take it when we aren't looking. It's like they rip it out and by the time we realize it, the damage is done."

"Is that how you feel about your father?"

"In a way. It's like we were an okay family, and then, before I even knew that we were broken, he'd already stolen something from me. Something I couldn't get back." He looks off into the distance behind my shoulder, lost in time, falling silent for several seconds before he turns his eyes back to mine. "The thing is, we can still survive. Even if pieces are scarred. Or dead. Or even missing. We can *still* survive. We can still *live*."

I glance down at my fingers where they fidget in my lap, clasping and unclasping, clasping and unclasping. "I'm not sure I'll ever really *live* again. I feel like the star of a fairy tale that went wrong. So, so wrong. Like Beauty *turned into* the beast. In the blink of an eye. So much more than just my skin died in the fire that day. I lost everything."

"Katie, look at me," Rogan insists, his finger tipping my face up toward his. "You're not a beast. You're still one of the most beautiful women I've ever seen. Your scars don't change that. The problem is, you won't take my word for it. You don't believe it. And unfortunately, I can't make you see it. *You* have to find it in the mirror, and you need to. You survived, but now you need to *live*. Because when you aren't living, you're dying a little more every day."

I feel my chin begin to tremble against his finger. "I'm trying. This . . . *you* are the closest I've come to living in a long time."

"Then let me bring you back to life," he whispers, brushing his lips over mine in a kiss even softer than his words. "Inch by inch, day by day, touch by touch." I close my eyes and let him soothe away the worry, the fear, the ash that I've carried in a bucket where my heart used to be. "Will you? Will you let me?" My eyelashes flutter up to find his jewel-like green eyes staring intensely down into mine. "Please," he breathes. I more *see* the word on his mouth rather than hear it.

The Katie I've fashioned from the remains of who I used to be hesitates, but within seconds, the lonely shell of the girl I *was* sighs into Rogan's descending mouth. "Okay," I manage and then his kiss turns into fire.

Monday. It's incredible what a difference a couple of days makes. I can't remember a better weekend. Ever. Granted, it had a few rough patches, but the good more than made up for the bad. Even as a child, when practically every day was loaded with some kind of happy memory of my parents, I can't remember feeling so whole and optimistic. It almost worries me, like I should be waiting for the world to cave in around me and demolish the little glimmer of hope I'm beginning to glimpse.

I don't know what kind of future Rogan and I could have, if any, but just the prospect, just the *consideration* of a tomorrow with someone is a huge step for me. I truly thought I was going to be alone. Forever.

There's a hitch in my step as I walk through the door to work. Nearly every morning since I've been here I've run into Ronnie first thing. We share our little ritualistic greeting and then go on with our day. Only today, things are different. And not just because of Rogan.

My carefree, happy morning just took a stressful turn as my eyes scan the hall for Ronnie. I don't see him anywhere.

But who I *do* see is Rogan.

My lips twitch up into a small, relieved smile when I spot his tall physique. He's clad in the rattiest jeans I've ever seen, along with black boots, a black tee, and a wicked grin that makes me blush. He didn't leave my house until almost dawn. Said he wanted to be there when his brother got up so he could fix their breakfast, as was his habit. Of course I didn't argue, even though I was loath to see him go. Much more than I would've expected when we've only really known each other for a few weeks. That alone should be a warning sign.

His sparkling green eyes watch my every step until I stop in front of him. "Mornin', darlin'," he drawls.

Butterflies beat their gossamer wings against the walls of my stomach, of my chest. I forgot what this feels like—this intimate feeling of *knowing* someone, of being close to them in a way that binds you, that turns every glance, every smile, every brush of the hand to delicious innuendo. To carefully controlled passion, biding its time until it can be unleashed.

I'm reveling in the moment, in the sensation, right up until Rogan begins to lean toward me. It shakes me from my fantasy world and I take a step back, glancing left and right.

I clear my throat, meeting his frown with another smile. "Good morning." When the wrinkle between his eyes deepens to a trench, I continue. "I'm glad you're here."

"You sure about that?"

I glance around again to make sure no one is watching or listening. "I'm positive. I usually run into Ronnie first thing in the morning."

Rogan's skeptical frown disappears in a blaze of fury that burns across his handsome features. "That asshole knows better than to get near you. He won't look at you, talk to you, talk *about* you ever again. Hell, he'd better not even *mention your name* if he knows what's good for him."

My grin widens. God, I love that he's protective. It's so nice to feel like someone cares, like someone *is caring for* me. I haven't felt like that since the accident when my parents died. "Even though I couldn't let you do anything to him, I love the sentiment."

"I love that you think you could stop me."

That gives me pause. "It would make things hard for me here. At work. You *do* understand that, don't you?"

I can see that he does, but he doesn't like it. "Yeah. I get it. But still, he'd better be very careful." As his anger dissipates, I see his eyes narrow. "Is that why you're keeping your distance? Because of work?" Reluctantly, I nod. He drops his voice in response. "Because it seems that just a few hours ago, we were about as close as two people are able to get. Chest to chest, belly to belly, my co—"

I clear my throat very loudly, interrupting him even as my cheeks blaze with color and heat. "So, you're early again, *Mr. Rogan*. You must be a morning person." I feel all flustered now. In the best possible, albeit most disconcerting, way.

"Oh, I'm very much a morning person." His wink reminds me of how he left me in the wee hours—sated, boneless, with the imprint of his body still fresh and warm on mine. Yes, he's definitely a morning person. And a night person. And a noon person.

I widen my eyes, a silent plea for him to stop his suggestive teasing, but all the while my lips are trembling. It's a struggle to suppress the girlishly delighted giggle dying to get out.

"What's the matter, Beautiful Katie?" he murmurs just loud enough for me to hear. "You look flushed. Dirty mind?"

Oh God! Dirty mind, indeed.

With a slight shake of my head and a tightly controlled smile, I make my way around Rogan, who falls into step beside me. I can feel his masculine gloat hitting me like waves of heat, causing my skin to feel dewy and hot from head to toe.

Rogan starts to whistle. It's a happy sound from a happy man.

Or at least he seems to be happy. There's a glimmer to his eyes, and they want to crinkle at the corners, like he has a secret. Or maybe a wink on deck. And *that* makes *me* happy. I shouldn't care about his state of contentment. But I do. *I* feel so good that it would seem far less "good" if *he* weren't good, too. But he seems good. We both seem good. And *that* is very good.

Although I keep my attention focused straight ahead, I'm aware of the sidelong glances we are getting as we make our way along the hall to my little cubby. I'm not at all surprised when I walk through the door to find Mona standing in the center of the room, arms crossed over her ample chest, toe tapping in agitation. She looks like a stripper dressed in school-teacher attire. She's wearing a pencil-slim black skirt and a white blouse that's at least two sizes too small. Her long legs are encased in fishnets and her feet in stilettos. All she needs is a riding crop, some smart glasses and hair that's piled messily on top of her head so she can whip it down dramatically.

"What's wrong?" I ask, taking in her petulant expression and rigid posture.

"I'm feeling very disenfranchised," she explains.

I glance over at Rogan, who's already smiling and shaking his head.

"Word of the day?"

She cracks a grin. "Yeah, why? Did I use it wrong?"

"Depends on what you were trying to say," I tell her as I walk past her to lay my purse on the counter. I turn back to her, feeling both pleased and nervous when Rogan comes to stand beside me, leaning his tall body against the counter next to me and crossing his arms and ankles. I can literally feel the warmth from his body. It teases me, beckoning me closer. I plant my feet and make a point to stand up straight, not giving in.

Mona's eyes are narrow now as she looks back and forth between Rogan and me. I can see the wheels of her romance book–polluted mind going a mile a minute. Finally, her posture eases and her face lights up with glee. She taps the tips of her fingers together in a tiny clap.

"Eeeeeee," she squeals in a hushed voice. "Okay, I'm not mad anymore."

She knows. I don't even have to ask about her reaction. I know how to interpret it. It's nothing that I really want to talk about with her, though, especially not in front of Rogan, so I steer the conversation elsewhere. "If that's what you were trying to say, then yes, you used the word wrong."

Mona waves me off, her expression saying she couldn't care less now. She's got something else to think about. And the thing is, Mona is like a dog with a bone. She won't be letting this go until she can talk to me about it. In great detail, I'm sure. "I don't care. Today is a good day. We should celebrate."

Before I can respond, Rogan speaks up beside me. "Maybe tomorrow. She owes me a lunch and I'm collecting today."

My insides beam with happiness and I try not to smile. "I guess that takes care of my lunch plans," I tell Mona casually.

"I want to buy her a piece of pie," he adds, a bit too softly. I want to look over at him, but I don't. I'm afraid I'll see something naughty in his eyes and I'll get all flummoxed.

Her face splits in the world's biggest smile and her eyes bounce back and forth between us. "Well, in that case, I'll just make other arrangements. Maybe tomorrow," she offers as she starts to back out of the room.

"I'll arm wrestle you for it," Rogan says, making Mona giggle delightedly.

"God, you two are *too cute*." And then she's gone, her excited squeal trailing behind her.

Rogan waits for a few seconds and then walks to the door. He closes and leans against it. His eyes meet mine and electricity lights up my stomach. I know perfectly well that if we were any number of other places, he'd start undressing me. And I'd let him.

He holds my gaze as he walks his sexy walk back toward me, not stopping until his hands are gripping the counter on either side of me and his face is about two inches from mine.

"What are you thinking?" he asks in his low, velvety bedroom voice.

I can't think past honesty. "That you make my stomach feel like the fourth of July."

He grins and laughs, an evil, satisfied laugh. Moisture rushes into my panties. God, this man!

"What are *you* thinking?"

"That I didn't realize how hard this is gonna be," he admits.

"How hard what's going to be?" I play dumb, but I know *exactly* what he means. I just want to hear him say it.

"Seeing you, being so close to you yet not being able to touch you." As he speaks, he leans in to rub his cheek against mine, his lips brushing my ear and causing chills to spread down my arm.

I clear my throat and swallow so that I can speak through the desert sand that has filled my mouth. "Well, you'll just have to make do, won't you?"

"Mmmm," he responds noncommittally as he presses his lips to the space beneath my ear and then drags them down the side of my throat to nip my collarbone with his blunt teeth. "Or maybe I'll just have to think of something else."

"Like what?" My voice is already breathless.

"Like where I can find you alone, for just a few minutes, so I can reach up under your skirt and find out if your panties are wet."

Before I can think to reply, Rogan reaches up under the knee-length edge of my skirt and slides his hand up between my legs, cupping my damp skin through my underwear.

"Oh *shit*, that's hot," he moans just before he covers my mouth with his own.

His kiss is meant to incinerate. And it does. My limbs burn with the need to wrap themselves around him, to hold him close as he buries his body inside mine. My back arches, an unconscious admission of my inner turmoil.

All of a sudden, Rogan backs away. My eyelids flutter open reluctantly and I focus on his handsome, passion-filled face. He looks flustered.

"Damn," he breathes, running a hand through his short, sandy hair. "Just . . . *damn*."

I grin. I can't help it. This big, gorgeous man wants me. *Me*. The shy one. The short one. The dark one. The scarred one. In a sea of tall, thin, beautiful people, he wants me. I might never get over that. This *is* the land of make-believe, though. Within the walls of this studio, the unlikely happens every day. On film. So maybe, just maybe, it can happen for me, too.

Rogan reaches down to smooth my skirt. It's such a sweet, familiar . . . intimate gesture, my heart gives a great heave of contentedness, like a sigh. "So, I guess you gathered that I'm taking you to lunch today. Do you think you'll have time to come and watch me film?"

I want to. God, how I want to! "Probably not this morning. Mornings are always busier because everyone has to be in makeup. But maybe this afternoon. If there aren't a lot of touch-ups and specialties . . ."

He grins, that sexy, lopsided one I love. "Then I'll look for you."

"Are you sure you won't be too . . . distracted?" I ask, running my finger along the placket of my shirt and looking up at him from beneath my lashes. I feel gratified when I hear the air hiss through his gritted teeth. It's been a long time since I felt the power of my sexuality, my femininity. It's hard to feel feminine and beautiful and powerful when you're hiding such ugliness. But somehow, Rogan makes me feel beautiful. Almost like my scars didn't happen. Almost.

"You're evil," he says softly.

I laugh as I straighten, tipping my head toward the makeup chair. "Have a seat, *Mr. Rogan*. If I don't hurry up and do you, I'll be running late all day."

I hear a low growl coming from behind me as Rogan takes his seat. "You're really gonna have to watch what you say."

And so begins the light, teasing, flirtatious tone of the day. And I've never been happier.

TWENTY-FOUR

Rogan

It isn't exactly *easy* to concentrate, but considering the kinds of scenes I'm taping for the next few days, thinking of Katie keeps me in the right frame of mind for them. I only wish that it was her lips I was kissing, her body I was smashing up against mine.

"Cut!" Tony yells, and I step away from Rayelle. Her eyes are wide and glazed.

"Shit! I'm going to need my vibrator since you won't rehearse with me," she says with a pretty yet annoying pout.

To this, I say nothing. Only smile.

"Lunch, you bunch of hacks," Tony teases as he stretches and makes his way over to me. He claps me on the shoulder. "Good job today, Rogan. I take it you got to run lines over the weekend."

"I did. It helped."

Tony grins as he glances between Rayelle and me. "I can see that."

I don't disabuse him of the notion that I can plainly see he's getting. The less I say, the less attention will be drawn to Katie, which is how I know she wants it. Me personally, I don't give a damn who knows, but . . . this isn't just about me.

"Later," I say briefly before I make my exit to go find Katie.

When I reach her little room, she's wiping off the counter, humming to herself again, hips swaying inside her chaste skirt. I love it when she does that. It's a soft, soothing sound and, for some reason, I get the impression she only does it when she's happy. And I hope she's happy. I sure as hell am.

"Wha'cha hummin'?" I ask, leaning against the doorjamb to watch her. This time, I can't identify the tune.

She whirls around guiltily at the sound of my voice. "Uhhh . . ." Her cheeks pinken, which intrigues me. Why wouldn't she want me to know what song is on her mind? "Just a tune that's stuck in my head," she hedges.

I just grunt my acceptance, willing to let her off the hook. This time.

She tosses her wipe in the trash and takes her purse out of the drawer she keeps it in. As she walks toward me, I have to ask, "Was it called 'I Wanna Get Naked with Rogan'?"

She grins, which I've seen her do more of in the last two days than I have in the last four weeks. "I don't think I've heard that one."

I stuff my hands in the pockets of my black "set" slacks, resisting the urge to wind my arms around her tiny waist and pull her to me. "Maybe I'll sing it for you tonight." We haven't made plans, but I figure this is a good way to test the waters without pressing her.

"You sing?" she asks, scooting past me out into the hall.

"For you, I'd sing like a mockingbird."

She blushes prettily again, something I could get used to.

I keep my hands in my pockets the whole way to the diner so that I don't touch her. It seems so natural to want to be in contact with her that I don't trust myself not to reach for her by accident. It's like my hands gravitate toward her, my palms itch for her, my fingers burn for her. They have a memory of their own, one that can't forget the way she responds to me, the way her body comes alive for me.

I focus more closely on what she's saying when I feel my dick stir in my pants. *Shit!* Why can't we be going somewhere private? Or some place where she doesn't care who sees? Like back in New York, where everyone is anonymous.

For a few seconds, I'm lost imagining a version of Katie where she'd risk discovery just to be with me. Where she'd risk some sort of legal penalty just to feel me hike up one of her prim little dresses. I can imagine just such a scene—Katie looking out over the edge of the Empire State Building at night, me easing my cock into her silky smooth pussy from behind, her coming so hard she can barely enjoy the spectacular view.

Shiiit!

"Are you okay?" Katie asks. I'm standing on the sidewalk in front of the diner. My hand is on the handle of the door, but I haven't opened it yet. I'm just staring down into the eyes that I see even when she's nowhere around.

Her forehead is wrinkled in concern. God, I want to touch her cheek, put my hands in her hair. Kiss her. But I don't.

"Yeah, I'm fine. I was just . . . thinking."

"About what?" she asks, slipping through the door when I finally have the presence of mind to open it for her.

"You don't wanna know," I caution. When she glances back at me, I wink and her eyes widen a fraction. "But then again, maybe you do."

She's stopped just inside the tiny, retro restaurant and I'm less than six inches away. I feel the magnetism between us like a tangible thing. There might as well be hands on my back, physically pushing me toward her. I feel the pull *that* strongly.

"Maybe you can tell me about it later," she says softly, glancing around nervously. When her eyes find their way back to mine, they're like coals of fiery want in the shy field of her face. She's the most amazing contradiction I've ever met. I could explore her for days. Weeks. Her body, her mind. Her soul.

"Promise?"

Her answer is a single nod and a slight curve to the corners of her mouth. So prim. So bashful. Such a little vixen when my lips are on her skin.

My balls throb in agreement.

"We'd better order," I say, my teeth gritted in determination. "Before I throw you over my shoulder and carry you out of here."

From the corner of my eye, I see her lips twitch up into more of a grin. I love teasing her. But I might love making her smile even more.

After we are seated, the waitress brings our drinks. "You ready to order, sugar?" she asks. For most other women, that would sound too . . . *old*, but somehow this cute, young blonde pulls it off.

I smile politely. "I think I'll have the double bacon cheeseburger with fries and a side salad."

"That's enough protein, even for a man like you," says the waitress, eyeing me appreciatively. I don't think much of it. It happens a lot.

She watches me for a few seconds longer before she finally drags her eyes over to Katie. Her demeanor cools considerably, which pisses me off. I know how catty women can be, especially ones like this waitress and most of the conceited starlets I work with these days, but it rubs me the wrong way to see *anybody* treat Katie with *anything* less than kindness and respect.

"And what'll you have?"

Katie's small smile is the same polite, hollow gesture I've seen all too often. "I think I'll have the Cobb salad. Ranch dressing, please."

She puts her menu back in the stand, but I tack on dessert for her. "And a piece of pie."

"What kind?" the waitress asks when she turns to me, all warm and smiley again.

I look to Katie. "The green kind?" I can't imagine what flavor it might be. Pistachio? Key lime?

Although still small, her grin turns more genuine, this time reaching her eyes. "How do you know I like the green kind?"

I don't answer; I simply nod to the waitress. "The green kind."

"One piece of key lime it is."

"With extra whipped cream," I add before she walks off.

"The cream is the best part," the waitress says, looking back over her shoulder.

I ignore her in favor of bringing my attention back to the fascinating creature seated across from me. Her eyes are slits as she studies me.

"How did you know about the pie?"

"The day I was in here and Victoria found me, you were eating right over there," I say, pointing to the booth she and Mona sat in. "You were right in my line of vision. I watched you eat your whole meal, but when you got to the pie . . . Holy. Shit."

"What?"

"That first bite you took . . . *God!* You slid that fork into your mouth and closed your lips around it. Your eyelids sort of fluttered shut and you pulled the fork out so slowly, like you were already enjoying the taste on your tongue. You didn't chew for a few seconds. You just sat there with your eyes closed, the expression on your face something like it is when you slide down on my cock. Like it's so good you wanna savor every second of it. *God! Damn*, it was so hot." Despite the fact that we're in a greasy spoon, surrounded by people, blood gushes south to bring my dick to life. I shift uncomfortably. "I've never wanted to be a piece of pie so bad in all my life. To feel those lips wrapped around me . . . to feel that tongue licking my skin . . . Hell, I'd do almost anything."

Katie's chest is rising and falling more quickly. She leans back, folding her hands together primly in front of her on the tabletop. "Well, we'll see what the afternoon holds," she says, avoiding my eyes. "I like more, ahem, flavors than just key lime," she adds, reaching for her water and taking a sip. Despite her refusal to meet my eyes, despite her unaffected manner, I know she's feeling this, too. Her hand trembles as she sets her glass back on the table.

I smile. I'm sure it looks wolfish. It *feels* wolfish. "I can't wait."

Her lips curl. Just at the corners. So demure. So deceiving. I know what lies behind it now.

And I've never wanted her more.

TWENTY-FIVE

Katie

I wasn't ready for lunch to end, but the bright side is that if I don't get to see Rogan on set, I'll evidently see him tonight. He hasn't yet said when, but he talks about it as if it's a foregone conclusion.

Some feminists might take offense at that, but I don't. I like that he makes it obvious that he wants me, that he wants to spend time with me. It's not like I'm really man or dating savvy anymore. I mean, I had no clue that Ronnie would attempt what he did at the lake. I guess I'm to the point now where I kind of need things spelled out for me.

I glance at the clock on the wall. It's two forty-five and I'm caught up with my work for the moment. I think of Rogan's last words to me when he left me at my door after lunch. He had a hungry look on his face that made me ache to feel his skin against mine.

"Come to the set if you get a chance. You . . . inspire me."

He reached out and brushed his thumb over my bottom lip, like he couldn't *not* touch me anymore. He did it so quickly that I couldn't complain, and then he was gone. My lip felt warm and tingly for at least half an hour after he left.

I don't know why he wants me to come and watch him, but I'm inclined to go, mainly because I want to see him. A few minutes this morning and an hour at lunch isn't enough. It seems the more I see of him, the more I *want to* see of him.

Throwing caution and my over-thinking ways to the wind, I lock the drawer with my purse inside and head to the other end of the complex, to the stage where Rogan is filming. I sneak in without much notice. Whether because I've perfected being unobtrusive or because I'm as unnoticeable as a wallflower, I don't know, but no one seems to be attuned to me, especially not the way Rogan is.

I'm standing along the back wall, watching the part of the scene that followed what Rogan and I rehearsed. I could only assume that there would be a steam after it. I mean, the dialogue seemed to be leading up to it, but also because it's a cable show. Liberties are taken to add some naughtier material. I knew this. I just never knew what it might feel like to watch Rogan.

He's saying his lines a little more stiffly than he did with me, but I cease to notice when he leans in and kisses Rayelle. God, it's like someone stabbed me in the chest with a broadsword. I have to look away for a few seconds to collect myself and remind my heart that this is all for show. It's fiction. Make-believe.

I drag my eyes back to the actors. They are separated now, still in character, and when Rogan's eyes sweep out as he gestures, they stutter, flying back to meet mine before he continues on. His hesitation was barely noticeable, but it was enough to cause Tony, the director, to cut the take and reshoot it.

I see Rogan's jaw flex, but then his eyes are on mine again, heated and a little possessive. He and Rayelle take their places again for yet another take. I watch, even though I dread what's to come.

This time, Rogan says his lines much more smoothly, much more convincingly, but he also dives into his kiss with Rayelle much more . . . enthusiastically, too. As hard as it is to wait, I don't leave until the take is over. I'm not surprised when Tony commends them on it. They certainly had me convinced.

I don't wait for Rogan's eyes to find me again before I make my exit. I'm not sure I want to see them darkened with desire. Especially after kissing someone as beautiful as Rayelle.

My feet feel heavy as I make my way back to my little place of peace in the makeup and entertainment world. I'm almost glad when a tech brings in an extra for a retouch on makeup. It's fairly involved, what with their being blood and some torn tissue written into the scene. It takes up a nice chunk of my afternoon, keeping me from replaying Rogan's scene over and over in my head.

It's as I'm cleaning my station, preparing to leave for the day, that one of the set assistants gives a swift knock on the door frame and moves inside just long enough to hand me a folded note. "Mr. Rogan asked me to bring this to you."

The note is short, simple and to the point.

Don't leave yet. Wait for me.

–R

It's written in a slanted, masculine scrawl that somehow suits him. And it makes my stomach clench against a little pinch of hurt. I caution myself not to make too much of what I saw, repeating the mantra, *It was contrived, it was contrived, it was contrived.* But for some reason, that doesn't ease the vaguely nauseous feeling swimming in my gut.

The assistant smiles politely and takes off without another word.

I fold the note and stick it in my pocket, turning back toward my daily cleanup duties. And I wait.

Time ticks slowly on. Absently, I listen to the sounds of everyone else leaving for the day as I continue cleaning, anything to keep my hands busy. I glance up at the clock, then out into the darkened hallway. I don't know how much longer I should wait, or if maybe he forgot about me.

Another pang registers in my chest at the thought.

I turn back to my furious scrubbing and I block out sound and thought and feeling as much as I can as I concentrate. That's why I don't hear Rogan until the snap of the door shutting startles me.

I turn around to find him approaching me much as I imagine a starving lion might approach his prey—quickly, savagely and with purpose.

One moment he's striding across the room, the next he's pushing me up against the counter, driving his hands into my hair. He kisses me with all the abandon of a wild animal. I'm elated and skeptical and overwhelmed by his passion.

I drag my mouth away from his. "Rogan, wait. Please." I struggle to catch my breath as dark green eyes devour my face.

"I thought thinking about you would help with my scenes. And it did. Right up until I kissed her. She wasn't you. No one else is you."

And just like that, all my insecurities, all my pain, all my niggling fears are washed away in the tide of his desire. This is for me. All *that* was for me, too. Whether or not I can see *why*, Rogan wants me.

"I thought . . . It looked like . . ." I stammer, feeling silly now.

Rogan cups my face. "When are you going to realize that *you're* the one I want, Katie? The *only* one I want."

"But . . . it just doesn't make any sense," I argue.

"It does to me," he says, bending his head toward mine, spreading kisses over my face to punctuate his sentences. "The shy way you look away from me when I watch you. The sexy way you lick your lips when you concentrate. The delicious way you pant when you're gettin' ready to come." Rogan's hands slip around the tops of my thighs and lift until I'm sitting on the counter. My skirt is hiked up and Rogan is standing between my knees. "Your midnight eyes, your lush tits, your perfect ass. You're all I can think about most days. And now that I've been inside you . . . *God!*" Rogan spreads my legs farther and pulls me toward him until we are pressed intimately together. He grinds against me and I grip the counter, leaning back and holding on. "My body craves you."

He dives into my mouth like it's an oasis in a barren land. His tongue swirls around mine in a ravenous rhythm that's like a drug. And I'm drugged. Out of my mind under his influence. "My hands feel you. Even when you're not around." As if to prove his point, Rogan backs away just enough to slide his hands under my skirt and up the outsides of my thighs. He runs his fingers under the edge of my panties, tracing the elastic to the damp material between my legs. Frantic and not thinking, I reach for his zipper. I need to feel his hardness. I need to *feel* that he wants me. I need to have it in my hands, a tangible thing. When I wind my fingers around it, it jumps against my palm. "And my cock . . . it throbs to be inside you," he says, moving his fingertips into my crease. He moans loudly as he spreads moisture over my clit and gently massages it.

Flexing his hips toward me, Rogan covers my fingers with his own, gripping his length and guiding it toward my body. He nudges my legs farther apart and rubs the head between my folds, the silken knob gliding smoothly over my clit.

Back and forth, he moves over me, pushing me closer and closer to the edge. "If I could make a living finding new ways to make you come, that's all I'd do. Every day for the rest of my life." He teases me with the wide crown of his shaft, the friction unbearably delicious. He eases down toward my entrance and then moves away again, a dance meant to torture. And that's what it's doing. "My mouth waters when I think about the way you taste. Better than pie," he says hoarsely, reminding me of our lunch conversation.

Suddenly urgent to mark him with moments and phrases and memories like he's marking me, I push against his chest until he releases me, and I drop to my knees on the floor in front of him.

Reaching around and sinking my hands into his firmly perfect butt, I lick the glistening head and then ease my lips down over Rogan, taking as much of him into my mouth as I can, which isn't nearly all of him. I taste the essence of me mingled with the flavor of his skin, a salty, intoxicating cocktail that has heat and more moisture gushing into my panties.

I moan against him and Rogan threads his fingers into my hair, hissing his approval as I consume him with mouth and hands, even running my tongue along the crease between his heavy balls. "If you were on the pill, I'd spread your legs and come all over you," he growls, rocking his hips against me.

I work my way back up his shaft, sucking and licking until I feel him tighten against my palm. "I'm gonna come," he breathes with great effort. A tingle of satisfaction ripples through me and when his warmth pours into my mouth, my sex throbs with need.

I take every drop, savoring him as the ache between my legs increases. And then hands are reaching under my arms to pull me upright. Rogan's mouth covers mine in a savage kiss as his fingers find my core, thrusting into me and stealing my breath. "Oh God!" I cry, my knees going weak.

Rogan wraps one strong arm around my waist and lifts, carrying me the few feet to my makeup chair, where he deposits me, dropping one leg over the arm, leaving me wide open to the assault of his mouth. It's his turn to drop to his knees, push my panties aside and bring me racing toward the precipice, sucking and thrusting me all the way over it.

Pleasure crashes through me like a violent electrical storm, innervating my every muscle fiber. My back arches, my feet flex, and my fingernails dig into the armrests as Rogan penetrates me with his tongue, licking my release as it pours out for him.

Slowly, his aggressive penetration turns to soft, leisurely strokes as though he senses exactly where I am and what I need. I lie limply in the chair before him as my body drifts down from the hazy heaven of my climax. After two long, languorous minutes, Rogan begins to rain butterfly kisses across my stomach, which is partly bared by the drastically skewed position of my skirt.

"That's what I've been waiting for all day," he says, glancing up at me as he rights my panties and tugs my skirt down to cover me. "Can I give you a ride home?"

"Yes," I breathe, giving in to the urge to smile.

Rogan, about to rise, stops and leans forward to run his forefinger over the curve of my bottom lip. "And *this . . . this smile* is what I'll wait for all day tomorrow."

Neither of us says another word as I cut off the lights and Rogan leads me from the building.

TWENTY-SIX

Rogan

"You're sleeping with the wrong brother. You know that, right?"

Sitting at the bar, munching on a carrot as I finish making dinner, Katie's mouth drops open and her cheeks turn bright red at my brother's comment. I kick the back of his chair.

"You're an ass, man."

"What?" he asks, like there's nothing wrong with his comment. "Oh, I forgot. It's Wednesday. Therefore I cannot speak the truth."

I shake my head. "Sore loser," I mutter.

"I didn't lose. Hell, you didn't even give me a chance to get in the game. *Some of us* are stuck here all day instead of on a television set kissing hot actresses and lying to beautiful makeup artists."

I see the little frown that appears between Katie's eyes as she listens. "I don't lie, you dickwad."

"Everybody lies."

"Somebody didn't get his nap out today," I needle, knowing that will piss him off so bad he'll just leave. And he does. Kurt whirls his chair around to face me, his expression filled with bitter resentment.

"Sometimes I hate you," he spits, and then he wheels himself around the bar and down the hall to his room where he slams the door shut.

"Is he okay?" Katie asks cautiously.

I shrug. "He's just got issues. That's all."

"Is he always like that? I mean, the first time I met him . . ."

"He was on his best behavior. Smitten, I guess you could say. But yeah, that's more his normal state of douchiness."

I'm matter-of-fact about it because I'm used to it. Kurt feels like he has a million reasons to hate and resent me. I only understand one of them.

"Why does he resent you so much?" Katie's eyes are puzzled. Then she starts to stammer, like she regrets her question. "I—I mean, he *seems* to, anyway. Not that it's any of my business." Her voice trails off as she drops her gaze down to her hands where they're fiddling with her napkin.

I laugh, reaching across the bar to still her fingers. "Hey, it's fine. You can ask me anything."

"Okay, then why does he seem to resent you so much? Is it just because of his handicap?"

I resume assembling the salads that will accompany the filets I'll be grilling. I lay slices of cucumber on each one as I answer her. "He thinks that the reason I never went to the cops or social services, the reason that I kept my mouth shut, was because I was weak. He thinks I didn't love him enough to get him out of there. I never told him that everything I did I did to spare him."

I hear Katie's gasp. "But why? Why would you let him believe that? When you sacrificed so much for him. Why?"

I glance up to meet her horrified eyes. "Because it would've eaten him up with guilt—knowing that I stayed around because of him. Knowing that I kept taking a beating so that he wouldn't have to. And I didn't want him to have to carry that around for the rest of his life."

"Oh God, Rogan," she whispers. Her face is pale, like she can literally feel the pain of it all.

"It's fine," I tell her with a smile. I'd rather blow it off than this end up in pity. It's probably dangerously close already. "We both survived."

"You never said what happened to your father." I can tell that she wants to change the subject as much as I do.

"He's gone. Long gone." Before she can ask more questions or fumble through platitudes, I slap my hands together. "All done," I tell her, setting the full salad bowls aside and pouring each of us a glass of red wine. I come around the bar and push one stem into Katie's fingers as I take the platter of seasoned meat. "Come on. Let's go grill."

Each day that has passed this week has brought on a new sense of urgency to enjoy every second that I can with Katie. Things in Enchantment are different. This place seems separated from reality, like the real world is on a parallel plane. Real, but not *here*. Somewhere else. Somewhere that can't touch us, can't touch what we have together. I feel like once I leave here, I can never come back. Like I will have lost Katie and whatever this is between us.

We live such different lives normally. That they intersected *at all* is a miracle, so what could be next? I don't know if Katie could survive in my regular life.

That's how I've come to identify my existence. Before, during and after. Past, present, future. The life I've led up until Enchantment, the life I lead here, and the life I'll continue to lead once I leave it. Is there a way to take the now with me? To make it a part of tomorrow? Or is it impossible for the two to ever peacefully coexist?

My phone bleeps with an incoming text. I glance at Katie, sitting on one of the poolside chairs with her feet tucked up under her. There's a serene look on her face. I love seeing it there.

She smiles at me as she sips her wine. I hold her gaze for a few seconds before she turns her attention to the waterfall that cascades down a rocky landscape before splashing delicately into the pool. I wonder what she's thinking. I wonder if *she* wonders what *I'm* thinking. Or if she knows.

I check my phone when it makes a second alert. It's my agent, reminding me of the arrangements his assistant made for my flight back to New York. I have a fight in three days. It was postponed until taping for this show was complete. Both for filming and aesthetic purposes, obviously. I knew it was coming, but in a way it almost feels like it signals the end.

But I don't want this to end.

I turn the grill flame to low and close the lid to allow the steaks to finish up. I walk to Katie and squat down in front of her, taking her free hand in mine.

"Thursday is my last day of taping." The statement hangs in the air. Like a cloud of inevitability.

Katie nods once, her face expressionless as she eyes me.

I figured she knew. She gets set notes, too.

"I've got a fight on Sunday. Kurt and I will be flying out Thursday night. The match is in New York. Come with me."

Her expression doesn't change, but her eyes search mine. I don't know what she's looking for, what she's thinking, and she doesn't say anything that might clue me in.

"New York is . . ." She trails off. Even if I couldn't sense the hesitation in her words, I could detect it in her body language. She's shrinking away from me. It's almost imperceptible, but I can see her pressing her back into the cushion.

I'm as honest as I can be. It's the only way I know to fight her hang-ups. "I'm not ready for this to be over yet. I want you with me."

Just as I nearly missed her pulling away, I could've missed her relaxing back toward me if I hadn't been paying attention. But I was. When it comes to Katie, I'm always paying attention.

"And then what? I'd have to be back here to work on Monday."

"I know. I'll make sure you're here."

I can see the indecision in her eyes, but I can also see that she, too, is eager to prolong our . . . whatever this is.

Finally, she nods her agreement. "Okay. I'll come."

I smile and lean forward to kiss her. When she weaves her fingers into my hair and slides her tongue along mine, I consider abandoning supper in favor of hauling her tasty little ass off to my bedroom. But then she pulls away, breathless.

"I'll never get used to that," she states, winded.

I wink at her. "I don't want you to."

TWENTY-SEVEN

Katie

Thursday

I wake conflicted. Part of me is ecstatic to be going to New York with Rogan. It feels like we haven't had enough time together, like this is coming to an end too soon. I'm glad he feels that way, too. And I'm glad I could get the time off to go with him.

Right now, I refuse to even think about what comes after Sunday. It makes my chest tight just to consider it. If I weren't such a coward, I'd probably admit to myself that I've fallen in love with him, fallen in love with a man who lives life in a way that scares the crap out of me. He never backs down. He seizes every day. He lives life to the fullest. He's everything I'm not. But he makes me want to be more, makes me want to *do* more, *risk* more.

Another part of me, however, is terrified to return to New York. I haven't been back there since Calvin. Since my parents died, since my life was burned away. My last memories of the city are of painful months in the hospital, recovering, and equally painful months afterward, trying to pick up the pieces of a life that had been reduced to ash.

But I'm going.

For Rogan.

For Rogan, I'm jumping into the fray when I've spent the last five years avoiding it. For Rogan, I'm going public with my relationship to a star when I've purposely perfected the art of hiding in plain sight. For Rogan, I'm attending a brutal fight when I still have nightmares of what it feels like to be pummeled with angry fists.

If I'm ever going to learn to fight to live, not just to survive, it has to start here. I don't know why, but instinctively I'm absolutely certain that this is crucial. That *he* is crucial.

Rogan.

Each morning, I've awakened to the feel of his body pressed to mine. Each morning, he's been waiting for me when I get to work. Each morning, he's watched me as I put on his makeup.

After that, the hours of each day have marched on like a thousand soldiers with feet of lead. Until he comes for me and we fall into a world consisting only of us. The world where there are no scars, no boundaries, no past and no people. There's just Rogan and me and the fire that burns between us.

And today is the very last day of it all.

Thursday.

Normally this day of the week is of no consequence to me. The only difference is that it's near the end of the week when I won't have to work for two days and I get to watch *The Walking Dead* in thirty-six more hours. Those are the landmarks of my life.

But *this* Thursday is different. *This* Thursday marks the last day I'll put makeup on Rogan, the last Thursday I'll wake up in his arms, the last Thursday that I feel a million other things that I don't want to examine too closely—love; acceptance; to be wanted, cherished, protected.

So it's with a reverence that I will go about every moment of my short-lived new routine. The next time Thursday rolls around, it won't feel like this. And Rogan will be gone.

"Wha'cha thinkin' about?" Rogan asks, curling around me like a hot octopus and pressing his lips to the curve of my neck. "New York?"

He thinks I'm excited. Or nervous. Both of which are true. And I'll let him think that's *all* that I'm feeling.

I nod, not trusting my voice.

"Don't be nervous. Kurt will be there, too. With his calming influence." His derisive snort makes me smile. A watery smile, but still . . .

I feel him start to roll out of bed to go and tend to his brother, as he's done every morning. Only this time I reach for him.

His eyes meet mine in the receding dark. I crawl up onto my knees and stare at him for a few seconds, memorizing this moment, this feeling, this man. I stroke my fingertips down his cheek, enjoying every prickle of his early-morning beard against my skin. I don't ever want to forget what it feels like to touch a star. Not a star in Hollywood, but a star in my otherwise black sky. Bright and warm and oh-so-fleeting.

A tiny frown flickers between Rogan's dark, glistening eyes. He turns his face and presses his lips to the center of my palm. As always, his kiss kindles a flame, one that, if left unchecked, burns its way into a raging inferno that only he can extinguish. It never dies, though. Not really. It always seems to be waiting there. Glowing embers, just beneath the surface, waiting for him to come along and bring them back to blazing life. Like he brought *me* to life.

I'm glad that he takes the time to make love to me once more before he goes, but I feel guilty when I see him scurrying about, rushing to get home to his responsibilities. I'm a selfish, selfish woman. Kurt will give him a terrible time if he's late, I'm sure. But I can't fully regret him staying with me a little longer. I could never regret a moment spent with him, no matter how awful the consequences.

Hours later, Rogan is there when I push through the doors at work. His smile shows no evidence of a bad morning with his brother. His smile never shows anything other than his easygoing, "take life by the balls" attitude. I'll miss it. I'll miss *him*.

After our normal odd conversation with Mona and her word of the day, I take my time putting makeup on Rogan. I relish the feel of his eyes on me, of his skin beneath my fingertips, of his closeness. And when he's walking out my door with the tech, I fight back tears.

It's as I'm cleaning up, preparing for the next person to fill my chair that I get a visit from Victoria. My stomach twists into a resentful knot when I see her. I hope my smile is as coolly polite as always, though.

"So, you enjoying your last day?" she asks.

I frown. "Pardon?"

"Your. Last. Day," she repeats, barbs in her tone as she enunciates each syllable like English is my second language.

"My last day of what?"

"Being Rogan's pretend girlfriend."

"I'm not—" I stop myself. I'm not going to discuss Rogan with this pit-viper of a woman.

"Awww, you're going to deny it? How nice of you to think that I care, but you can save it. Because I don't. People like you don't even register as a blip on my radar." Her top lip draws back from her teeth, a sneer of disgust that clearly belies the sugar of her words. "I think it's sweet that he took pity on someone like you, but I don't want you to think it'll last. He'll be back with me before next weekend." My heart is a sluggish thump behind my ribs as her face suddenly breaks into a blinding smile. "Okay, well, see you Monday."

She slinks back through my door, turning her nose up to the man she passes. He plays a mafia don on the show and he's next on my list for the day. He's older and not very attractive, *far* beneath her notice, but he's a nice guy. Too nice to keep company with the likes of her, anyway, even if she wanted to. But I still hate to see her treat him like his importance ranks somewhere just beneath that of gum on the bottom of her shoe.

I smile my same polite, professional, distant smile as he takes the chair and I go about my job. It takes all my concentration to hold my mask in place, a mask that says the dark cloud over my head didn't just get a little bit darker.

"Did you bring your umbrella?" Rogan asks when the stewardess leaves to fetch our drinks at just after six Thursday evening.

"Yes. I packed it, but are you going to tell me why I'm bringing a polka-dot umbrella to New York when the forecast isn't even calling for rain?"

Rogan's lips curve into that lopsided, sexy smile that I love. "Oh, it'll rain. You'll see."

The stewardess returns with two flutes of champagne. "What are we celebrating?" I ask as I inhale the sweet perfume of the bubbly liquid.

Rogan's smile wanes as he watches me until he glances down at his glass. His expression takes on a hint of sadness. "More time."

My heart! Oh God, my heart!

I can't find a smile to give him, so I'm glad that he isn't looking at me for one. "To more time."

When he looks up to clink his glass against mine, his temporary melancholy seems to have lifted. He winks and takes a long sip of the delicious fizz.

"Where the hell is Patrice?" Kurt blares from behind us.

"Maybe she, ohhh I don't know, has a day off now and then. Ya think?" Rogan calls back in sarcastic response.

I grin when I hear his brother mutter, "Asshole."

"He's so spoiled. Just a few flights on a private plane and he's a diva. 'Where's Patrice?' 'Bring me peanuts!' 'Somebody pull this stick out of my ass!'" Rogan mocks in his best, low-key Kurt impression. He seems gratified when I laugh. I know he likes it. He's said as much.

A man who likes to see me smile and make me laugh. Was it ever possible that I wouldn't fall in love with him?

I think I know the answer to that. Falling for Rogan feels like it was as inevitable as the sun rising or the stars shining.

"So, is this *your* plane?" I ask.

"Nah. I don't fly enough to justify one. It's leased by the agency that represents me. I guess when you're dumb enough to get in the ring with some of the world's deadliest fighters in order to make them millions of dollars, they figure the least they can do is give me a comfortable flight."

"The very least. And do they have someone on board to give you a foot massage, too?"

"Not this flight. I thought if there was any . . . *massaging* to be done . . ." He wiggles his eyebrows suggestively and I roll my eyes, even though my stomach does a flip at his insinuation.

"You're not going to say something about the mile-high club, are you?"

"I *wasn't*, but now that you brought it up, I'd love to fill you in on the, ahem, package."

I smother a laugh, resisting the urge to look back over my shoulder and make sure Kurt isn't listening.

"I'm sure your brother wouldn't have anything to say about that *at all*."

Rogan scowls, as though he'd forgotten about his brother *that* quickly. "Damn it."

"I guess you'll just have to be on your best behavior today. Just this once."

Rogan huffs loudly. "Fine. I guess we can watch a movie." Reaching for my hand, Rogan kisses my knuckles and then looks into my eyes. "You know, of all the informative little tidbits that I so pleasurably dug out of you over the last six weeks, there's one thing I never asked. What's your favorite movie?"

"How could you be so remiss?" I gasp in mock horror.

"I was too busy being smitten to think about movies."

My pulse stutters, but I do my best to ignore it and act natural. "But not too busy to find out what kind of facial hair I prefer on a man?"

"Hey, that's a legit question. Sometimes I get the urge to grow a goatee. I needed to know where you stand on the matter."

"Why? It's not like you were going to be around very long."

A shadow passes over his face, a mirror of the one that has hovered over my heart all week. More inevitability.

Too many things are inevitable, it seems. Love, loss. Ecstasy, heartbreak. To have, to have not.

"Don't say things like that. It's like you're not even giving us a chance."

I'm surprised by the snap in his voice.

"It's not that. It's just . . ." I trail off, looking down to study my fingernails as I ponder which way to go with this conversation. We both know what's happening, but maybe we don't need to discuss it.

Maybe we can just pretend. For a little while longer. I quickly decide not to mar what beauty might be left in our last hours and days together. I do my best to recover outwardly. I lean my head back against the plush leather seat back and turn on a bright smile for Rogan. "I'll give us every possible chance."

His face relaxes into its normal happy façade. "Good. I didn't want to have to kidnap you. Now, where was I?" Rogan brings his lips back to my fingers, kissing each fingertip before softly reminding, "Favorite movie?"

God, I wish I could stay in this bubble with him forever, with things exactly as they are right now. Just me in a confined space with Rogan and his wonderful smile, his tender touch.

"*Judge Dredd*," I say, deadpan.

Rogan's reaction is comical. His head jerks up and his face scrunches. "*What?*"

"Yep. Cinematic genius, that one."

His mouth hangs open limply as he stares at me like I've sprouted horns. "I'll drop you off in Philly as we pass. I hope you're good with a parachute."

I laugh outright. I've never even seen *Judge Dredd*, but now I'm pretty sure I never will. "Fine. How about *Gremlins*?"

"Philly."

"*Pretty in Pink*?"

"Philly."

"*Blade Runner*?"

"Good God, when were you born?"

"All right, all right," I say dropping my gaze. "I guess *The Man Without a Face* would be my all-time favorite." When Rogan says nothing for several seconds, I sneak a peek up at him. He's watching me with a sad smile.

"What's your *second* favorite movie?"

I don't hesitate. "*Phenomenon.*"

Rogan drops his forehead onto my hand where he still holds it inside his. "You're killing me! Don't you like any movies that won't make me want to flush my head down the airplane toilet?"

I giggle. "You should've specified and asked what my favorite movie *that you might like* would be. Because in that case, I'd probably say *World War Z. Rocky. Iron Man.* Shall I go on?"

Rogan smiles broadly. "Now we're getting somewhere." He releases my hand to reach for a bag that rests on one of the two deep swivel chairs that face us. The plane is laid out with four captain's chairs facing a central table and, toward the back, two small sofas on either side of the aisle. Kurt is behind us, stretched out on one of those listening to music, with his wheelchair parked beside him.

Unzipping the bag, Rogan produces nearly every movie I mentioned, except for *Pretty in Pink.* I wouldn't expect a guy to have that one, but the fact that he has *this many* tells me there's a spy involved. Even though I was joking about them being my absolute favorites, they are the movies that come to mind most often. Well, except for *Dredd.*

"You cheated," I tell him, not the least bit angry, but rather touched instead.

"Blame Mona. That girl's tongue is loose at both ends."

"This was her idea?"

"No, this was my idea. She loved it, though. At least I guess she did. She acted like she was about to cry when I explained to her why I wanted to know."

"Yep. That sounds about right."

"So, what'll it be?"

I notice that the bag isn't empty. "What else do you have in there?" I ask, now curious as to what he brought that had nothing to do with me and my loud-mouthed friend.

I reach for the bag and Rogan's hand flinches, almost as though he was going to prevent me from looking inside, but then changed his mind.

I flip through several war movies. I don't even have to ask about those. They have Kurt written all over them. It's the one that rests on the bottom of the pile that intrigues me.

"Who's this for?" I ask, removing the DVD of *Beastly* and holding it up for him to see.

Rogan actually looks sheepish, an expression I've never seen him wear, which only further piques my curiosity. He clears his throat before he answers. "I, uh, I saw that one night on cable a few weeks back and thought it was a pretty decent romance. I mean, a guy needs to keep on top of shit like this, too, right?" His little grin tells me that he doesn't expect an answer. "But then when I got to know you . . . especially when you showed me *all of you*, I went and bought it. I've watched it more times than I care to count."

His eyes flicker to mine and dart away, flicker to mine and dart away.

I swallow hard, not knowing what to make of this association. It's plain who the beast is in our situation, but I'm trying not to jump to conclusions. I just want our last time together to be perfect, not . . . something less.

I could kick myself for being so nosey.

"Is . . . is this what you think of me?" I try to sound unconcerned, I try to *be* unconcerned.

Too late. My heart is already breaking.

He looks stricken. "No! God, no! I just thought it was appropriate because we've both struggled with our scars. We've both felt like the beast. Still do, sometimes. But that doesn't mean that other people see us that way or that we can't fall in love or be loved in return because of it. I guess this movie was just, like, *proof* of that or something." He shrugs to add an air of nonchalance to his statement. Meanwhile, I'm dumbstruck, my brain circling his reference to love like bees circling a honeycomb.

I don't know what to say, how to respond. I want to ask questions, but then again I'm afraid that the answers won't be anywhere near the ones that are making my pulse race and my heart soar right now. Instead, I go with, "Let's watch this one," and I hand him *Beastly*.

One side of Rogan's mouth pulls up, putting his single dimple on display. "Seriously?" His eyes are a light, happy green, a few shades darker than grass.

"Seriously," I confirm, forcing the words past the lump of emotion clogging my throat.

I watch as Rogan walks to the front of the cabin and fiddles with some electronics in a well-concealed cabinet and then comes back to sit next to me. A flat screen descends from the ceiling just as the movie begins to play.

We recline our chairs and Rogan leans toward me. I rest my head on his shoulder and we watch *Beastly* together.

He plays with my fingers the whole time, stopping occasionally to kiss my palm or my wrist, but then he resumes, always touching me. It's like he realizes how limited our time is and he wants the contact just as much as I do.

So we touch and glance and kiss and enjoy, all in an unspoken agreement to make the most out of what's left of the "us" that was born in Enchantment and will soon die in New York City. There's nowhere for it to go. Rogan's life is in Texas or New York or . . . wherever his fights or his acting gigs might be. And mine is in a tiny town called Enchantment. Our paths crossed for a few magical weeks, but now our trajectories go in opposite directions. His out toward a world that adores him, mine inward, toward the only place I feel comfortable.

Just over two hours later, when we land, I have to fight back tears as Rogan leads me off the plane. I want to turn around and climb back on, to suspend time indefinitely. But I can't. The end is coming whether I want it to or not.

TWENTY-EIGHT

Rogan

I had my agent put Kurt in a different room so that Katie and I would have the entire suite to ourselves. And I'm glad I did, because by the time we walk through the doors, all I can think about is getting her naked.

As soon as the bellhop sets our bags in the closet, I tip him and practically shove him out the door. When he's gone, we are surrounded only by absolute quiet and the insatiable chemistry that fills the space between us.

I take her hand and softly invite, "Come look at the view."

We walk to the floor-to-ceiling windows and I push open the sheer curtains. Spread out before us like a galaxy of twinkling stars is the city that never sleeps. Standing in front of me like a siren of unmatched beauty is the woman who never lets my mind sleep.

"It looks exactly the same, like time stood still."

"I think it's never looked more beautiful," I tell her, burying my nose in the exposed side of her neck. She still insists on keeping that one thick wave of hair swept around to cover the other side where her scars are located. "Then again, I've never seen it with you standing in front of it."

She looks up and back at me, her eyes all wide and sparkly. "You know just what to say."

"I only speak the truth."

"Your truth makes me . . ." She trails off in a wistful sigh.

"Makes you what?" I ask, circling her tiny waist with my hands before I run them up under her shirt to cup her breasts.

"Makes me . . ." She trails off again, this time on a breathless note, her eyes drifting closed as I rub her hard nipples between my fingers.

I release them to unbutton her top, stepping away from her only long enough to pull it from her shoulders and slip off her bra.

I knead the firm mounds as I move her forward a few inches. I lean into her, watching her nipples pucker as they near the cool glass of the window and then flatten against it.

"Can I share you with New York?" I ask, rhythmically pressing into her back so that the glass stimulates her nipples. It frees my hands to slide down her stomach.

"What do you mean?" Her voice is already raspy and shallow.

"I want to tease them with what I get to touch, what I get to taste. What they can never have."

I ease one hand beyond the loose waistband of her jeans and into the front edge of her panties. I find her slit with my index finger and I slip inside. She's slippery wet and hot.

"God, you're so wet. Is this all for me?" I ask, rubbing my finger in her moisture before leisurely stroking the firm little ridge of her clit.

"All for you," she breathes, letting her head fall back against my chest.

With my other hand, I unbutton and unzip her pants and push them down her legs along with her panties. She steps out of them and leaves her thighs spread for me.

My cock is straining against my own jeans. I unfasten them to free it, guiding the tip to the crack of her lush ass as I press her chest tighter against the glass.

"Aren't you supposed to start your period soon?" I ask, feeling a drop of precome ooze out to coat the smooth skin of her cheek. I grind my teeth together, my erection nearly painful as I think of all sorts of wicked things I'd like to do to this girl.

"Yes," she says, swiveling her hips against me as she reaches back and grips my thighs, digging in with her fingers as my pace on her clit increases. "Why?"

"Would it be safe to have sex without a condom this close to it? I want to feel you with nothing between us. Just this once."

I run my finger down to her entrance, teasing her by popping it in and out in shallow thrusts as my palm massages the rest of her sex. She grunts and my cock jumps. *God, she's amazing. Hungry. Like me.*

"Y-you don't have to worry," she explains. "I went after work the night you had to shoot late and got an IUD."

My balls contract in anticipation. "Are you serious?"

She nods, pressing her cheek to the window, her eyes still closed. "I was going to tell you, but I . . . I . . ."

"It's okay," I tell her. There will be plenty of time for talk later. Now, all I want to do is shoot come so far up into her that she can taste it in the back of her throat. "What do you think the people down on the street would think of this pussy if they could see it?" I bring my hand around to her hip and push her pelvis up against the window, too. "Every one of those bastards would kill to be me, just to have this beautiful body underneath them one time."

I slip my hand between her legs from behind, finding her slick core and thrusting two fingers as deep as they'll go. She rises up on her tiptoes and her mouth rounds out into a silent O.

"Just thinking about someone seeing us, someone watching me put my fingers in you, put my cock in you, watching your come drip off my balls is just . . ."

It's all too much—the thoughts, the words, the anticipation. The urgency of being inside her while I still can.

I spin Katie toward me, covering her mouth with mine as I lift her by her legs and press her back to the glass. I enter her in one smooth motion, stopping when I'm buried to the hilt in her tight little body and her gasp in my ear is the only sound I can hear.

"Fuuuc . . ." I groan, forcing myself to concentrate so that I won't come. "Holy shit, Katie!"

I pull out, leaning away just enough to tongue a nipple into my mouth and suck hard. When I've regained control, I slam up into her again, going even deeper. Katie loses it. I feel the tremble of her muscles right before they contract, squeezing me until it almost hurts it feels so good. Her sweetness pours over the head of my cock and down to my balls, and it's more than I can take. I'm done. Finished. Spewing into her in record time.

Finding her mouth again, I drive my body into hers over and over and over again until I can't tell whose come is whose. And I don't give a shit either. The only thing that matters right now is the woman in my arms and how I don't want to be anywhere but inside her.

And that I love her. Damn it, I love her.

Shit.

TWENTY-NINE

Katie

Friday

I don't know what I expected that we'd do two days before the fight, but Rogan has been much busier than I anticipated. Evidently, because he hasn't been training like he should, he has to go through a series of challenges to prove to his trainer, Johns, that he won't go into the ring and get himself killed. Johns says that his acting, or "playing" as he calls it, just makes him weak. And according to him, Rogan needs to be at his best for this particular opponent.

"This ain't some pussy from outta nowhere, some random jack-hole who fights like a girl. This kid's got something. I wanna see you eatin' him for breakfast, not the other way around," the crusty, graying fifty-some-year-old explains in his smoker's growl.

I listen to Johns taunt Rogan with barbs as he pushes him through the most grueling workout I've ever seen. Not once does Rogan falter. Even as he grunts with strain, even as he grimaces in pain, he doesn't slack off. In fact, Johns seems to have a way of driving him to work even harder, so maybe this is just their dynamic.

From my perspective (once I got used to Johns's way of needling Rogan) it has been fascinating. Not just their relationship and the whole "gym" scene, but Rogan himself. Watching his muscles flex beneath his shimmering skin, seeing him press beyond the point of most human endurance, listening to his breath heave with his exertion—*good Lord!* My knees are weak and my panties are a wet mess.

This man is delicious in any setting, whether dressed in jeans and a tee with his cute grin and wicked wink, or dressed in a pair of shorts and dripping with sweat. He takes my breath away.

This makes me respect his physical conditioning and fighterly prowess, too. Rogan is a deadly machine. It seems he's perfect. Top to bottom, head to toe, inside and out.

"Told you I was keeping up better than you thought," Rogan tells Johns as he guzzles from a liter of vitamin water.

"Like I'd take your word for it, pup," Johns replies, slapping Rogan's shoulder. He calls him that a lot—pup. Seems like their affection for each other runs deep, far beyond this man's gruff exterior.

"Get some rest. I'll pick you up at eight." Before he disappears around the corner, the brusque old man calls back to Rogan, nodding to me, "And explain to her what needs to happen on fight day. And what *doesn't need to happen* on fight day."

With a wry grin, Rogan salutes his trainer and then turns to me, slinging his still-dry towel over my head to collar me and pull me toward him for a kiss. "I don't want to touch you and get you all sweaty," he says, keeping every body part except his lips at bay.

"I've been watching this sweaty body for the last four hours," I tell him, running my hands down his granite stomach and leaning into his chest. "I *want* it touching me."

The black of his pupils swells within the green forest of his eyes and I barely hear him breathe, "Damn you, woman."

Looking left and right to make sure no one has inadvertently stumbled into the private gym that his trainer rented, I give a startled yip when Rogan suddenly bends and throws me over his shoulder, trotting off toward . . . somewhere.

The next thing I see from my perch atop his shoulder, facing the floor, is the carpet turn to tile. When Rogan puts me down, we are in the bathroom. That's the last thought that registers before his hands are all over me, his lips are all over me, and I find out first-hand what happens when you get a fighter all worked up.

It's amazing.

An hour and a half later, we are in the back of the limo, retracing the streets to our hotel. I'm lying, boneless, against Rogan's side, my head on his shoulder and his arm draped loosely around me. He seems distracted. Happy and satisfied, but still distracted.

"What did Johns mean about what to expect on fight day?"

I hear Rogan's huff of laughter rumble through his chest and vibrate into my ear. "He has always insisted that a very specific ritual should be observed on fight day and he never deviates from it. Ever."

"And just what does this ritual entail?" I ask, picturing everything from the blood of a live chicken to wearing a jockstrap that hasn't been washed since 2009.

"Sleeping until seven. A big breakfast at eight. Stretching at ten, followed by a massage and lunch. He has pretty much the whole day planned out. What he forbids, no questions asked, is sex. Thinks it makes a fighter weak, distracted."

Bummer.

"And what do *you* think?"

I feel his lips brush the top of my head. "I think my mind is always on you, so I'm not sure abstaining will make any difference."

Now I feel guilty. Deliriously happy, of course, but also guilty. "Well, this is important. Maybe we shouldn't mess with what works."

"Well, this isn't a title fight, so . . ."

"But still. If you lost because of me . . ." I sit up and look at Rogan. His eyes are lazy yet hooded. I want to ask what's going on behind them, but I don't dare. If he wanted me to know, he'd tell me. And maybe *I* don't *really* want to know.

"I won't lose," he assures me with a quiet confidence. He kisses my forehead and the tip of my nose. "I'll win for you. Because you'll be there watching me."

"That's something I wanted to ask you about," I begin, toying with the neckline of his V-neck tee. "Will I have to sit in a certain place? I mean, I'd rather not . . . I don't want people to . . ."

Sexy lips quirk into a knowing grin as Rogan hooks a finger under my chin to raise my eyes to his. "Why do you think I wanted you to bring the umbrella?"

I frown. "I don't know. Why did you?"

He brings his smiling mouth to mine and teases my lips with a short kiss. "You'll see. But don't worry about anything. I've got it all taken care of." When his tongue flicks out to trace my bottom lip, I find it hard to worry about much of *anything*. "Until then, we've got a lot of hours before fight day. I hope you don't have plans."

I think to myself, while I can still think at all, that I don't have any plans other than to be devoured by this gorgeous man. There are no better plans than those.

Sunday, Fight Day

As I'm chauffeured from the hotel to the arena, limo-style, I reflect back on the day. When Rogan said he had it all taken care of, he wasn't kidding. Maybe it was because he knew I was nervous to be back. Maybe it was because he knew he would hardly see me. Or maybe it was just because he's thoughtful and kind and wonderful. I don't know, but he had the entire day planned out, right down to the minute.

We didn't leave our room at all yesterday. I lost count of how many times we made love. We both fell into an exhausted sleep sometime in the wee hours, but when I woke this morning, he was gone.

Room service was delivered to my room, promptly at eight. It consisted of eggs, bacon, hash browns and the most delicious pancakes in the history of the world. But the best part was what rested beside the tiny, swan-shaped cake of butter—*The Walking Dead: Season One* and a one-word note that read *Enjoy*.

Which I did. All the way through lunch, which was delivered to my door at precisely twelve o'clock. And then, again, right up until the phone in my room rang at three fifteen to inform me that my masseuse was on her way up for my three thirty appointment.

I've never had a massage before. Obviously, at this point in my life, I'm not terribly fond of people touching me, but I didn't want to send her away and make a big deal of it and embarrass both Rogan and myself, so I jacked my chin up and decided I'd suffer through it. I mean, from what I've seen, there's a hole in the table that you can actually hide your face in. It's perfect for someone like me. At least she wouldn't know of my shame. But as it turns out, Rogan even had *that* organized to the finest detail. She came in, asked me to change and wrap myself in a sheet, and then she proceeded to give me my massage right through the sheet. My hair stayed swept over my shoulder as I lay, face down, staring at the carpet. Well, until I got so relaxed that I closed them. Then I wasn't staring at much of anything other than the backs of my eyelids.

After that, I slithered off her table and made it to the couch, where I collapsed in front of the last episode of *TWD* until suppertime, which was again delivered to my door. The only way the day could've been better is if Rogan had been with me for all those hours. But if I had to be in New York and spend them alone, that was certainly the way to go.

I suppose I could've called Kurt, but somehow that didn't seem like it might be a very good idea, so I refrained. If Rogan had wanted him to be part of my day, he'd have penciled him in.

So now, here I am, walking into a packed arena, just a few minutes before the fight starts. My polka-dot umbrella is in hand, although I have no idea why.

My palms are sweaty, even though there's no good reason for them to be. I guess it's just the fact that I'm out of my comfort zone, out of my shell after hiding inside it for so long. But I have to admit that it's been a nice change of pace.

There was a man waiting for me at the curb when the limo pulled up. He opened the door and asked, "Ms. Rydale?"

I nodded and he offered his hand, which I took and let him help me out. He then led me inside, past all the outer bands of security and ticket-taking hot spots, right to a seat that borders on what people call the nosebleeds. I'm not sitting up in the rafters, but I'm not ringside, either. Not that I wanted to be. Too much attention.

Surprisingly, I have an excellent view. I'm nearly eye-level with the ring, which is a big, fenced-in octagon, just farther away.

I sit down, taking in the energy of the people around me. Many are standing, watching the ring expectantly, and many, especially the women, are carrying umbrellas, which I find odd. Odd, both that they're carrying umbrellas when it's been gorgeous outside (and is supposed to remain gorgeous until Tuesday according to channel six) and odd that there are *so many women* here. I mean, this isn't exactly the kind of sport I would expect a lot of women to love, but . . . who am I to judge?

When the announcer walks to the center of the ring, the crowd goes wild. I'm not sure why, but since I'm the newbie, I figure it's better to just go with it. I'll probably never experience something like this again.

I give a muted little *whoooo* in an effort to blend in. I'm immediately more enthusiastic about this venue when I see that no one pays me the least bit of attention. A place where I can go completely unnoticed, in a crowd this size, is right up my alley.

A minute or so later, I see people start to point and a preternatural hush falls across the arena. Seconds later, a guitar riff starts to strain loudly through the speakers. It plays for several seconds, like an intro, and then, when the horns of *Battle Without Honor or Humanity* kick in, a deafening roar erupts from the crowd. Heads turn and people start to jump up and down, but I can't see what's going on. I can't see anything except umbrellas popping open everywhere, being held aloft and shaken to the beat of the music.

Scrambling for mine where it resides under my seat, I open it as well, standing along with the rest of the crowd, looking for the source of the excitement. My gut (and the umbrellas) tells me it's Rogan.

I finally see him when he reaches the edge of the ring. He's cloaked in a black satin robe that has a huge green R on the back and what look like raindrops falling through it. Even though the hood is up, I'd recognize him anywhere. That walk, that posture, that mouth and chin, barely visible in the slice of light shining in on it.

It's Rogan.

I know it.

Stripping off his hood with a flourish, Rogan bounces on the balls of his feet and holds up his thinly gloved hands. He nods to each section of the stadium as he turns a slow circle. Each one goes even wilder when he does. Women screaming, men hollering, everyone chanting. It isn't until the music starts to die down that I can finally make out the rhythmic words of the fans. They're crying, *Bring the rain! Bring the rain! Bring the rain!*

Rogan turns to enter the fenced ring, but just before he ducks inside, he stops and scans the crowd in a more purposeful way. As his eyes pass each section surrounding the octagon again, I even hear a few propositions, girls offering to do everything from have his baby to lick his abs and a few other less publicly appropriate declarations.

He seems to ignore them all as he searches the masses. When he turns in the direction of my section, my heart stutters in my chest and I hold my umbrella steady. Now I understand why he wanted me to bring it. In a sea of black and green umbrellas, my polka dots stand out like a sore thumb. Something he should easily be able to spot from a distance.

And he does.

I know it the second he sees me. I feel his eyes on my face like a touch. It's as though there isn't a field of people between us, as though there aren't a million eyes on him. For a tenth of a second, it's just Rogan and me. Our connection sizzles with electricity as he brings one fist to his mouth, kisses the knuckles and holds it out to me.

To *me*. He holds that kiss out *to me*.

Everything inside me melts. Even as people turn to see who he's giving such a public nod to, my heart thunders, my pulse races and my face breaks out into a smile that I can't stop. It comes from too deep, it speaks of something too beautiful to hide.

This man. God, this man!

I don't know whether to laugh or cry. Or do both.

How can he do this to me? Make me feel so much with such a tiny gesture?

After a few seconds, he drops his hand, bumps his fists together and smiles that cocky, lopsided grin that makes my stomach turn flips. And, judging by the response of the ovary-possessing portion of the crowd, I'm not the only one. There are a couple of girls sitting close to me that I worry might faint. I wonder briefly if they think he might've been motioning to one of them. I don't know, of course, but a guy tells one of them to sit down before she falls down. When she does, I see that her face is pale and streaked with tears.

This fan business is some serious stuff.

As the two fighters enter the ring, the announcer explains that this is a fight to benefit a charity called A Way Out, a safe haven for abused children, and that no title will be awarded, yada yada yada. I'm even more anxious for Rogan to win now, now that I know why the charity is so close to his heart.

After that part, the announcer starts to become more animated, drawing out certain words as he gives the information on the challenger, Daniels. He goes through weight and titles and his nickname. I think everyone is as impatient as I am for him to get to Rogan.

When he does, the announcer pauses, like he knows the anticipation is rising to fever pitch. I can almost feel it vibrating through the bodies in the stadium like a living thing.

"And in the corner to my left, weighing in at two hundred nineteen pounds, wearing his signature black and green, the reigning UFM heavyweight champion of the world, Kieeefer 'The Rain' Rooooooogannnnnnn!"

Another deafening roar as Rogan bounces out, turning three hundred and sixty degrees in the center of the ring before facing off with his opponent. The guy who I'm assuming is the referee gives them some kind of "protect yourself and listen to me" speech before asking them to tap gloves.

As the fight starts, I'm recalling the research I did about this sport. I watch them dance around each other, taking shots called jabs, I think, and kicking out with their knees. Not much is connecting yet and, based on the grin Rogan is wearing, I'm guessing he's not overly worried that any might. It seems as though he's toying with his competitor.

I read that this guy, Daniels, will be one of the next in line to challenge Rogan for the heavyweight championship, but this particular bout doesn't count. This is more of an exhibition type thing, just for charity. But it's still strong in the back of my mind what Johns, his trainer, said about not wanting to see this kid eat him for breakfast. That must be why my fingers are curled into such tight, nervous fists that my knuckles ache.

My eyes are glued to Rogan when, all of a sudden, like lightning striking a tree, he steps in and punches Daniels. The blow is so hard that it whips his head viciously to the right. Obviously Daniels wasn't expecting it. He reels backward, shaking his head to try and clear it. The crowd cheers Rogan on, but he doesn't take the bait. He just grins at them and steps back, giving his opponent time to recover. I'm sure this isn't the way he normally fights. The point would be to take advantage of Daniels's addled status and take him down. But since this is for charity, I'm sure Rogan wants to give them a good show.

Daniels finds his way back to the center of the ring, his left hand raised to protect his face from Rogan's potent right hook. They engage in their dance again, advancing and retreating, Rogan the fierce cat playing with his prey.

Daniels punches at Rogan several times, but he doesn't land even one strike. Rogan dodges each one like he can see it coming just a fraction of a second before Daniels decides to throw it. Rogan's muscles bunch and shift under his skin a moment before Daniels attacks, moving him out of the way as smoothly and effortlessly as water flowing over rocks. He's quick and graceful. Fluid. Amazing to watch.

Rogan's opponent reaches in to grab Rogan around the neck. I'm a bit puzzled at first as to why Rogan would let him, but the guy beside me yells excitedly, shouting, "That's just where you *don't* wanna be, asshole!"

I return my attention to Rogan just as the crowd starts to shout again. *Bring the rain! Bring the rain!*

I can see just enough of Rogan's fierce expression to know that he isn't playing with Daniels anymore. Things just got serious.

Both men are still in the center of the ring, Daniels gripping each side of Rogan's neck, Rogan's hands on Daniels's shoulders. They hold each other like that for several long seconds. The chanting, the anticipation, the energy of the crowd—it all collides to bring my nerves to a jangling crescendo. And then, in a movement that is so perfectly executed, so blindingly fast, Rogan kicks with his knee, slides his other foot behind Daniels's and has him on his back in the blink of an eye.

They are a writhing mass of slithering limbs and grappling hands, and I'm unable to make heads or tails of their form until Rogan pushes out with his legs. I hear the excited cries and shouts of the people surrounding me. I see them coming to their feet and cheering, so I know something significant is happening. Then I see Rogan stretch out nearly full length at an angle to Daniels's body, his legs wrapped around his opponent's upper body and Daniels's arm being pulled up between them. Rogan, holding tight to his opponent's arm, continues to stretch back, a little at a time, bending the joints in a way that makes them look deformed. Daniels's face is bright red as he reaches toward Rogan with his free hand, punching haphazardly.

Something happens and Rogan loses his grip, Daniels's arm slipping out of his grasp and almost free of him completely, but Rogan bends forward, smashing his fist into Daniels's face in four rapid-fire strikes. Even from a distance, I see blood fly as Daniels's head bounces against the mat with a thud I'm sure I could hear if the crowd wasn't so wild.

My stomach clenches and, for a moment, I'm caught in a time and a place where I felt the impact of fists, where I was held down so that I couldn't escape. The fear, the incapacity, the remembered pain flood my body with a sick adrenaline that causes my hands to shake and perspiration to pop out across my forehead.

I blink my lids, forcing my eyes to focus on the present, on where I am, on the fact that I'm safe. But the feelings are still there, too intense to be part of my past. It's like they leapt out of my nightmares to become a reality to me again.

My chest feels tight as I watch Rogan regain control of Daniels and pull his arm through his legs again. "Arm bar! Arm bar!" the man in front of me yells. Rogan shows no mercy this time. He stretches back, his face a stony mask, and relentlessly contorts Daniels's arm.

I see Daniels tap the mat with his free hand. The referee makes a gesture and says something that I can't hear, causing Rogan to release his opponent and jump to his feet. He won.

His stance says he's the victor. The crowd says they had no doubt.

I study Rogan's face. Gone is the fierceness of only seconds before, replaced by the confident smile that won my heart. He never had any doubt either. He's in his element when he's in battle. And I'm in my own personal hell.

I've never been more conflicted.

THIRTY

Rogan

Victory. It surges through my blood. I can taste it on my tongue, sweet and tangy. I can smell it in the air, mingling with sweat. There is no feeling in the world like winning. It makes me feel alive when, for a lot of years growing up, I wasn't sure I'd survive.

But I did.

Against the odds. And here I am, on top of the world.

My first conscious thought as I do a slow turn of triumph in the center of the ring is of Katie. I squint past the bright lights, scanning the sea of faces for hers, but I can't find her. My gaze drops to the first row, to where my brother is parked in his wheelchair. I frown my question at him, nodding to the upper rows. He shrugs. He doesn't know where she went, even though he was supposed to keep an eye on her.

I feel a thin thread of unease unraveling in my gut. I don't know why she would leave her seat like that. My agent was supposed to

bring her to me in the locker room in another ten or fifteen minutes. Now I don't know where she is. Maybe the bathroom . . .

I pull my attention back to getting through the next hour. After
all the regular post-fight shit, I can disappear back into a world where
it's just Katie and me. For as long as we've got left.

As usual, my trainer joins me in the ring. I'm surprised when
my agent, my publicist, my benefactor and Victoria Musser show
up as well. Surprised and pissed off. No one told me Victoria would
be here. And why the hell is she? She has no place at my side.

I hide my irritation, putting on a polite smile for the cameras. I
hate everyone touching me and posing with me, though. All they
want is a photo op. Pieces of shit.

As flashes go off in every direction, I think to myself that it's
probably not *that big* of a mystery why they're all here. It's great press
for my agent; my publicist; and Senator Sims, my benefactor; and
his son. And, of course, it's a great photo op for Victoria. Not to
mention a convenient plug for the show on which I'll be starring at
the beginning of the season. I guess it's even logical. For media
whores, that is.

If anything, their presence only makes me *more* anxious to get
away, to find Katie. She's like an island in a sea of sharks and suck-
erfish. It seems she might be the only person on the planet who
wants nothing from me except . . . me. My time, my attention, my
love, my touch. And I'm more than happy to give her all those. For
as long as she'll have me.

The circus continues, following me all the way to the locker
room where they hover at the door, pounding me with questions.
Senator Sims, who has now been joined by his wormy son, is proudly
answering questions to my left when a beaming Victoria wiggles her
way in at my right.

I have to make myself hold steady and not lean away when she latches on to my side. The media, always observant, doesn't miss the way she drapes herself over me. I grit my teeth when it takes the questions in a different direction.

"Victoria, does this mean you and Rogan are back together?"

"Rogan, you were at the top of your game tonight. Did that have anything to do with Victoria's presence?"

"Rumor has it that you two patched things up on the set of *Wicked Games*. Is that true?"

"Victoria, the word was that Rogan dumped you. What made you take him back?"

"How about your relationship? Is it open? Our sources say that you two have expanded to include Rayelle Parker."

As if on cue, the corps of reporters parts and Rayelle comes slinking through, making a beeline for me. With a kiss to Victoria (on the lips, I might add), she insinuates herself between Senator Sims and me, stretching up to kiss the side of my neck. It only takes me a few seconds of both women hanging themselves on me, running their hands up my bare stomach, to realize what the hell is going on.

Publicity for the show.

This is all a publicity stunt.

That's when I look up and see a familiar dark head. It catches my attention, bobbing at the very back of the throng of paparazzi. It's Katie. I see her shrinking away from all the commotion, backing down the hall with my brother trailing along in her wake. Her face is as pale as a ghost.

THIRTY-ONE

Katie

I'm nauseous, paralyzed. If I thought the remembered fears of my past were incapacitating, this feeling, this *horror* is enough to bury me where I stand.

It's extremely upsetting to see Victoria and Rayelle rubbing themselves all over Rogan, to hear insinuations being dispensed left and right. It's extremely upsetting that Rogan is doing nothing to remove himself from the situation or disabuse anyone of the conclusions being drawn. But none of that is as agonizing or confusing as the presence of Senator Sims and his son at Rogan's side.

I've known Senator Sims for years. I've hated him for almost as long. He's responsible for the police declaring the fire that disfigured me an "accident." Seeing him turns my blood cold, yet it's nothing compared to how the man to his left makes me feel.

Calvin Sims.

My ex.

The guy I thought I loved. The guy who had a dark side that I didn't see until it was too late. The guy who broke hearts and bones and spirits like some people break bread. The guy who, in a fit of rage, set me on fire. The person who has inhabited more of my nightmares than the boogeyman.

And they're both standing beside the man I let myself trust, the man I confided in. The man I fell in love with.

My head spins. My heart shrivels.

How? Why? How could this be?

Suddenly, I feel claustrophobic. It's as though the train of my life has flown off the tracks and all its cars of past, present and future are colliding. Everything is piling up into one big mess, a heap of twisted truths and inconceivable realities threatening to crush me under their weight.

My lungs are failing. My head is spinning. My oxygen is running out. Slowly, I back away from the fervent crowd as it encroaches on Rogan, pummeling him with questions.

Across the tops of their heads, jewel-green eyes lock on mine. He stares at me for a few intense seconds, something unfathomable darkening emerald to jade. My stomach flips over and my chest constricts. I thought I knew this man, but I knew nothing. I only saw the façade. And the unfortunate truth is that there's nothing beneath it, no more to him than this. Lies. Cameras. Action.

When I'm far enough away that I can no longer feel the body heat of the horde, I inhale sharply, ready to bolt back down the hall. Why did Kurt come to find me at the front doors when I'd left for air? And why the hell did he bring me here? Did he want me to see the real Rogan? Or did he just want to hurt me? Maybe that's who he is, too. Just a cruel, cruel person. Like his brother.

An internal alarm blares when I hear a short pause, a hush almost, followed by a barrage of questions.

"Who's that, Rogan?"

"Is that the girl from the stands?"

"Is she the one you saw before the fight? Who is she, Rogan?"

Panic. That's exactly what I feel when I see every eye turn toward me. After that, it's just chaos. Voices raised, people clamoring, everything closing in on me.

Before I can get away and before Rogan can get to me, Victoria somehow slips through the crowd and appears at my side. She loops one arm around my shoulders and hugs me to her.

I don't move away from her. Having someone, *anyone* familiar close to me is somehow comforting, like a buffer.

I shrink against her side, wishing I could disappear entirely. I feel like a deer in headlights, frozen. Terrified.

Then, as though every facet of my worst nightmares are coming to life in a single evening, Victoria reaches up with the hand on my shoulder and gently sweeps my hair away from my neck, exposing my scars for the flash of cameras, for the fodder of the media.

I'm so shocked, so completely taken aback by the gesture, I simply stand there, mortified and stunned. I can't even lift my arm to cover my shame.

"Guess who told me all about your little secret," Victoria hisses next to my ear, her smile never faltering as she looks into my eyes and then presses her cheek to mine to pose for the multitude of pictures being taken.

Guess who told me all about your little secret.

Agony rips through my insides. Rogan. He told her. He told her about my scars. The ultimate betrayal. How could he do that to me? *Why? Why* would he do that to me?

It's like I don't even know him. Like I never did. It was all just an act to get the girl who no one else could get. And I let him. I let him in, let him close. But I was misled, deceived. On every possible level. By the first person I've trusted in years. By the first person I've loved in forever.

Flash, flash, flash. Cameras being shoved in my face, microphones being held out to me, curious onlookers dissecting my every word and move.

"Are you affiliated with the charity?"

"Are you a representative at the benefit?"

"How do you know Rogan?"

"Are you a victim of abuse? Do you have a story to tell?"

With my mind spinning, I listen to their questions, still too stunned to move. I can only assume they're asking about abuse because the charity is one for abused children. I'm sure that, by the look of my scars, they think I might very well be one. I can understand their rationale, and perversely, I almost wish it were the case. Somehow it doesn't seem quite as humiliating as the truth. But still, my lips can't form an answer, my throat can't utter a sound.

I look up for Rogan. He's gone. I look at Calvin. His face is contorted in a sneer that I remember all too well. I look to my side at Victoria. She's as smug as I've ever seen her.

"Told you he'd be mine," she whispers, winking at me for the reporters, even though they can't hear what she's saying.

I urge my numb legs into motion, taking one step back. It feels so good I take another. Then another. The closer I get to freedom, the farther away the faces get, the more my muscles cooperate. Three, four steps later, I'm running through the maze of halls behind the stadium, looking frantically for a way out. Any way out.

I see a red *Exit* sign up ahead and I lunge for it, pushing through and out into the cool, dark night like a woman possessed. I run in a straight line, aiming for the lights of the street in front of me. When I reach it, I hail a cab, a skill I'm glad I never lost, and I give the driver the airport as my destination. I don't care that I have only the clothes on my back. I don't care that my belongings are still in the room I shared with Rogan. I don't care that I'm acting irrationally. I have to get out of here. I can't be in this city anymore. For the second time in my life, it's taken from me everything I hold dear.

Everything.

THIRTY-TWO

Rogan

I've felt protective before. Over Kurt. Over my comrades in Delta Five unit. I'd fight to the death for them. But even my feelings for Kurt, my damn *brother*, don't hold a candle to the almost violently protective surge that's pumping through my veins right now.

Katie.

Seeing her expression just now, seeing the sheer panic on her face when this bunch of nosey asshole reporters saw me notice her . . . God, I just wanted to tear through them like teeth through meat, ripping and tearing and killing.

But I know better. I know better than to start something that could go sideways with her caught (physically *and* emotionally) in the middle. She could get hurt, and I couldn't live with myself if that happened. So, without a word, I turn and run through the locker room, heading for the door that leads into an anteroom and then out into the hallway. It should empty out somewhere behind Katie, some place that I can get her and get her the hell out of here.

But when I burst through the door, there's no Katie. The hall is full of the same reporters, all as voraciously curious as a tank of barracudas who've caught the scent of blood. Besides them, there is only Victoria. No Katie. Even Kurt is gone.

Unconcerned with niceties or worrying about the damn cameras, I reach through the crush of bodies and grab Victoria's arm. She turns a blinding smile on me that only serves to piss me off even more. I'm not playing her games right now. "Where's Katie? Where'd she go?"

"How am I supposed to know? She was here one minute and then she was running down the hall like a scared rabbit the next. I guess she freaked out over those scars."

Scars? For about a tenth of a second, I'm confused. What happened while I was coming for Katie, while I was running through the back rooms?

I don't ask because I already know the answer. I see it on Victoria's face. The satisfaction, the malice. I wind my fingers around her stickish upper arms and haul her up against my chest, hissing down into her face, "What the hell did you do?" She doesn't answer me, just smiles. "You *bitch*!"

I've never hit a woman. Never even considered it, but looking down into these smug eyes tries my patience like never before.

"She's not right for you, Rogan. She never was. You just needed a little help in seeing that."

"If you've hurt her, so help me God . . ."

Victoria has the audacity to arch her back and make this into an even worse spectacle. "You know I like it rough, baby."

I throw her away from me like the trash that she is and she stumbles backward. "You know, Tori, you're the only woman I've ever known who I can truly say I hate."

Without another word to her or anyone else, I take off down the hall, praying that Katie's waiting for me back at the hotel.

Only she's not.

After a twenty-minute ride because of traffic, a ride during which I'd done nothing but hit REDIAL on Katie's cell number, I took the elevator up to an empty hotel room. I feel a pang of panic when I see that all her stuff is exactly where she left it, but she's nowhere to be found. Where the hell could she be? If not here, where else would she go?

Fear clenches in my gut, a cold fist wrapping around my stomach. What if something happened to her? What if she got railroaded by the press somewhere else at the coliseum? What if she got hurt somehow?

Sweat breaks out on my forehead, but I push all that emotion down, deep down. I have to think. I have to find her.

Rational thought brings Kurt to mind. He's gone, too. He was supposed to keep an eye on her. Maybe he knows where to find her.

Furious with myself, my brother, my nasty bitch of an ex-girlfriend, I dial Kurt. He answers after the first ring.

"Where is she and why the hell weren't you keeping an eye on her?" I preempt the instant he picks up.

"I checked the hotel and she's not there."

"No shit. That's where I'm at."

"You just need to calm down. There's—"

"Don't tell me to calm down. She's upset and I need to find her. I need to find her because *you* couldn't do the one simple thing I asked you to do."

"I'm at a little bit of a disadvantage, if you haven't noticed," he replies bitterly.

"Not this time, Kurt. I give you that excuse practically every day of our lives, but not this time. All I asked was for you to keep an eye on her. Your eyes work just fine, damn it."

To this, he says nothing. Silence is my only answer.

"I have to find her," I growl in frustration.

"Have you checked the airport?"

The airport. It makes perfect sense. She's scared, upset, humiliated. She'd want safety, security, the comfort of the familiar.

"I'm on my way, but until I call and tell you that she's okay, you get everyone you can find on her ass. I want her found and I want her found *now!*"

I hang up, throw on a pair of jeans and a shirt, grab my wallet from the room safe and retrace my footsteps back down to the lobby, where the bellman hails a cab for me. I'm in too much of a hurry to wait for the limo. I'd take a motorcycle if they had one, but . . .

In the back of the cab, I resume dialing and redialing Katie's number over and over and over, all the way to the airport. If she's not there, I don't know what I'll do. I don't know where else to look. I brought her here, to a city I know she mostly hates, and then I lost her. She could be anywhere.

I leave only one message for her, hoping that wherever she is, she'll listen to it. "It's me. I don't know what happened, but I need to find you. You're scaring me. Call me back. God, baby! I . . . I . . . Just call me back, Katie. Please."

At the airport, I'm encouraged to find that the next flight back to Atlanta leaves in forty minutes. If she's here, she'll be on that flight to get back to Enchantment. I don't hesitate to buy a ticket and make my way through security and on to the gate. I'm deflated when I scan the few faces I see lounging in the concourse chairs. I don't see Katie's. My heart is galloping as I spin and look in all the other fairly close chairs for her, too. No dice.

But then, tucked in a corner right next to the window, nearly out of sight, is a familiar head. My chest gets tight just looking at her. She's holding her cell phone to one ear, her eyes cast down. Even though I can't see much of her face, I can see enough of it to know that she's still pale and that she's been crying.

I don't call out to her when I spot her. I just exhale, relief flooding my muscles, making me weak. Suddenly I feel like Daniels won that fight, not the other way around.

I make my way across the short carpet to where she's sitting. When I get within a few feet of her, she glances up from under her eyelashes. Her eyes are big pools of dark blue misery. I watch them fill with tears and something that looks an awful lot like hate.

I slow down, approaching her cautiously. "Are you okay?" I ask softly.

"You need to leave, Rogan."

"Not without you."

"I'm going home. Alone."

Alone. A lurch of my heart.

I gulp.

"What happened?"

Her eyes spit fire. "Don't you dare. Don't you dare pretend you don't know." Her voice is low and calm, but there's venom in it. She's livid, but I can tell how hurt she is, too. It slices between my ribs, through cartilage and muscle, right into my heart, like a scalpel.

"I swear to God, I don't know. I don't know what I did to hurt you, baby, but you have to know I'm sorry. I'll fix it if you let me. Just tell me what I did. Tell me what happened."

She glares up at me. "Don't lie to me."

"I'm not lying. I looked up after the fight and you were gone. Then when I saw you in the hall outside the locker room, you were so pale. I must've missed it when I was coming for you. You have to know I'd never let anyone hurt you. Never."

She makes a noise, a strangled noise like a wounded animal. She's struggling to hang on to her anger, but she's struggling *hard*. She wants to just be mad, but I can see that somehow I've ripped her heart out. Even though I don't know what I did.

"Stop it, Rogan. Please. Don't make me relive it. Just let me go. We don't belong together."

Her words cut like pieces of shattered glass. "Please don't say that." I knew that we might have some problems trying to make this work, but I was willing to try whatever I could. Anything. And I'd only do that if I thought we really belonged together. Which I do. But then to hear her say that we don't . . .

I swallow hard. I search for the patience to handle this delicately, like I know she needs me to. What I *want* to do is pick her up and carry her out of here and then sit her down and make her talk to me, but that won't work with Katie. In fact, if anything, it would only push her farther away. So I'm going slow. I'm being patient. As difficult as it is, she's worth it.

"I don't believe that," I confess. "And I didn't think you did either. What changed your mind?"

Her chin starts to tremble. "Haven't you done enough? Do you really need to hear me say it?"

"I guess I do."

She stares at me for several long seconds, a thousand emotions swirling in her eyes. But then I see her ball her fingers into tight fists and I know her anger is taking the front seat again.

THIRTY-THREE

Katie

I reach for calm. I grasp at control. I search for distance. "I shouldn't have been with you anyway. You're a fighter, for God's sake. Watching you pound your fists into that guy tonight just brought back too many memories for me. I don't need violent men in my life. I should've trusted my gut and stayed away from you from the first day that I met you."

"My fists?" I try not to let the look on Rogan's face affect me. He looks like I physically slapped him. "God, Katie, I would never, *ever* hurt you. Ever!" He raises his big hands up in front of him. "These hands will never touch you in anger. I'd rather die than see fear or pain on your face. How could you think otherwise?"

It burns in my chest like acid, that he could still, after all this, make me feel anything but disgust for him. And yet he does. He looks heartbroken that I would even suggest such a thing. And see-ing *him* this way hurts *me*. Even though I hate him right this minute, and even though what he's done is unforgiveable, I still don't want to see him hurt.

"I'm not saying you would ever hit me. I'm just saying that I can't watch things like that. I can't cheer you on while you beat the crap out of another human being for money or fame or beautiful women. Or for whatever other reasons you do it."

"I told you why I fight, Katie."

"I know, but . . ."

I trail off, hoping he'll just take that as enough explanation and go. Just go.

But he doesn't.

"That's not it, though. Or at least that's *not all*. I saw you in the hallway. You turned so pale. I saw it. Something else happened."

My stomach turns in on itself, like it's going to eat a hole all the way through my spine, leaving me hollow in the middle. As hollow as I feel.

"Everything happened. Everything happened and everything fell apart." It kills me that my voice is so deplorably small. Once again, my anger has abandoned me. As quick as that, as quick as his question. The agony of betrayal is the only emotion available to me now. Even when I'd rather hold on to my fury, I can't find it beneath all the hurt. "I watched you pose with two women, like some sick love affair. I watched you smile with the man who had my case dismissed as an accident. And then I watched you have your picture taken with the person who set my car on fire." Rogan's brows knit together for a few seconds before he pales beneath his tan. I see how my words affect him, but I don't stop. I can't stop. I can't give him an inch or I'll crumble. "And then, as if that weren't enough, Victoria played her hand and exposed my scars for all the world to see. Scars that she said *you* told her about."

I hate that my voice trembles. I hate that my chin quivers. I hate that he can see how weak I am, how weak and pathetic. But this will all be over soon and I'll be on my way back to Enchantment. There, I can hide. There, I can lick my wounds in private. There, I can disappear until I find a new way forward. Until I can get away and start a new life.

Again.

Rogan shakes his head as though to clear it, like he's overwhelmed. I guess he didn't think he'd get caught *so* red-handed. Or maybe he just thought he'd never get caught at all.

When he finally collects himself, he drops to one knee in front of me, his eyes trained steadily on mine. "Katie, listen to me. I don't know what she said or why she'd tell you that, but as God is my witness, I never told Victoria your secret. I've never told anyone. I would never do that to you. I thought you trusted me."

Again, he looks wounded. And again, it kills me to see his hurt.

I remind myself that it's probably not even real, though. It's probably as fabricated as everything else has been between us. Facts don't lie. And I'm drowning in facts right now.

I can't give in. I can't trust him. That's why I'm in this position to start with.

"I *did* trust you, Rogan. And look where it got me."

"I don't . . . I didn't . . . Katie, I swear I—"

"You're the only one who knew except Mona. And even if she were going to betray me after two years, she *certainly* wouldn't tell Victoria of all people."

Rogan bows his head in defeat. I won. Only I don't feel like the victor.

After several seconds of quiet, his head snaps up and his wide eyes lock onto mine. "Ronnie. Ronnie knew. From the night he

attacked you. And I've seen him talking to Victoria on more than
one occasion."

I frown. I had forgotten about the incident with Ronnie. He most
definitely knew my secret, saw my scars firsthand. And as much as I
would love to refute the accuracy of what Rogan is saying, I can't.

Even in my tiny little world inside the studio, I've heard the
rumors floating around about Ronnie's fascination with Victoria.
If he knew how she felt about me, maybe he gave her some dirt to
get in her good graces.

"I'm sure neither of us rank high on his list of favorite people,"
Rogan adds, watching me with hopeful eyes. "Please, Katie. You have
to believe me. I would never, never do something like that to you."

Like he's been able to do from the day we met, I feel Rogan softening me, taking the edge off my anger, soothing my hurt. Breaking
down my defenses. But it's no matter. The fact remains that he can't
be trusted. His associations prove that.

"Fine. I'll give you that one, but what about Senator Sims? And
Calvin? How could I ever trust someone who's in league with men
like that?"

Sadness steals over Rogan's handsome face and stabs at my
heart. "They're just business associates, Katie. Nothing more. I had
no way of knowing what they'd done to you."

"But you can understand why I can't have anything to do with
them. Nothing. At all. Ever. Right?"

Rogan gazes intently at me. His silence might be more painful
than anything else. Something tells me that this is the one thing
he can't explain away. Can't fix. Can't or won't.

He looks defeated.

"Yes, I completely understand. And as much as I hate them both
for what they did to you . . ." I see his jaw flex as he looks away from

me, like he's resisting murderous impulses. "As much as I'd like to tear them both limb from limb, there's nothing I can do about it. They're . . . I can't . . . There's just nothing I can do."

Suddenly I feel desperate, desperate for him to explain it away in terms that won't rip me apart. But I'm terrified that he won't. "But why? What are they to you?"

"They're . . . well, Senator Sims is my benefactor."

I guess, when it boils down to it, I was secretly hoping that Rogan would be able to explain away his association with the two most awful men that I know. Part of me even expected that he might chase me down in Enchantment and explain it all away and we could pick up where we left off. But reality isn't like a romance novel. Sometimes there isn't a happy ending to be had. Sometimes things just don't work out.

"So this is about money? You'd keep people like that close to you for *money*? Knowing, now, what they did to me?"

I'm incredulous. I'm confused. I'm devastated.

"It's not about the money."

"Then what *is it* about?"

Reaching out to take my clasped hands in his, Rogan closes his eyes and drops his forehead onto them. "Katie, please. You just have to trust me."

You have to trust me.

That's not an answer. Not a denial. Not an explanation. Not a promise or a platitude. Because it's the truth. He can't even deny it. He has no quick excuse or story to tell. So he's hedging. The fact of the matter is Rogan has a price. A literal price. And nothing is worth more to him. Not even me.

"Trust you? *Trust you?* How can I trust you? I feel like I don't even know you."

There is a physical tightening of everything from my sternum to my navel. It feels as though an excruciating weight is bearing down on me and I'm struggling to resist. My muscles tremble with the effort not to be crushed.

I just want to fold over, to curl into myself and vanish. How could I be so wrong about someone?

You were about Calvin. Now it's happening again.

Rogan releases my hands and leans into me, cupping my cheeks. I feel the tears that I can't hold back stream from the corners of my eyes to pour over his fingers. His expression is urgent, determined. Desperate.

But he's an actor. To be fooled would make me foolish.

"Katie, you know me. You *know* me. Better than probably anyone in my life, you *know me*. Please just trust me. One more time. I promise you I'm not like them. If there was anything I could do, any other way . . ."

I reach up to wind my fingers around his wrists and tug them away from my face. "There's always another way. You just have to want to find it."

Rogan drops his hands and leans back before running his fingers through his short hair, sending it shooting out in twenty different directions. "Katie, please! You have to believe me. Can't you just . . . Rrrrah!" With that growl of frustration, Rogan straightens and turns away from me, lacing his fingers behind his neck as he paces. When he swivels back to me, he just looks . . . beaten. "I know you want me to fix this, but *I can't*. I wish there was something I could do, but there's not. This is beyond my control. Please, just give me the benefit of the doubt. At least give me some time to figure something out. Please."

I take a deep breath and bolster myself against the desire to crawl into a corner and die. I gave my heart away and this is what it's come to.

I'm resigned. The least I can do at this point is try to retain some amount of dignity. I stand to my feet, legs shaky, knees wobbly, and I pray for strength before I speak. "It won't matter, Rogan. We're just too different. We were kidding ourselves to think otherwise. Go back to your people. And I'll go back to mine. All I ask is that you stay away from me. If you respect me or ever cared anything about me, you'll do this one thing for me. Please."

I'm glad my voice stayed strong through the end. I'm glad I was finished speaking, too, because, as I shoulder my purse and walk past Rogan, I'm overcome with the feeling that I can't breathe, much less speak. Yet I walk on. I walk to another seat at the farthest end of my gate and I take it. I slip into it, my only thoughts of the door that will lead to the airplane that will take me away from here, away from Rogan. I just have to make it home in one piece and then I can fall apart.

And I will. But this time, I'm not sure the pieces will be big enough to put back together again.

Thankfully, they board the plane within minutes of me walking away from Rogan. I don't look back until I'm seated in coach, staring out across the tarmac, waiting for takeoff. Only then do I give in, albeit reluctantly, to the urge to sneak one last glance behind me, at where I've been. I don't expect to find Rogan. I figured he'd have already left. But he hasn't. And I have no trouble spotting him.

There, standing tall and strong in front of the enormous wall of windows that faces me, is the love of my life. The betrayer of my last bit of trust.

Although his eyes are fixed in my general direction, I know he can't see me. Maybe he never did. If he had, he'd know why we can never be together. Not after this.

Tiny droplets begin to pepper the thick, oval glass between us. For a few seconds, I can't tell the difference between the water in my eyes and the water falling from the sky. But then it starts to rain harder. According to the forecast, there was no chance of rain, but they were as deluded as I've been. There's *always* a chance of rain, no matter how small.

After a few minutes, my window is nothing more than a highway of rivulets that turn Rogan from real and solid into a wavy hallucination. Soon I can barely see the terminal at all.

Kiefer "The Rain" Rogan. Yes, he brought the rain. And if I'm not careful, I might well drown in it.

THIRTY-FOUR

Rogan

My legs feel tired. As I walk back through the airport, I'm aware of every muscle, every tendon, every ligament, and they all just feel . . . tired. Like I fought the best, most important fight of my life, and I lost. And, even though I won, I *really did* lose. I lost *everything*.

The ride back to the hotel is uneventful. When I try to think about past the now, it seems that everything feels the same way—uneventful. The night, the morning, next week, next year—all uneventful. It's like everything I had to look forward to got somehow twisted around and wrapped up in a shy wisp of a girl. And without her, there's just . . . nothing.

Uneventful nothingness.

At the hotel, I'm pissed to find Kurt in my room. "How the hell did you get in here?"

"Being your brother has *some* perks. Being handicapped just helps my case."

I don't reply. I don't take the bait. I'm just not interested in Kurt right now. Actually, I'm not interested in much of anything except sleep. I just want to sleep.

Ignoring him, I walk into the bedroom to get some clean lounge pants, and I head for the bathroom. I cut on the shower and turn to find Kurt parked in the doorway. "What?" I snap.

"Did you find her?"

"Yeah."

A pause. "And?"

"And what? She's gone."

"You're the dumbest asshole I've ever met. Why would you let a woman like that go?"

"It's what she wanted."

"Well, I gotta give her credit for making the smart choice, but I'm surprised. I thought she was pretty into you."

"Maybe she was, maybe she wasn't. Doesn't matter now. It can't work."

"What kind of a defeatist attitude is that? Did it ever occur to you that you might actually have to *try* with some people?"

I clench my fists to keep from sending him back into the bedroom on his ass. "I tried, you shitdick. There are just some things that I can't change, things that she can't live with. That's it. If I could fix it, I would, but I can't."

"Why? What's so bad that it can't be fixed?"

If you only knew, I think harshly. But I don't tell him that. As I've done for years, I protect my brother. Mostly from himself.

"Just forget it, man. Back up," I say, walking toward him to force him out of the doorway. "I need to shower."

I close the door in Kurt's face as soon as his lifeless feet are clear of the jamb.

"You're making a big mistake, dude," he says from outside. Unless I'm mistaken, there's actually a note of regret in his voice. But not nearly as much regret as what's in me. Nowhere close.

THIRTY-FIVE

Katie

I couldn't face Monday. I called in sick and stayed in bed all day. Mona called at least six times, but I let them all go to voice mail. I knew I'd have to tell her eventually.

Today, Tuesday, is "eventually."

As was her custom when Rogan was my first client of the day, Mona is in my "office" waiting for me when I arrive. Her face wreathed with a smile that's so brilliant it rivals that of the sun. Until she sees me, that is. I watch it fall into an expression of concern.

"Kitty! You look terrible! What happened?"

She rushes across the room to take me in her thin arms. I resist the urge to literally cry on her shoulder. That's not my style. Or at least it wasn't until recently. For the last thirty-some hours, I feel like I'm no longer in control of my tear ducts. They've been over-taken by evil spirits or something. They don't even care whether I'm asleep or awake. Each time I've fallen asleep, my own sobs have awakened me.

Somehow I manage to keep it together until Mona releases me. I give her a tight, polite smile and plead, "Do you mind if we just not talk about it?"

I can tell that's tantamount to asking her to bite off her own tongue and swallow it, but still she nods in compliance. I walk past her to slide my purse into the drawer where it lives during the day. "Just know that when you're ready, I'm here."

I don't turn to face her. I just nod. I don't trust myself to speak.

THIRTY-SIX

Rogan

I have a lot of reasons to be angry. I had an abusive father who never once tried to hold his temper with me. I enlisted in the Army and got to see, up close and personal, the evil that men are capable of. My team has been betrayed by someone we trusted. We just haven't found out by whom yet. I've been on the receiving end of hundreds of punches and kicks from various opponents, both professional and otherwise. I've been burned, cut, whipped, thrown, slammed and insulted more than I care to remember, but never, not once in my life, have I ever wanted to hurt someone as badly as I do right now.

As badly as I have since I found out who he is.

Calvin Sims. Katie's ex. The man who tried to burn her alive.

Every time I think of Katie, I think of him. And that happens almost as often as I breathe.

He doesn't deserve to live. Lots of people don't, I'm sure, but I've never really wanted to take a life. Not even when it was part of my job in Delta Five.

Until now.

But I want to take his. He stole everything from Katie and then he stole *her* from *me*. He stole our future. He stole any chance we might have. I can't blame her for drawing the line. Unfortunately it's a line I can do nothing about. So I'm angry. No, I'm furious. Livid. Irate. All the time. And it's eating away at me like cancer, gnawing at my guts. Always gnawing.

I've been in front of a speed bag, a punching bag or a sparring partner three or four times a day since the morning after she left. I beat on them like I want to beat Sims. Only I can't. Because my hands are tied. And no matter how many other people or objects I take out all my aggression on, it never makes me feel any better.

I just feel worse.

More trapped.

More hopeless.

Less alive.

Every day I wonder how much longer I can let this go. Not that I'm letting it go. I'm holding on to it. Tight. With a death grip that feels like it's only killing me. Slowly. Day by day.

At least I tell myself that's what it is. But deep down, I know that it's really not what's killing me. Grief is. I die a little bit more every day. Every day without Katie.

THIRTY-SEVEN

Katie

Days creep by. The week is punctuated only by the arrival of my belongings on Friday afternoon. Everything I left in New York, packed neatly into my bag, brought by messenger to my door. No note. No Rogan. No hope. Just a suitcase full of stuff that I couldn't care less about.

I've never hated Friday more.

Slowly, the days turn into a week. One week into two. Two into three. And then a month has elapsed. I'm firmly back in my shell, hiding from everyone except Mona. It seems everyone is hiding from me as well. I've become a bit of a pariah, from what I can tell.

Two days after returning to Enchantment, the disastrous post-fight interview aired on Sports Central. I didn't immediately know, of course, since I have ovaries and therefore do not live and breathe sports. It didn't take too long for me to figure it out, though. The men who saw it asked the women they knew about it. Then the women talked among themselves over lunches and drinks and workplace water coolers. Eventually, word got out and the video made its way around the studio.

I wasn't surprised by the strange looks that followed the circulation of the video. I'm the resident freak show, after all. I'd been living right here under their beautiful, flawless noses all this time, unbeknownst to them. But even so, that doesn't mean I'm not hurt by them. Hurt and humiliated.

The *Ew, what happened to her?* and *Gross! What's wrong with her skin?* looks were both hurtful and humiliating, but not nearly as much as the ones that showed pity. Those are the ones I have little tolerance for. They're the ones that hurt the most. They say I'm the pathetic girl who fell for a guy way outside her league. They say I was a fool to ever think he could really be interested in me. A freak. A scarred, backward, freak who used to be somebody but then basically died in a fire. Only a few human parts remain and they fled the moment I left Rogan at the airport.

Rogan.

Even now, after a month, it hurts. I thought it would get easier, but it hasn't. It seems that the gaping hole in my chest is ever-widening. I've had these recurring nightmares where I'm sucked into oblivion by the vacuum that exists within me. Only sometimes, it's a dream rather than a nightmare. In a way, I'd welcome an end to this misery.

Victoria has kept her distance. She didn't come out of that video looking like a very nice person. She did the smart thing and just hung her head like she was ashamed. Now she's laying low until it blows over. As for me, I hope I never have to see her again. Despite the fact that this is a small studio and an even smaller town, I've gotten really good at avoiding. Life, people, the outside world, I avoid it all. I go to work, I come home. Sometimes I go to the store. Sometimes I take Dozer to the park. Other than that, I eat (sometimes), I sleep (sometimes) and I work. That's it. Even Mona has become accustomed to eating in my "office" with me rather than venturing out to the diner.

All in all, it seems that Kathryn Rydale has died yet again. That's twice now, twice that I've suffered the death of who I am in some way or another. Kat died in a fire, and only a tiny part of her was resurrected in Katie. And most of Katie died in New York after a mixed martial arts charity fight. She still lives in the same house and works at the same job, but all the pieces of her that were living are mostly dead now. I can't even seem to find happiness in the few trivial things that I'd managed to enjoy as Katie. There's just nothing left for me. Just . . . nothing.

I foresee me living out my life as a walking, talking corpse. A zombie. Someone who used to have a heartbeat, but is now just going through the motions.

The phone is ringing when I unlock my door. My landline rings so seldom that I forget that I even have one most of the time. I give Dozer a quick scratch and head for the kitchen to grab it before it stops ringing. I can't even imagine who might be calling me on it. Probably a telemarketer.

"Hello?"

The pause is so long that I'm getting ready to hang up when I hear the baritone voice that I'll likely never forget.

"Hello, Kat."

Chills break out on both arms and my skin feels both cool and hot at the same time.

"What do you want, Senator Sims?"

"You used to be such a pleasant girl," he remarks.

"You'll have to excuse me if I can't find any pleasure in hearing your voice."

He ignores that.

"I've got a proposition for you."

"I'm not interested."

"You don't even know what I'm going to say."

"It doesn't matter. I don't care what you have to say. The answer is no."

"Even if it could save your friend?"

There's a hitch in my pulse. It feels like my heart almost stops for a second. "My friend?"

"Yes. Kiefer Rogan. He *is* your friend, isn't he?"

Air freezes in my chest like wedges of thin ice. "And what does he need saving from?"

"Not *what*. *Whom*."

I'm quickly becoming irritated with his vagueness. "Why don't you just tell me what it is that you want, *Mr. Sims*," I say, emphasizing a title he will feel is disrespectful.

If it needles him, however, he hides it well. When he resumes speaking, it's as though he's embroiled in polite conversation with an old friend. "Kiefer Rogan is a man of secrets, secrets I'd be willing to bet he's never shared with you."

If he's hoping to hurt me, it's working.

"Everyone's entitled to their secrets."

"In any case, they're not really entirely his secrets to share."

"What's that supposed to mean?"

"Did Rogan ever tell you how his father died?"

A lump of dread forms in the back of my throat, making me feel for a few seconds like I can't breathe. I focus on drawing air in and out of my lungs slowly. Steadily. "No, but I think you already know that."

"I do, but there's no reason I can't enjoy this." His tone is smug and it sets my teeth on edge. But he's got my attention, so I hold my tongue until he continues. "There was an unfortunate accident involving his younger brother. He had enlisted in the Army just before graduation. His father found out and tried to cripple him with a crowbar. Kurt hit him in the head with a baseball bat. Killed him instantly. Kiefer wasn't willing to trust his brother's future to the fickle legal system in this country, but he trusted his coach enough to tell him what had happened, to ask his advice. His coach came to me. He knew I could help, that I could make things . . . go away."

My stomach feels like a ball of lead is sitting in the bottom of it. I know just how adept he is at making things go away. At letting criminals go free. "Why should I believe you? Why should I believe *any* of this?"

"Because that's why Kiefer will do as I ask, no matter what. When I wanted him on a Special Forces team that my senate committee oversaw, he enlisted in the Army. When his brother was injured and discharged, Kiefer came home and went back into the ring to fight for me. He's smart enough to know that I hold the keys to his brother's past. And his future."

This is too much information, too fast. "Wait, what? Rogan was in the Special Forces?" He'd mentioned the Army, but not Special Forces.

"He didn't tell you that either?" He's smiling. I can hear it. He's enjoying torturing the girl who dared dump his son. He probably blames *me* for Calvin setting me on fire, like it's somehow my fault his son is psychotic.

Obviously the apple doesn't fall far from the tree.

"No. He didn't mention that."

"Don't feel too poorly. There's not a lot he would even be permitted to tell you about, but pillow talk can be quite an effective . . . relaxant. If the partner is good enough."

Another knock at me, as if to say that I wasn't good enough in bed to worm all of Rogan's secrets out of him. To hear this man, this disgusting monster of a man, degrade the beauty of what we shared makes me crazy.

"Why don't you just get to the point?" I snap. "And why is it, exactly, that you think I'd care about helping Rogan?"

"It's obvious you have strong feelings for him and he for you. Since you're the problem, I knew you could be the solution as well. You see, if he continues moping around and postponing his fights, if he continues putting all his time and resources into investigating my son *on your behalf*, he's liable to run into some very . . . significant and unexpected health problems. Do you understand what I'm saying?"

A threat. A viable threat. I of all people know how dangerous dealing with the Sims family can be.

"Yes, I understand." My voice is cool. Hard even.

"Then you understand that if Rogan isn't *able* to fight, he won't be a benefit to me at all. I need a hearty-and-hale Rogan. Otherwise he and his brother will no longer be any of my concern. Nor will they be under my protection."

My stomach lurches at the thought of what kind of atrocities this man is capable of.

"What do you expect me to do about any of this?"

"Well, if you care about Rogan, you'll help me to get him back on track."

"And how do you propose that I do that?"

"By removing yourself, and *the hope of you*, from his life."

"I'm already removed from his life."

"Not as much as you could be."

I don't know how I could be any farther from him, physically or emotionally. I feel the loss of him, the absence of him every day. I'm *definitely* removed from him. And he from me.

"How do I go about that, then? How do I remove the hope of me from his life?"

"You get back together with my son."

This time, I think my heart really does skip a few beats. I have the sudden urge to wrap my arms around myself and hold on tight to keep myself together. To keep myself from falling into a thousand tiny pieces.

"*What?* Have you lost your mind?"

"No, it's quite genius actually. And this will be only a public reconciliation, not a private one. I just want to give Rogan reason to move on, maybe even fight harder. In addition, this will provide my son with some . . . insurance, if you will. Just to make sure you can never try to bring your . . . unfortunate accident to a place that could hurt him. And neither could Rogan. No one would believe you if you decided to make an issue of what happened. Not after you're seen dating again. I mean, what kind of sick individual would *date* a man who set her on fire?"

I'm not convinced of his logic. Many abused women reconcile with their abusers, but I think he's right in that it would make it much less believable if I ever tried to tell the truth about Calvin. I mean, he set me on fire! I *would* have to be pretty sick to ever willingly put myself in his company again. Pretty sick or desperately in love with someone I'm trying to protect.

"So this isn't as much about Rogan as it is about protecting your precious son."

"Oh no. It's about both. Don't be confused on that point. Rogan is a champion. He's making me a great deal of money. But just like most wild animals, he needs a leash. And I'm not sure his brother's fate is enough to keep him in check anymore. Not since you. So I'm giving him reason to move on. To let it go. To let *you* go, so that things can return to normal."

I try to swallow, but my mouth is bone dry. This feels so wrong, so screwed up, but I just don't see a way out. Now I know how Rogan felt. My hands are tied. Unless I give him over to this ruthless man, something I would never do. "Wh-what do you want me to do, specifically?"

"I want you to meet with Calvin, take a few happy, candid photos, have a nice dinner. Spread the word that you two have reconciled. Really sell it. And that should be it. Other than keeping your mouth shut about all this, of course."

Of course. There's always that. My eternal silence in exchange for his despicable help.

But his help is needed. He holds all the cards. Rogan isn't protecting himself. He's protecting Kurt. But who's protecting Rogan?

I might be the only one who can. I'm not sure this is the best way to do it, but agreeing with him will at least give me some time to think.

"So you're saying that if I do this Rogan will be safe? That once he sees these pictures, he'll move on and fight for you and all will be well? You'll keep Kurt's secret and keep Rogan safe?"

Even to my ears, it sounds ridiculous. Almost too simple. Just a few pictures and lies to ensure Rogan's safety and the protection of their secret.

Only it's not just a few pictures and lies. It's me. With Calvin. Even if it's just pretend, it's Calvin. *Calvin.*

"I believe he will, yes. When he sees that you and Calvin are back together, he'll move on. He won't risk hurting you by hurting Calvin. And most likely, when he fights, he'll be out for blood. Anyone's blood. And fights like that make a lot of money."

"I think you might be overestimating how Rogan feels about me. Did you ever consider that when planning your diabolical extortion?"

"Don't be silly. That boy loves you. Unfortunately for him, it's just not convenient for me."

That boy loves you.

My heart soars. Right before it takes a nosedive.

The small kernel of hope that took root is dashed as quickly as it sprung up. It never really had a chance of survival anyway. Although I now understand why Rogan's hands were tied, this doesn't change anything. It's not like we can be together just because I know what he was hiding. If I do this to help him, he'll think I'm back together with Calvin. That will destroy any chance we could ever have had. But if I don't do it, Rogan himself could be destroyed. It's a lose-lose situation for me.

But not for Rogan.

Not for the man who I fell in love with. Not for the man who held me so tenderly and kissed my scars so sweetly. Not for the man who has given so much for the people he loves.

I have the power to help him *and* his brother.

If I'm tough enough to go through with it.

As I consider the Senator's words, I think of letting Calvin back into my life, even in this controlled way on a temporary basis. The thought makes my physically ill. My belly roils with nausea and remembered fear. My skin feels cold and clammy, and my hand shakes where I hold the phone to my ear.

Let Calvin back in. When I practically had a panic attack just seeing him after Rogan's fight. How can I do that? How can I stand to be near him? How could I smile pretty for a camera like I'm not shriveling on the inside just being in the same room with him? How could I do that? When he took so much from me—everything, in fact—how could I do that?

I fold over so that blood can rush to my dizzy brain. I squeeze my eyes shut like maybe when I open them, I'll be somewhere else. Maybe some*one* else.

But then I see twinkling green eyes and a lopsided grin. They pop into my mind as if by answer.

How could I do that?

Rogan.

That's how I could do it. For those eyes, for that smile, for that *man*, I would do almost anything. But does that include *this*?

"My offer is not without its time restrictions, you understand," the Senator says when I suppose I've been silent for too long, drowning in the idea of a misery I'm not sure I can face.

"I . . . I just . . ." I'm finding it hard to breathe even considering this. It's as though the fire of my past is consuming all the oxygen from the room of my present, leaving me no air. Saliva pours into my mouth and my chin trembles with emotion. But despite my body's reaction, my heart remembers only one thing. *Rogan.* I can do it for Rogan.

Or would the truly strong, truly *tough* thing to do be to find another way? To outwit the Senator and his son? To beat them at their own game and save Rogan *my way*?

Liquid steel pours through me, strengthening me in all my hurt places, reminding me that I've come so far and that I'm better than this, stronger than this. They can't rule me anymore. I'm not the victim anymore. This time, *I* will win.

"I'll do it."

"You're smarter than I gave you credit for. Maybe you'd have been a good match for my son after all."

"You can go to hell, because when this is over, I don't expect to ever see either one of you again. Not as long as I live."

I hear a smile in his voice again, one that causes a shiver of apprehension to ripple down my spine. "That can be arranged," he says in a snakish way. "I'll be in touch."

The line goes dead, leaving me alone in my kitchen with a combination of bad memories and rock-hard determination.

THIRTY-EIGHT

Rogan

I'm not sure how I've made it through the last month. I've tried everything from exhaustion to redirection, and nothing seems to work. I even tried to get the Colonel to let me come and help him, help him find the man who's targeting our team, but that didn't work either. Couldn't get ahold of him. Not that I'd be much help anyway. My focus is shit right now. Hell, I could be the next target for all I know, and I'd be a pretty easy one since I'm out of hiding in Enchantment and distracted as shit. But still, it's the farthest thing from my mind. At least Katie is safe from that threat. We weren't together very long and we were never public, so she was never in any danger.

Katie.

The only thing that's getting me through the days is rage, I suppose. I've let it consume me. Well, I don't know if I've *let it*, so much as it just *has*. It's that or go completely batshit crazy. I didn't realize what an important part of my life Katie was until she was no longer in it at all.

But I'm stuck. Trapped.

Some of it has been my own doing, some not. The thing is, I can't change the past. As much as I wish I could, there are too many things beyond my control, things that have nothing to do with Katie. Yet everything to do with why I'm not with her right now.

I jerk off my sparring gloves and throw them aside in a fit of temper. I turn and walk off the mat, running my fingers through my wet hair. Damn it! If I'd only known that the two men who hurt her most in the entire world were two people that I was forced to work with . . .

But then what? Would I have kept it from her? Not told her I knew them, worked with them? Maybe I'd have told her elaborate lies. Or just never let her find out.

No.

Hell no. I couldn't do that to her. I couldn't live with myself knowing that I'd taken away her right to choose like that. Even if I knew that choice would mean the end of us. And that's just what it cost me—her. Us.

She thinks I'm a pile of shit for associating with the Simses. Actually, I couldn't agree more. But it's not just me who would suffer if I cut ties. And that's what makes me stuck.

If it were just me or my career, or even my ass on the line, I'd choose her over them so fast it would make their heads spin. But it's not. Only she can never know that. No one can. It's a secret I have to keep.

That doesn't mean that I'm sitting idly by, letting those two bastards get away with what they did, though. I've been having that shithole Calvin followed since the morning after Katie left. I'll get him for something. I'll nail his ass to the wall. For Katie. Even though no one will know that it was *me* who did it or that *she's* the reason. That doesn't matter, though. *I'll* know. And that's how I'll be able to sleep at night. Well, what little bit of sleep I actually get without Katie.

THIRTY-NINE

Katie

I wake with a pounding heart and a heaving chest. My dream . . . it was so real. I was at work with my back to the door, putting away some new products, when Calvin walked in. I turned to find him just a few feet away, watching me. As big as life. As big as my nightmares.

I realize now that he hasn't changed much. I didn't really notice at Rogan's match; I was too stunned by his presence to note much of anything. But I relived it all in my dream, and I saw. I really saw. Saw the handsome exterior. Saw the monster underneath.

His hair is still dark sable and cut short. He's got the hair of an aristocrat. And why not? He's like political royalty because of his father. His face is still handsome even though I'd much rather see it after a truck tire rolls over it. His eyes are still the same greenish blue, but in my dream, the pretense was gone. There was not a shred of kindness in the cold depths. He'd stopped playing the game. We'd come to an understanding. I know just what lies beneath the surface and he's not going to waste his energy trying to convince me that I don't.

I shudder involuntarily as I think about glancing down at his hands in my dream, hands that brought me such pain during the year we were together. Hands that ultimately stole everything from me with the simple flick of a match.

Even as I curl onto my side under the covers, I still feel every single emotion as if I'd actually experienced the whole thing. In a way, I guess I did. It was as if I'd actually gone through with it. But this . . . *this* is why I have to call Rogan. I have to fight this. I can't trust them. I *won't* trust them. Not with my life. Not with a day. And certainly not with Rogan's future.

No, this is my only choice. Today I have to call Rogan.

FORTY

Rogan

I'm already irritable, as it seems I always am here lately, when I pull up to my house to find a rental car in the driveway. "Who the hell is this?" I bark at the quiet interior.

I get out and walk up the front steps, slinging open the door. I stop dead when I see Jasper, one of my Army buddies, standing in the kitchen talking to Kurt.

He turns when the door slams shut behind me and then I see a woman peek around his shoulder. She's practically hidden by him. I recognize her. She's the Colonel's daughter. We met a few weeks ago when the three of us—Jasper, Tag and me—went to Atlanta to discuss Reid's death and who's targeting our team with the Colonel. His daughter, Muse, was there. Not a name *or* a face I'm likely to forget. She's gorgeous as hell.

But she's not Katie.

"Hope you don't mind that we dropped by," Jasper says. His voice is dark and deep, like always. He was the more . . . intense of the four of us. Even now, though his comment is casual enough, there's something about his expression that tells me this is no casual visit.

I cross to them, looking first at his companion. "Muse. It's nice to see you again." She returns my smile and I lean down to kiss her cheek. Seems like the right thing to do. She *is* the Colonel's daughter after all.

"Rogan, right?"

I poke my elbow in Jasper's ribs. "See? I told you I was unforgettable."

His smile is barely there. As always. But that doesn't surprise me. What surprises me is the way he looks at Muse.

"She's heard me talk about you enough."

I back up, nodding. Understanding. "So, it's like that."

He nods once. "It's like that."

I examine him a little more closely. Under the dark look of whatever brought him here today, I see subtle differences. Good differences. "I'll be damned. You're in love with her."

This time Jasper actually laughs. It's a sound I'm not sure I've ever heard before. He really *has* changed.

"It's a good thing she already knew that or I'd kick your ass for telling her."

"You sly bastard! Congrats, man!" I pull him in for a dude's hug and slap him on the back. When I lean away, I can see that what I'm seeing on him is happiness.

And I'm envious as hell.

"Thanks. I wish that was the only reason I was here."

Right to the point. Just like Jasper.

"Let's go into the study," I tell him. I glance at Muse. "Kurt'll get you something to drink, Muse, but feel free to make yourself at home."

The grin she gives me tells me that she probably wasn't planning on sitting this one out. But she nods at me and winks at Jasper, which assures me that she's okay with it, though.

"This way," I tell Jasper, starting off back toward the foyer. As I pass the door, I see another car pull up, some anonymous dark blue sedan. "Who the hell is this?"

I feel like I'm asking that too often today. But then I see my other buddy, Tag, get out and start up the drive. I glance back at Jasper. He's watching me. He doesn't say a word. But then again, he doesn't have to. The only reason we'd all be here is the same reason we were all at the Colonel's safe house.

Reid Sheridan.

The fourth one of us. The one who was killed. The first of us to be betrayed.

I open the door for Tag. He comes in. He smiles, but it doesn't reach his eyes. He knows why we're here. This is serious shit. We didn't dick around on our missions. We took out terrorists. We neutralized threats. We took lives. We assassinated leaders. But for the right reasons. On orders from our government. Not like what happened to Reid. He was targeted. Betrayed. Sold out.

"Don't you shower anymore, brother?" Tag asks.

I take in his expensive shirt and slacks. "You afraid I'll wrinkle you, ya pussy?"

We hug and then he and Jasper shake hands before we all three head for the study.

When the door is closed, I lean up against one side of the desk, Tag against the other, and we both face Jasper. He wastes no time. "The Colonel got a name. He found out who's behind Operation Napalm."

A name. Finally. The person responsible for the death of Reid. The person responsible for the death of Jasper's mother. The person responsible for putting our team in the crosshairs.

That's why I couldn't reach the Colonel. Seems he was busy uncovering a dirtbag.

"Who? Who is it?"

Jasper glances at Tag and then looks long and hard at me. "Senator Sims."

Holy. Hell.

No one says anything for a few seconds. We all know who he is. And I guess it makes sense. He knew us. Knew all about us. He would be one of the few people who could manipulate us fairly easily. Mislead us. Set us up.

His committee is the only one that knew about us, the one that authorized our missions. Black Ops shit. High risk. Highly classified. Ugly business. Things that had to be done, things no one else wanted to do.

I'm probably the only one who knows what he's like in real life, though, Senator Sims. The only one who knows how much of his cutthroat politics bleed into his personal life.

"But why?" Tag asks. His gray eyes are stormy. I remember that look. With Tag, much like with the rest of us, you're asking for trouble when you mess with the unit. Or anyone he cares about.

"He's making a run for the White House. Turns out he has skeletons. Several of them. That job we did in Syria, taking out Assad's second-in-command . . . it wasn't government sanctioned like the Colonel thought. Sims was just covering his tracks. He'd been brokering arms deals for that asshole for his own personal gain. Made millions. I guess presidential campaigns are expensive. But he had us take him out. Now we're the only loose threads. *We* are his last remaining skeletons."

Tag's jaw is tight. "So he's taking us out. Cleaning up the mess."

"He's trying."

"He's taking out everyone he thinks can be a threat, right down to people we might've told. Like family. To someone like him, no one is off limits, but to us . . . to us that's sacred ground. You don't go after family. You just don't. We knew what we were signing up for, but not them. Not them," Jasper says somberly, his mother having been killed already. Caught in the crossfire and blown up by a mercenary wannabe who knew about Jasper's past.

The wheels of my stunned brain come to a screeching halt.

Family.

Loved ones.

Cleaning up messes.

Skeletons.

An image of Katie pops into my mind, the one of her face when she saw the Simses at the fight. She knows what they're capable of. *I* know what they're capable of. And after the way I reacted to her at the fight, they now know what she is to me.

"What is it, man? And who's Katie?" Jasper asks. I didn't even realize that I'd said her name aloud.

"I think she's one of his messes, too."

I know they won't understand. They don't know about Katie. They don't know about what little Sims did to her. Or how that might look for a father if it came out during a bid for the presidency.

My palms start to sweat. It all makes sense now. How could I not have seen it? How could I not have known?

Mother of God.

He's going to turn his son loose on Katie.

As if on cue, my phone rings. I see the familiar number and my insides clench.

"Katie?"

"Rogan?" she replies. My whole body, even my blood, sags with relief.

"Are you okay?"

"Uh, yeah. Why wouldn't I be?"

"I . . . I just . . . I saw something on the Internet." I try to come up with a plausible response without revealing the truth. "Something about you and Calvin Sims. I was just worried. That's all."

There's a long pause before she responds. "Actually, that's what I was calling about. I need to talk to you. It's about what the Senator is trying to do. To you."

"Stay there. I'm on my way."

I hang up before she can argue and I look up to two pairs of eyes watching me with varying degrees of fury. After a few seconds, Jasper merely steps out of my way and nods toward the door.

"Let's go. We've got work to do," he says.

I nod and lead the way. I've never looked forward to hurting someone more than I do right now. Not even my shitty father.

FORTY-ONE

Katie

As I leave the studio, I realize that as anxious as I am to get away from work, I'm not very enthusiastic about going home. Work used to be just a job, neither good nor bad. Now it's the place where I spent the happiest days of my life with Rogan and the most humiliating days of my life *after* him. And home . . . home used to be my sanctuary. Now it's just pure hell. The memories of Rogan . . . they chase me. Haunt me. Refuse to give me a moment's peace. Even to sleep.

Nights are the worst. They're nearly unbearable. I toss and turn rather than sleep, and everywhere I look, I see and feel Rogan. With perfect clarity, I can picture him asleep on the pillow next to me. With excruciating precision, I can feel his hands on me, his mouth, his body. *Oh God!* What I wouldn't give to forget, to just have my memory wiped clean of all traces of Rogan. But there's no such mercy for a girl like me. He will live on in my head and in my heart until I reach the only escape I'll ever have from him—death.

When blood stops pumping through my veins, maybe then I'll finally be over him.

And now I'm going to see him again. I know it will set me back. Maybe even right back to square one. But I have to do this. I have to talk to him and tell him what's going on.

I unlock my front door, pausing to look for Dozer like I do every day. When I see that he isn't in front of the door, I push it open to step inside. It's as I'm closing it that I feel the niggle of someone's presence behind me. But not soon enough.

I'm turning to face him, door still ajar, when Calvin grabs my upper arms and backs me into the living room, slamming the door shut behind us.

I struggle to free myself from his grip, but his fingers are like iron shackles. A bolt of fear flashes through me. Among the memories of his punches and kicks and slaps, I'd forgotten how easily he could overpower me. But it's all coming back to me now. Too fresh, too clear.

I reach for bravery. I reach for boldness. I reach for tough. I don't want him to see that he can still rattle me. Even though he can.

"What are you doing here? Get the hell out of my house!"

On his face is a sneer. "What? Change your mind so soon?"

"Change my mind? About what?"

"About seeing me again."

Sweet God! I'd told the Senator I'd do it, but I didn't say when. No arrangements were made. And certainly none for this soon. It has only been a day, for God's sake!

"What's the matter? *Kat* got your tongue?" he asks, using my old name.

"No, I . . . I, uh, just wasn't expecting you this soon. And certainly not *here*."

"What's the matter, Kat? Afraid to have me so close to your bed?"

His leer coupled with the smell of alcohol on his breath gives me a surge of adrenaline. My heart thunders and every subtle nuance of this moment is carving itself indelibly into my brain.

"Hardly. You disgust me!" I hiss in a burst of bold and brave honesty.

His expression turns furious and he grabs me by my upper arms. "So he's so much better than me, is that it? That piece-of-shit fighter. Where is he now? If he's so much better than me, where is he? Why am I here with you when he's not?" A dart of fear pierces me. He was always much worse, much more forceful and unpredictable when he was drinking.

I keep my calm, at least outwardly. "You're drunk, Calvin. You need to leave."

"So anxious to get me out of here. Why? Is *he* coming? Will he be warming up that pussy tonight?"

His temper flares and his fingers bite into my arms, making painful indentations.

"Let me go, Calvin. I'm not kidding." Part of me wants to cower in the face of his anger, the memories flooding me like salt water flooding a hole in the sand. But another part of me, a tough and slightly reckless part, wants to face him, wants to stand up in his face and scream that I'm not afraid of him anymore.

He stares down into my face and I see the battle waging. Stay or go. Lash out or calm down. Stay and fight or walk away. I see his pupils swell and I know which way the tide is turning.

The muscles along his jawline flex as he grits his teeth. He jerks me up close to his face so that I can feel the heat of his temper. And I do. I feel it. And I know what's coming.

"I tried to forget you after the fire. I thought it would burn you out of my blood. And for a while it did. But when I saw you again . . .

with *him* . . . Damn you for making me feel this way again! Damn. You."

Before I can respond, Calvin straightens his arms and sends me flying across the entryway, a tangle of flailing limbs.

I look up to see him pushing the unbuttoned sleeves of his dress shirt up his forearms, like he's preparing to get messy. I know that gesture. I remember it like I remember the bone-jarring ache of being punched in the ribs. Or kicked in the back of the head.

Courage flees me. Calm abandons me. And terror, pure terror turns my blood to ice in my veins. After a time, I knew Calvin had a bad temper and that he was prone to violence, but never would I have suspected that he might set me on fire. Yet he did. That's when I realized that I had no idea the depths to which his mental illness extended. He could be capable of anything. Even murder.

With speed uncommon in someone as lanky as Calvin, he lunges for me before I can react, grabbing me by the front of my shirt and pulling me to my feet to sling me across the dining room table. I go skittering along the top before I crash down onto the chair at the end and topple it to the floor, the edge of the seat cracking against my hip. I gasp in pain, my fear nearly blinding me as I scramble to get my bearings.

"I'm sorry, but I'll have to punish you, Kat. For leaving me. For making me hurt you. For spreading those legs for someone else. You're mine, Kat. You always will be."

My addled mind spins with solutions and scenarios, for any possible way out of this without getting myself killed. He set me on fire last time. I can't give him the chance to hurt me again.

I stall until I can find a way, find something with which to defend myself. "I didn't think you'd want me with all my scars," I tell him. I swallow past the balloon of fear that inflates in my throat and I scoot into a sitting position.

Calvin frowns. I'm not sure what to make of it. Is he confused by my tactic? Disgusted by the mention of my disfigurement?

"I thought you knew how much I loved you. Yes, I hate the scars, but I'll pay for plastic surgery to get rid of them, and you'll be my beautiful Kat again. At least for a little while."

For a little while? That sounds . . . ominous.

Absently, I push scraps of the broken chair out of the way so that I can find my balance and make my way to my feet. I pause as my eyes settle on one of the splintered legs. For a few seconds, I zone out of the present as I stare at it, as I think of the implications of it. As I look at it, I drift into a strange place of calm.

The jagged wooden end holds my attention, almost as though it's beckoning me. Calvin's angry voice is nothing more than a distant backdrop to the peculiar trance I've stumbled into. In this peaceful world, I don't distinguish between Kat, Kathryn or Katie. I don't live a life as splintered as the chair leg I'm gazing at. I'm simply a girl who's tired of hiding, who's tired of being hurt. Who's tired of only surviving. I am a woman who needs to stand up. To fight back. To get the missing part of myself back. To be whole again.

In the fuzzy recesses of my mind, I realize that if I don't stand up now, if I don't start to live now, I never will. Just like Rogan said, I'll die a little more each day.

Fight to survive. Fight to live.

I've fought to survive. For years now, I've survived. But I need more. It's time to fight to live.

It's time to live.

My movements have a slow, surreal quality to them at first, almost dreamlike. I reach for the makeshift stake. I curl my trembling fingers around it. I use my free hand for balance. I come carefully to my feet. And I face Calvin.

Although fear is still with me, it's muted by this strange calm and, somehow, I'm bolstered by the feel of the cool wood of the chair leg against my palm. I flex my fingers around it, rubbing the sharp tip against my thigh as I study Calvin.

"If you leave me again, it'll only be worse, Kat. I didn't think I could hate you as much as I loved you, but I was wrong. You made me see that. God, you were such a bitch! What you did to me . . ."

I tilt my head as I watch him. His face is bloodred as he rants, a single vein standing out like a thick rope right in the center of his forehead. I wonder briefly that it doesn't burst and send him face-first onto my floor to drown in his own blood. I actually smile at the vision.

Calvin stops talking. I notice only because his lips cease to move. All I hear is the beat of my own heart, pounding in my ears.

I see spit on his chin. I focus on it for a few seconds, oddly fascinated by the foamy little drop. I notice only in the most absent of ways that it begins to get closer. It's that minute detail that shakes me from my thrall.

Taking a step back, I hold out one hand and raise the other, wielding the stakelike piece of wood like a weapon. A weapon that I will use if I have to.

"I want you to leave, Calvin. Right now. And never come near me again. You and your father can go to hell. Stay away from me. Stay away from Rogan. Let this drop or I swear on all that is holy, you'll regret the day you ever met me. Get out, Calvin. I won't ask you again."

At first he looks confused. Then stunned. Then, when his eyes bounce from me to the stake and back again, almost insulted.

I raise my chin defiantly. My cards are on the table. I'm taking my stand. And it feels good. *I* feel good.

But then he starts to laugh.

"Oh, Kat! You can't be serious."

Surely the girl who took his abuse for months wouldn't fight back.

Surely the girl who he set on fire wouldn't dare to stand up to him. Surely the girl who he murdered in all the ways that count couldn't have found a reason to live.

Surely not.

The hell you say!

Righteous fury explodes from my chest like a bomb, raining adrenaline into my blood. It's like rocket fuel. It propels me into motion. Offensive motion.

I lunge forward, slicing in a downward angle at Calvin's chest. I feel the tip of the pointed stick tear through something. Not flesh, but something.

When I step back, I see Calvin staring down at his torn shirt, at the bloody scratch that mars the smooth skin of his chest. The eyes he raises to mine are homicidal.

A needle of fear pricks my bubble of bravado, piercing it. For a moment, what *was* and what *is* collide, leaving me confused and frantic. I inhale sharply, my body mobilizing its fight-or-flight response as Calvin comes at me with an ear-splitting roar.

His aggression drowns out the loud clap of the front door flying open and ripping the hinges out of the frame. It doesn't, however, drown out the image of Rogan racing toward Calvin like an avenging angel, come to save me.

At the last second, Rogan's feet leave the floor. He's airborne for only a few seconds before he comes down on Calvin like a two-hundred-twenty-pound hammer, driving his elbow into the top of his head. Calvin weaves and wobbles, dazed, before he stumbles back into me. I move to my right, barely escaping his falling weight, as Rogan comes after him again.

Kneeling, one knee on Calvin's chest, the other on the floor, Rogan smashes his fist into my monstrous ex's face in four punches of blurring speed. When he pauses, Calvin is oozing blood from his nose, mouth and the corner of one eye, and mumbling something about his daddy.

"I'm not thinking about your *daddy*. And neither should you. You should be listening to what I'm telling you right now, because I won't say it again. If you ever, *ever* come near her again, I'll kill you. I. Will. End you. I'll break your neck, throw your body into a river and disappear before anyone can find me. And if you think I'm kidding, just ask your shithole of a father about me."

Calvin rests on my floor, his head rocking back and forth as he drools blood onto his cheeks. Rogan stands to his feet, spitting on Calvin before turning to me. His expression is fiercer than anything I've ever seen. It softens the instant his eyes meet mine, though.

He doesn't touch me, doesn't come near me. I'm not sure I even want him to. I just want to stand here, in his presence, and take him in. Bask in his being, in the knowledge that he came for me. That he saved me. Again.

"You're safe now," he declares quietly.

I don't know what to say. My tongue seems to be frozen to the roof of my mouth.

Behind him, I see Calvin stumbling to his feet. I gasp and Rogan jerks around, grabbing a handful of hair from the top of Calvin's head and pulling down until my ex's face meets the upswing of Rogan's knee. With a nauseating crunch, Calvin drops lifelessly onto the floor again.

Barely breathing hard, Rogan straightens, turning his head just enough that I can see his profile. "I'll be back after I take care of the trash," he says quietly.

He bends, tossing Calvin over his shoulder and walking slowly toward the door. He pauses in the opening, like he might turn to face me, maybe to say something, but then he changes his mind. I just stand here, numb and stunned, until he starts to move again. That jars me into action.

"Rogan, wait!"

He stops and turns toward me, his eyes eating me up as I close the distance between us. He looks relieved.

"The Senator . . . he was blackmailing me. He said if I didn't publicly date Calvin so that you would fight, he'd tell your secret. Kurt's secret."

He says nothing at first. Just watches me. "You know."

I nod. "Yes."

"Katie, I'm so sorry. I would never choose those snakes over you. If he hadn't held that over my head . . . over my *brother's* head . . . I swear to God, I'd have walked away and never looked back. For you. For you, I'd walk away from the world if it's what you wanted me to do."

My pounding heart soars.

As though Calvin is nothing more than the trash Rogan referred to, he drops him unceremoniously onto the floor and steps closer to me. His emerald eyes stare unflinchingly down into my face. "I'd rather die than watch you date Calvin Sims. I'm tough as hell and I've survived a lot in my life, but I wouldn't be tough enough to survive that. I couldn't stand it. I just . . . I couldn't."

His voice is raw with emotion and I feel belated tears well in my eyes.

"Then, Rogan, please tell me there's another way. Tell me that he won't win. I can't bear to see him hurt you. They've taken so much already. From me, from you. I can't give them anything else."

His lips spread into a thin, sad smile. "They won't take anything else from you. You have my word."

The statement sounds final. Definite.

"Wh-what are you going to do?"

"Something that could make you hate me. Something that you can't be a part of. But something that has to be finished. The Senator has done things. To you. To me. To the brothers I served with in the Army. We did a lot of covert ops. Things I can't talk about. Things the Senator shouldn't have ordered. Now he's trying to cover his tracks. He's having people targeted. Assassinated. *My* people."

I had no idea that Special Forces meant . . . this. The room has narrowed to a tunnel that extends from Rogan's eyes to mine and contains only the sound of his voice and the blood rushing behind my ears. Part of me thinks that I should be outraged, shocked. Afraid. But the rest of me . . . *most of me* . . . wants this, wants to be rid of him for good.

And knowing that Rogan is one of the men who has sacrificed so much for his country, for those he loves, for *me* . . . well, I could never hate him for that. Only love him more.

As if on cue, my heart swells with it, threatening to rip me open with the pressure of it inside my chest.

"I . . . I could never hate you, Rogan."

"It would kill me if you did, but I won't lie to you. I would never disrespect you like that. That's why I'm telling you. Senator Sims is guilty of war crimes, Katie, and he'll pay. It's the way it has to be."

"And Calvin?"

"I've got plans for him, too."

I nod. I don't know what else to do. Or to say. I want this. Even though it may not change things between Rogan and me, he'll be free. And so will I. At least we'll have that.

He backs away, bending slowly to throw Calvin the Trash over his shoulder and turn back toward the door. Things feel so . . . unfinished between us that I want to ask him to stay. But I know he can't. And maybe he shouldn't. But I want him to anyway.

"Rogan?"

He swivels to look back at me, a crooked smile twisting his lips. "I love you, Katie. I think I always have."

And with that, he walks right out the door and into the night, leaving me staring after, out into the inky darkness.

FORTY-TWO

Rogan

If I'd been a few minutes later, Katie could be dead. She was reliving parts of her worst nightmare, had gotten herself into a shitty mess, for me. She did that all for me. Hating them as she does, hating what I do as she does—as she has every right to—she was considering walking right back into that world to save me. She'd risk everything for me.

I know what I have to do next. What I *want* to do next. For her. All for her.

After I take care of this piece of shit, I think, throwing Sims's limp body into the back of my rented SUV and slamming the door shut. After I climb behind the wheel and start the engine, I dial Jasper's number. He's at a small airstrip for private planes on the outskirts of Enchantment. We all flew in separately, but our destination (as well as our mission) is the same.

He answers the phone with a question. "Do you have him?"

"I've got him. I'll make the call."

"Tag just checked in. He's at the airport."

"On my way to the location. He'll be there when you arrive. My flight is booked."

"I'll let you know when we're in the air."

"I'll be waiting. Be careful," I tell him.

"Check."

And with that the line goes dead. I start my drive through the dark and deserted streets of Enchantment.

The three of us devised a plan for taking care of the Senator. He thinks he's untouchable because of who he is, but he obviously forgot who *we* are—three men who were handpicked and trained by the government to move under the radar, to strike with silence and leave no traces. Removing threats is what we do. Or used to anyway. And Senator Sims is a threat. A murderer. On his order, lives were taken. All for his own gain. Some for money, as with Assad's second-in-command, and some to save his own ass, as with Reid and Jasper's mother. Senselessly, ruthlessly. Criminally. And there are consequences for those kinds of actions.

Even if you're a sitting senator for the United States of America.

Because of my public association with the Senator and now my association with his son through Katie, I can't be involved more than getting Calvin to the pickup spot. From there, Jasper and Tag will take care of them. Or, more likely, just Jasper. He's the only one still in the game. Plus, his mother was killed as a result of all this. We all lost our friend, but he lost even more. And I wouldn't want to get in the way of his . . . reckoning. It's the only thing he can do for his mom at this point.

We all have to do what's best for us, for the people we love, which makes me think of Katie. Again.

She's chosen to live a quiet life, one as far from violence as she can get, and I feel like I've brought everything she's tried to escape right back to her door. How could I ever ask her to be with me when what I do reminds her of such painful times?

I couldn't.

I won't.

But I don't want to live without her either. I've only got one choice as far as I can see, but it's an easy one when she's on the other side of it. Nothing is as important to me as Katie, and with Senator Sims out of the way, I'm free to do whatever I have to in order to win her back.

And that's what I'm going to do.

I dial Johns to let him know that I still plan to fight in Vegas on Sunday.

When the light turns green, I make a hard right to turn into the only gas station in town. I buy a plastic gas can and fill it up before getting back on the road. As I pull out of the lot, I wake my phone and punch in the number of Senator Sims.

"What is it?" comes the gruff voice that says I'm interrupting.

"It's Rogan," I announce flatly. Already, satisfaction is unrolling in my stomach, like butterfly wings from a caterpillar's cocoon. "I've got your son in the back of my car. He's unconscious, and in about fifteen minutes, he's going to be strapped naked to a tree in a very public park. And then doused in gasoline. I hope you can get here before I put a match to his dick at dawn."

I hang up and drop my phone in the cup holder, expecting it to ring back any second. And it does. But I ignore it.

I pull into the lot of the park I met Katie at. I figure it's poetic that he'll get a little, teeny-tiny bit of what's coming to him in a place that brings Katie so much joy. I'm not going to burn him alive. That would ruin the plan. I will, however, put the fear of God in him. I will make him sweat, make him wonder. Give him a few hours of pure emotional hell, wondering if he's going to burn to death, naked in a public park.

I cut the engine and walk around to the back of the vehicle, opening the hatch. Sims is waking up, rolling his head from side to side, moaning. I lean in and punch him in the jaw, putting him out for a few more minutes.

I grab his ankles and haul him toward me with a functional yank. I don't give a damn what I hurt or how sore this bastard is. The more he hurts, the better.

I toss him over my shoulder and slam the hatch shut before I carry him to a tree near the area where I purposely ran into Katie that evening. It was the first time I tasted those sweet lips.

I drop Sims in a heap at the base of the big oak and I set about taking off his clothes. Shoes and socks first, pants next. He's going commando, which saves me from the unpleasant task of taking off his underwear.

"Thanks for making it easy on me, asswipe," I mutter to the unconscious man.

Next, I take off his shirt and work on tying the long sleeves to his pants legs. I use his belt to restrain his hands behind his back before propping him up against the tree. Then I use his clothes to tie him to it. There's no way in hell he's getting out of this when he wakes up.

I stand back to admire my handiwork before I return to the parking lot for the gasoline can. I take it to the tree and wait for Sims to regain consciousness. It only takes about ten minutes for him to rouse. When he does, I slap his cheek a few times to help him focus.

"Got something to tell you, shit-for-brains. You listening?" I ask. I stand and kick the bottom of his bare foot. When he opens his eyes and sees me, I uncap the gas can. I want him to see. I want him to know. I want him to fear.

"I-I'm listening," he says, still addled.

"Good. Can you tell me what this is?"

I start at his head, dumping about a half gallon of gas onto his upper body. He sputters for a few seconds and shakes his head. I know the instant he makes the connection. His eyes open back up, wide and terrified. I can see the understanding, even in the low light of the full moon. That's when he starts to scream.

"What are you doing? What the hell are you doing? Hellllp!"

"Hey!" I say, kicking his foot again. "No one can hear you. The best thing you can do for yourself is commit to memory every word I'm about to say."

He's panting, struggling against his restraints. I pour another couple of splashes of gasoline on him, letting it run down his chest, and then douse his junk real good. He screams again when the cold liquid runs down between his legs. I can only imagine what he's thinking.

It's probably pointless to talk to him. Chances of him actually making it out of the next twelve hours alive are slim. But I'm going to say my piece anyway. For Katie.

"This is for Katie Rydale. No amount of suffering is enough, but this is a good start."

"What are you going to do?" he wails, panicked.

"Do you really have to ask?"

I take out a pack of matches and toss them up into the air, catching them and stuffing them back into my pocket. His eyes watch my every move, getting wider by the second.

"Oh shit, oh shit! You can't do this! You can't do this to me! You know who my father is! He'll have your ass if you do this!"

"Will he? Because I don't think even Daddy can save you this time."

Even in the dark, I see him turn white as a damn sheet at the coldness of my smile, of my words. He knows I speak the truth.

"Please," he begs, giving me some small bit of satisfaction.

"I bet you've never had to beg for anything, have you? I bet others have, though. Like Katie. I bet she begged for you to stop when you hit her. I bet she would've begged for you not to strike that match if you'd given her the chance. But I bet she wouldn't beg you for a damn thing now, would she?"

I see the piss trickle from the end of his shriveled dick and I spit on the ground beside him. "Yeah, you just think about that. I'll be back soon. With more gas."

The pathetic shit starts to cry. "Please, please, please," he chants.

"Maybe I should leave your fate up to Katie. You think?" I muse aloud, knowing nothing can change the course of events now.

"That bitch!" he spits in furious desperation. "Don't listen to that bitch! She's a fuc—"

I kick him square in the jaw, silencing words I have no interest in hearing. He doesn't deserve to speak them.

"Enough of that, asshole," I say, dumping the remaining gas on his head, making sure he's soaked from head to ass. When he's coming to, already whimpering like a little school-boy bitch, I put a hand in my pocket and walk off, whistling as I swing the gas can.

Back at the parking lot, I pick up my phone. I've got fourteen missed calls and two messages. I don't bother to listen to them. I want Senator Sims to sweat. I just type in a text to my buddies that reads one simple word: *Ready*.

FORTY-THREE

Katie

I'm drifting in that hazy place between sleep and wakefulness. My mind won't let me rest completely, so I've been lying here for hours, thinking. Drifting. Wanting.

The television is playing softly, the bluish light flickering against my closed lids. I'm not concentrating on the words, but the name gets my attention.

I raise my head and glance down at the flat screen. There's a small corner picture of Senator Sims, and a red banner at the bottom of the screen that reads BREAKING NEWS. Just below that are the words SENATOR AND SON FOUND DEAD IN WRECKAGE OF PLANE CRASH.

I sit up, fully awake now, my eyes wide and my pulse thudding. Am I dreaming? Am I hallucinating?

I stare at the screen, watching for more details. None come. Just that flash of news. Important news. News that could very well change my life.

People all over the country might be mourning their passing. I'm not one of those people. I feel only a sense of intense relief. And vindication. And freedom. I'm finally free. And so is Rogan.

The next thing to flash along the ticker tape at the bottom of the screen is a statement on the crowd's anticipation of a mixed martial arts fight being held in Vegas tomorrow.

It's Rogan.

On the one hand, I know I shouldn't go. Shouldn't even want to. But on the other hand, I desperately want to see him, to talk to him. To hear him say those three little words again. I want them to change everything.

But is that realistic? Is it possible? Is it possible for me to put the last few years behind me and move forward as yet another different version of myself? Or am I tough enough to embrace all the different parts and live as just me? Scarred yet whole. Free.

There's only one way to find out, of course. And to do it, I'll have to be brave. Tough. Tough enough to *live*, not just survive.

For the first time in what feels like a lifetime, I feel like I might be ready for that. Finally ready. Finally strong. Finally tough enough.

FORTY-FOUR

Rogan

I feel different. As Johns slides my gloves on, I know in my gut this will be a night like no other.

I focus on the music that I've heard before every fight since day one. I let it bring me to the present, where it's only me and my opponent. The pump of blood to my muscles and the burst of adrenaline through my veins. This time, my opponent is internal, though, and winning against him is more important than ever.

Above the music, I hear the *pop pop pop* of umbrellas opening all around me. I reach deep for my "The Rain" persona and I tap my fists together, throwing my hands up and dancing from foot to foot as I turn a circle and wordlessly thank my fans for showing up.

As my eyes scan the sea of mostly black umbrellas, I do a double take of the upper level of one section, my eyes stuttering over and then returning to a pink and white polka-dot umbrella. I stop and stare, trying to see past the bright lights to the face in the shadow, but I can't. Surely it's Katie. Isn't it?

But then I think that, after all the commotion when I spotted her and acknowledged her at the charity fight, the new thing might be for women to bring a polka-dot umbrella. How the hell should I know?

But still, the fact that it might be starts to eat at my stomach.

I enter the cage and listen as the announcer goes through his usual spiel. I resist glancing up into the crowd again.

I walk to the center of the ring, as I've done dozens of time. I listen while the ref gives us our instructions, as I've done dozens of time. But when it comes times to tap gloves with my competitor, I don't move. I don't touch them; I only stare at him. I asked for this fight. People will expect a show. Maybe this will be show enough for them.

I think of how I'm going to phrase what I'm about to say. Nothing eloquent or elaborate. I'll say the only thing I need to say. And the person who needs to understand it will understand.

The ref eyes me, as does my opponent, when I motion toward the ceiling for the drop-down mic. There's a hushed kind of chatter that spreads through the crowd. I try to ignore it, which is much easier this time. My focus is on one person, whether she's here or not.

When the mic drops down, I grab it and turn toward the umbrella that may or may not be hiding the woman I'm in love with. I gesture to her with my free hand and speak clearly to the waiting crowd.

"This is for you, Katie," I begin. Then, when the place is almost silent in anticipation, I continue. "Tonight will be my last fight. I'm officially retiring."

And then all hell breaks loose. Screams erupt, voices yell, cameras flash, and a mob of frenzied fans rushes the cage. The gate, still ajar until the fight begins, is pushed open and people rush in. Security forces their way through to my opponent and me, ushering us out of the stadium and back into the locker rooms. To safety. To calm. To the consequences.

FORTY-FIVE

Katie

I hit the release of my umbrella and shrink it as quickly as I can so that I can push my way through the crowd. When I get to the aisle, I run as fast as I can for the tunnel into which Rogan disappeared. When I reach a crossroads in the two main halls surrounding the arena, I spot Johns heading around a corner. He doesn't look happy.

My lungs burn as I launch myself toward them, frantic to get to Rogan before he does something irreversible. I skitter around the concrete corner and burst through the double doors at the end of the short hall. All eyes turn toward me, but I only see one set, the only set that matters.

They are the clear green of a princess-cut emerald being held up to the light. And they are focused on me.

"Don't do this for me," I blurt breathlessly.

"I want to," he says, edging his way toward me where I stand near the door. "This is me showing you that you're the most important thing in my life."

My heart slams against my ribs. "All you had to do was say so."

"Words aren't enough. You need to see that I'd do anything for you. I'd give up anything for you, I'd take on anything for you. I'd run, I'd fly, I'd fight. I'd do *anything* to prove to you that I love you. That I've always loved you."

I wanted so much to hear him say it again. Just one more time. Or a million. Or every day of forever.

I feel the sting of tears. I don't even try to hold them back this time. I'm too happy to hold them in. "I love you, too."

His shoulders sag and he drops his head. My heart stutters in alarm as I take in his posture. He doesn't look happy. He looks . . . defeated.

"God, Katie," he begins softly. "I wanted you to love me. More than I've ever wanted anything." He raises tortured eyes to mine. "But I knew I couldn't give you what you needed."

"*You* were all I needed. Only you. I thought it was the fighting. Then I thought I couldn't get past you working with Sims. But then I got a taste of life without you, of what it feels like to truly be dying inside. That's when I realized that I can do anything for you. That I'm tough enough to live now. Because of you. I was tough enough to stand up to the Simses. I was tough enough to fight back. And I was tough enough to come here. To you. Because you're all that matters to me."

"I don't ever want you to hurt for me. Ever. You've been through too much."

"I hurt for you when I'm not with you. I've been burned alive and I've never been in more pain than I was when I was without you."

His lips curling up into a small grin, Rogan moves toward me, not stopping until I have to crane my neck to look up into his gorgeous face. "Woman, you broke me. I didn't think I was going to make it."

I swallow hard, hating to think of him hurting, but at the same time loving that he was as miserable as I was. "Let's not do that to each other again."

He reaches up to tenderly cup my face. "Deal. Don't ever leave me and we'll be good."

"Done," I say with a smile, my heart lighter than it's been since I was a child.

Rogan brushes his lips across my forehead, down my temple and around to the corner of my mouth. My whole body is humming in anticipation of his kiss. I feel as though I've been starved of it for an eternity.

But it's not to be. A gruff voice interrupts our moment. "The cage has been cleared. Now damn it, get the hell out there and stop giving me trouble," Johns grouches. "I can't believe you'd pull this shit without telling me."

Rogan leans back and grins down into my face. "See what I have to put up with?"

"Poor you," I say. "Is there anything I can do to make it better?"

"Ask me after the fight."

"Rogan," I say, staring up into his eyes, as serious as I can be. "Please don't retire because of me. Don't make a choice like that because of—"

A long finger comes to rest across my lips, silencing me. "This part of my life is over. I'm ready to move on, to start something new. With you. Something where my body isn't sore unless you make it sore." The sparkle in his eyes and the smile on his lips bring a warm buzz to my muscles. My cheeks sting as I imagine Johns listening to our every word and rolling his eyes in displeasure.

"Well that's about the best damn excuse for retiring that I've ever heard. Now kiss her and get your ass out into that cage," Johns barks.

I risk peeking at him over my shoulder. He's grinning at us—at least I think that's what the expression is. He winks at me and then tips his head toward the door before he leaves us in a quick moment of peace.

"I love you, baby. With everything I am."

"And I love you, my tough fighter. Now go win something."

"I already won the best prize, but I guess I can throw in another little something for you."

I smile as he kisses my knuckles and makes his way toward the door.

"Come back sore. I think I can help you out with working out the kinks."

"I won't be long," he says, turning to jog out the door.

I'm standing in the same spot, staring at the last place I saw Rogan when the door flies open and bangs against the wall. Rogan makes his way to me in long, determined strides, takes me in his arms and kisses me for all he's worth. My heart, my body, my soul sings with relief. I don't know how he knew, but I needed this. Desperately.

When he has kissed me breathless, he leans back, brushing a strand of hair behind my ear. "I love your hair, by the way."

I feel the warmth flood my cheeks. For the first time in five years, I wore it up today. It's a loose, sexy style that I used to favor. Before. But now the only before and after I care about are before Rogan told me he loved me and after. All the many years of after. "I wanted to be tough today. For you. For me."

"Tough looks amazing on you. I always knew it would."

"Thank you," I say, casting my eyes down in an old habit.

As he's done dozens of times before, Rogan lifts my face toward his. "You never have to hide, especially from me. I love you just the way you are. Beautiful, perfect, *real.*"

"Thank you for fighting for me."

"I never stopped."

No, he didn't. And he never will. He's my fighter. My love. My Rogan.

EPILOGUE

Rogan

Five months later

"Good for you, Mona," Katie says from her seat. I glance over to see her typing something into her phone.

"What'd she do? Use 'onomatopoeia' correctly?" I grin just thinking about Katie's friend and her new love of the dictionary.

"No, she dumped White. She says she wants the dream now. I guess seeing how happy I am, how you treat me and how a good relationship works has made her see White for the cheating crapbag that he is."

"Cheating crapbag, huh?"

She giggles and leans her head back against the seat to smile over at me. "I got tough, but my words are still . . . mild."

"I think in this case, you could spare something a *little* tougher, don't you?"

"Sure. Mona's worth it," she says, straightening. "What did you have in mind?"

"How about 'shitbird'?"

"Yeah, White's a shitbird!" she says enthusiastically, her eyes twinkling. "A shitty, shitty shitbird."

I laugh outright. "God, I love you."

Her face takes on that glow she gets when I tell her I love her. It makes me want to take her to bed and tell her over and over and over again just how much I love her.

"Damn, you're beautiful."

Her cheeks stain pink and she stretches across to kiss my cheek. "And you're the most gorgeous man I've ever seen." She nuzzles my neck, pressing her chest against me as she rests her hand along my thigh.

"Okay, so we have two options. Either take your wicked lips and your delicious body back over to your side of the car, or stay where you are and reap the consequences."

"What consequences are those?" she asks around a husky laugh as she rubs her tits against my shoulder.

Damn her.

"They involve me pulling off the side of the road, putting my hands up that tiny little skirt you're wearing and probably embarrassing the shit out of you right here in front of my friend's house."

She turns around, wide-eyed and surprised to see that we have arrived. "I thought you were taking me to some rustic spot in the mountains," she says as she eyes the big stone house sitting at the top of the circular end of Chiara's drive.

"I am. We aren't quite there yet."

I park in front of the granite steps that lead to the front door. Tag is standing at the top of them, smiling. From the corner of my eye, I see Katie smooth her hair over her left shoulder. I shift into park and reach for her hand when it flutters back to her lap. "Don't be nervous."

She turns her dark blue eyes to mine. "I'm not nervous."

"You *are* nervous. You still pull your hair around when you're nervous."

Her lips part like she's going to argue, but then she just smiles sheepishly instead. "You know me too well. No fair."

"You have nothing to worry about. Tag's a great guy."

She smiles around a calming breath. "He has to be a great guy. And anyone worth your time is someone I'll love. Maybe I am a little nervous. I guess I just want him to like me because he's important to you."

"He's gonna love you. The only thing you need to worry about is Tag flirting with you and getting his ass kicked. That could really compromise the weekend."

Her lips ease into a more natural smile. "I don't think you're going to have to worry about that."

"Good. Then just relax. This is supposed to be fun."

"Fun business?"

"Yep. Fun business."

I kiss her knuckles then give her lips a short peck—anything more than that always gets me in trouble—before I get out and walk to her side of the car and open her door. We walk hand in hand to meet my friend.

He descends the few steps and gives me a bear hug. When he leans back, we exchange a look that says a lot. It says we're glad to see each other. It says we've been through hell together. It says we're both happy that the threat to our group is neutralized. Yet neither of us has to say a word.

When his gray eyes flicker to Katie, I turn and put my hand at her lower back. "Tag Barton, meet Katie Rydale."

I see his eyes sweep her appreciatively. He's my friend and I know he means nothing by it. It's a guy thing—checking a woman out that way. But more than that, it's a Delta Five thing. It's habit now, I'm sure, for all of us to observe, to take in details, to make all kinds of mental notes. It's part of our training.

I grit my teeth and suck it up, because he's my friend and this is important. What I'm *not* prepared for, though, is Katie's reaction. Her smile is small and shy, like it used to be for me, but her eyes flicker up to his and away, up to his and away. Like she can't stop looking at him.

I don't know why I'm surprised. Tag has always had that effect on women. With his jet-black hair, dark skin and silvery eyes, he makes quite an impression. Plus, he's always had this air of . . . I don't even know. Something different. But women love it, whatever it is. I guess I was just assuming that Katie would be immune to it.

"Such a pleasure to meet you, Katie. Rogan said you were beautiful, but not that you were *this* beautiful," he says charmingly.

I watch Katie's cheeks bloom with color as she shakes his hand. I have to ball my fists to keep from pulling her back.

But then, just before I end up doing or saying something stupid, she backs away on her own, curling into my side and winding an arm around my waist. When I look down at her, she's already looking up at me. Her eyes are pools of sapphire and her lips are curved into a smile, the smile that she only gives to me.

This is why I don't have to worry. *This* is why I don't have to be jealous. She's as nuts over me as I am over her. We were meant to be together and no one could ever change that.

I relax instantly, bending to press my lips to her forehead before I turn my attention back to Tag. "So, where are we starting?" I ask.

Tag claps his hands and then rubs them together. It's easy to see that he's enjoying this. "How about a tour first and then I'll show you to your cabin before we talk business. Sound good?"

"Sounds good," I say.

Katie thinks I'm here to look into buying a cabin, which I am. Sort of. It just so happens the cabin is part of this vineyard.

I pat my pocket as we follow Tag around the house and onto a well-worn path that leads through the trees. A small cabin is nestled at the end of it, resting in the dappled shade of a big oak. The sun is already turning red in the windows of the two dormers and I imagine that the view of it setting over the vineyard is spectacular.

Tag's steady monologue about the vineyard and the cabin stops when he opens the door and gestures for Katie to precede him. He winks at me as I pass and then closes the door behind us, making a quiet, unobtrusive exit.

In the quiet, I hear Katie's gasp. She's standing in front of the small dining table with her hands over her mouth. A white cloth covers the surface. On it, two white candles are lit in silver holders and red rose petals are scattered all around it. A silver wine bucket rests on a stand to the right, holding a chilled bottle of Chiara sparkling wine. From there, a trail of red rose petals disappears into the next room.

Katie glances back at me, her eyes shimmering with the suspicion of what's to come. I say nothing. I do nothing. I simply follow her as she follows the trail of petals.

They lead to a small bedroom. The king bed is draped in white and covered in rose petals. In the center is a pile of long-stemmed roses with a card propped in front of them. In calligraphy, it reads *Will you marry me?*

I hear the soft huff of her breath. She's crying, her hands still covering her mouth.

I step in front of her, meeting her glistening eyes, my heart pounding harder than any of my opponents ever have, and I spill my guts. "I never thought I'd meet someone who would become the focus of my world. I didn't think love like that existed. Until a beautiful makeup artist painted her image on my heart. Every day, I wanted her more. To see her smile, to hear her laugh, to feel her touch. One day I woke up beside her and realized that I couldn't live without her. I could only survive. Miserably. So I tried everything I could think of to make her mine, to make her love me like I loved her. And when she did, I brought her to a vineyard, one I hope to buy for us, to tell her that I'm giving her my life. And I'm praying that she takes it. It wouldn't be worth anything without her in it. That's why we're here. This is me, offering everything I'll ever be to the person who already owns me." I reach for her hands, taking them in mine as I sink to one knee. I've never cared so much about the outcome of a fight before. Because it's been a fight. Me fighting for her, her fighting to get her life back. Each of us fighting for the other. "Will you marry me? Will you stay with me today, tomorrow and every day after that? Will you let me make you happy, keep you safe and spend my life working to give you everything you've ever wanted?"

She's absolutely still. The only thing moving are the tears pouring down her cheeks. And then she nods. And then she nods again.

And then she's in my arms. Kissing me like she can't breathe unless her lips are touching mine. Touching me like she's never letting go. Hanging on like she's resisting gravity.

"I said yes before you ever told me you loved me," she confesses tearfully, tearing her mouth away from mine. "I've been yours all along. And I always will be."

It's more than two hours—two very heated, loud hours—later when Katie, curled up against my side, asks me about the vineyard.

"Tag was raised here. His father passed away a couple of years ago and his mother is sick now, too. He wants to buy this place, not just because he's spent most of his life here, but also because this is home for his mom, too. He wants her to be able to stay here the rest of her days, not having to worry about work. He could use an investor, and I thought it would be a good place to park some of my fighting money. This way, we can stay in Enchantment as long as you want, whether you continue working or not."

She turns her smile up at me. "So truly no more fighting?"

"No more fighting for me. I already have the only thing worth fighting for. I consider that a happy ending all the way around."

"I got my fairy tale after all."

"And I got you."

"You certainly do," she says, sliding up my body to plaster her lips against mine.

"I hope Tag has some ear plugs," I say, swallowing her throaty moan. Those are the last words either of us speak for a long, long time.

Turn the page for a special excerpt from the next
Tall, Dark, and Dangerous novel by M. Leighton

BRAVE ENOUGH

Coming soon from Berkley Books!

ONE

Weatherly

I'm surprised that I know the way back to Chiara. It's been years since I've visited our family vineyard on the outskirts of a small Georgian town called Enchantment, but I find that I know the turns even before the navigation tells me which way to go. When I was growing up, it was one of my favorite places in the world. Winding roads, lush green hills, and purple-gray mountains rising up in the background—it's like the best of every world, all in one spot.

Already I feel a little less claustrophobic just leaving Atlanta behind. Don't get me wrong; I love that city, but with my father and his old cronies bearing down on me, I had to get away. I can't very well come up with a plan to save myself if they're occupying all my time and hovering around every corner.

The lightly scented breeze whips through my hair like a lover's fingers as I slow my convertible to make the last turn. I barely creep along the serpentine road, taking my time to enjoy the sun filtering through the trees and the broken glimpses of row after row of grapevines. Being here feels like coming home. It always did.

Throughout my entire childhood, we would come here for two weeks every summer just before harvest. Dad would catch up on the vineyard business for the first couple of days, but then he'd relax with Mom and me. We ate meals together, we swam together, we played board games at night together. We acted like a normal family and I loved it. There were no pretenses to keep up, no important people to entertain, no pressures from the outside world. Just us in a mountain hideaway, protected by rows and rows of grapes.

Even now, I feel the stresses of my life draining away as I drink in the sweet scent of the air. It's as familiar as the bustle of city life, but as removed from it as east is from west. Although I haven't been here since before I went to college, time is already melting away as though I visited just last week. Here at the vineyard, little changes.

As I drive past the rows, a flash catches my eye. I slow to a stop and focus on a broad, sweaty back as a man drives wooden supports into the ground in front of a downed vine. I let my gaze travel over him. He must be new because I don't recognize the physique. And I think I'd remember if there had ever been a man built like this on Chiara grounds.

His shoulders are easily double the width of mine and he's probably almost a foot taller, just guessing. And I'm not short at five foot seven. As I start to pull away, I let my eyes linger on his impossibly narrow waist and hips, and the world-class ass that fills out the black denim.

I'd love to see if the face goes with the body. I'm very curious about him now, and about what the heck he's doing here. Maybe I'll run into him later. If I'm lucky.

I came back to Chiara looking for some peace and quiet, some time to find a way out. I would not be at all opposed to a handsome distraction, though. It's been too long since I've been able to want somebody just because I want him and not because of how he may or may not fit into my life. Maybe it's high time to go with my instincts. To go with someone who might be all wrong for me. To go with the passion. To throw caution to the wind.

As my dark hair flutters around my face, my optimism climbs with my speed. Maybe, just maybe, this little vacation will get a whole lot more interesting. It would be nice to get lost in something not planned and not political. Something real, something innocent to the ways of the world.

Is that too much to ask?

For my life, probably. But that doesn't mean I can't hope for it. Or try to have it. At least for a little while. A few weeks maybe.

When I pull up to the top of the circular drive, I shut off the engine and grab my smallest bag from the backseat. It has all I'll need right now—my toiletries and a change of clothes. I want to get the grime of the road off me before I unpack and get settled.

I glance at the ivy-covered stone front of the main house, a smile tugging at my lips. So many good memories here.

The front door is unlocked when I climb the wide front steps and test the knob. Maybe Stella is cleaning today. Although I didn't tell anyone I was coming (mainly because I didn't want my father to find me right away), she keeps the house ready at all times. That must be what she's doing.

"Hello?" I call when I step into the grand foyer with its Brazilian cherry floors, vaulted ceiling, and antique chandelier. My voice echoes around me, but otherwise I hear no sign of life.

I set my bag at the foot of the winding staircase and head off past the formal dining room to the kitchen at the back of the house. "Hello? Stella?" I call again. No answer.

With a shrug, I make my way back to my belongings and carry them up the stairs to the room I've always stayed in. It's just one of the guest rooms, but it has a charming window seat that I used to curl up in a lot as a little girl. In my head, that made it mine, so that's how I've always thought of this particular room—as mine.

I set my bag on the thick, beige duvet that covers the bed and begin taking out what few things I'll need. As of today, gone are the "presentable" clothes. These are the days of spaghetti straps and sarongs, flip flops and loose hair.

I eye the steam shower longingly, but as soon as my gaze falls on the oversized clawfoot tub, the shower is forgotten. A nice relaxing soak to sooth my stiff, road-weary muscles sounds like heaven.

I cut on the spigot and test the temperature with the backs of my fingers until it's a little warmer than what's comfortable and then I start stripping. I grab two towels, a wash cloth, my phone, and my organic soap and set them on the chair that sits near the head of the tub. Then I climb in.

Air hisses through my teeth as the hot water stings my legs and then my belly. I let my skin adjust to the heat before I reach for my phone and turn on some music. I wet the washcloth, drape it over my eyes, and then slide down in the tub. Within two minutes, I'm already feeling boneless.

I soak for a good thirty minutes before pulling the plug and draining half of the tepid water so that I can refill it with hot. I grab my soap and roll the silky bar in my hands, working up a rich lather to spread over my arms. The scent of almond and coconut permeate the air and I can all but feel it sinking into my skin.

I lather my hands again and set my fingers to my chin and neck, working toward my chest. I close my eyes, the image of the vineyard guy popping unbidden into my head.

I wonder what he might look like. What color eyes would go with a body like that? Something exotic, maybe. Something piercing. Something that would say he wants me without ever having to open his mouth.

My breathing picks up as my fantasy takes off in an unexpected direction. I massage the scented soap into the soft mounds of my breasts, dragging a fingertip around each nipple over and over, imagining what it might feel like to have the calloused touch of a manual laborer there.

"My birthday isn't for another week," a deep voice purrs, jarring me from my thoughts.

With a gasp, I sit up in the tub, covering myself the best that I can. I forget all about propriety, however, when I see the tall, insanely gorgeous man standing in the bathroom doorway.

Black hair, cut in a longish style.

Gray eyes that are almost silver they're so light.

Olive skin that matches the sweaty back I saw less than an hour ago.

It's the man from the vineyard. His build and his coloring are unmistakable. As are the black jeans that he's wearing. He fills them out as perfectly from the front as he did from the back, only this side includes a thick, tantalizing bulge behind his zipper placket.

Holy. Shit.

"P-pardon?" I stammer, my brain a jumbled mess. Between the little fantasy I was indulging, him catching me off guard this way, and his incredible good looks, I think I might've forgotten my name, much less that I should be prudishly insulted right now.

Only I'm not.

I'm intrigued instead. Especially when he grins.

If smoke could smile, this is what it would look like. Dark, mysterious. Sexy as hell.

Holy mother! What is a guy who looks like this doing working in a vineyard?

"My birthday," he repeats in a perfectly modulated, cultured voice that sounds like chocolate and cinnamon. Deep. Spicy. Delicious. "Isn't that what this is about?"

"Ummm, no. I don't know anything about your birthday."

"Damn. I was gonna thank the hell out of somebody." His eyes rake my naked upper body and chills break out across my chest, reminding me that it's probably extremely inappropriate for me to be carrying on a conversation with a perfect stranger when I'm in the tub.

But other than propriety, which I'm evidently not too concerned with right now, I can't think of one good reason to ask him to leave. Not one.

"I'm Weatherly O'Neal. My family owns this vineyard. Who are you?"

One black-as-night brow shoots up. "I'm Tag. My family works this vineyard."

Every cheesy book and movie about a rich woman and the cabana boy (chauffer, gardener, handyman, and a whole slew of other clichés) scampers through my head. Now I understand. Now I understand how it happens. Now I understand the draw. It doesn't matter that our stations in life are worlds apart. It doesn't matter that my father would have a conniption. It doesn't matter that it could never work out. All my body and my mind are thinking is that the way he's looking at me sets my blood on fire.

And I love it.

"Well, Tag," I say, enunciating the name that somehow suits him perfectly, "I guess I'll be seeing you around then."

He's still smiling. I don't think he's stopped since he showed up in the doorway. "I look forward to it. Very. Much."

With that, he skims me once more with his smoky silver eyes and then turns, very slowly, to leave.

When I hear the door to my bedroom click shut—the door I forgot to close—I rest back against the cool ceramic and exhale. I smile, too, as I think to myself, Yep. This little getaway is going to be just what I needed.

TWO

Tag

So this is Weatherly O'Neal, I think as I watch the stunning raven-haired beauty slide onto a lounger by the pool and tip her face up to the sun. She's wearing a tight camisole-type thing in red and a breezy wraparound skirt that shows off her long, slim legs when she sits down. Her skin glistens with a healthful glow after her bath. I can all but smell the sweet scent of her flesh from all the way over here.

It'll be a long time before I can get the vision of her out of my head, particularly the one of her in the bathtub. I watched her for a few seconds before I spoke. Her eyes were closed, her head resting against the curved edge of the tub, and her slim fingers were teasing the most perfect nipples I've ever seen. They were rosy and hard and my mouth waters just recalling the way they poked wetly from the lush mounds of some seriously great tits.

Damn.

I didn't get as good a look at the rest of her. Once I spoke and she sat up, all I could really focus on was her face. Heart-shaped, pale skin, plump lips just the right shade of pink. And her eyes . . . God, those eyes could make a man beg. If that body, with its round breasts, flat stomach, and smoothly shaved everything, wouldn't do it, those eyes would. They're a rich blue. Almost violet. They have an exotic shape to them that makes her look like she's turned on all the time.

That or she was turned on.

I grit my teeth.

Double damn!

Yeah, her arrival is definitely not going to make things any easier for me. But nothing worth having is ever easy.

And I'd be willing to bet having her would be worth a lot of trouble.

I saunter down the dappled path to the patio that surrounds the pool. Weatherly's head snaps toward me the instant my boot hits the hard surface and alerts her to my presence. Her mouth drops open the slightest bit and, for a second, there's nothing but steam between us. Hell, I'm surprised the pool water isn't evaporating.

I don't stop until I'm standing over her, my shadow shading her face. She pushes her sunglasses up into the smooth sheet of her straight black hair and focuses those amazing eyes on me.

"I'm sorry that I interrupted your bath," I say, pausing to inhale the decadent scent coming off her skin. "I'd have apologized at the time if I hadn't been so . . . distracted."

Her lips quirk, but just at the corners. "Distracted?"

"A bit, yes."

"Hmm, what on earth had you distracted?"

She likes to play. God, this is going to be fun!

"The local . . . scenery changed today. It became much more . . .

dazzling. Took my breath away, in fact. Made it hard for me to think. My manners went right out the window."

"That's understandable. I was a little, um, preoccupied myself."

"I thought you might've been. You looked deep in . . . thought."

Her lips spread all the way into a full-on smile this time, making her even more striking. The only sign of embarrassment is the tell-tale pink stains that appear on her cheeks.

"I was definitely . . . thinking."

The innuendo is as thick as the humid air seems to be. "Care to share what had you focused so . . . intently?"

"No, not yet."

"Not yet?" I ask. She shakes her head, mouth still curved. "Well, whenever you're ready to talk, I'd love to hear all about it."

"I might take you up on that."

I nod. "Will you be eating in tonight?"

"I will, yes."

"Is there something particular you'd like? I can let Mom know."

"Anything that goes well with a Chiara red. I'm in the mood for red."

"I see that," I say, nodding to her red strappy top. "Anything else you're in the mood for that I should know about?"

She shrugs her shoulders, drawing my eye to the crease of her cleavage. "A surprise. Surprise me."

"Oh, I can definitely surprise you," I reply with an enthusiastic grin.

"Will you be joining me tonight then? You and your mother, I mean?"

"Isn't it frowned upon to mingle with the help?"

"Nobody is here to care, is there?"

"Not a damn soul," I say. "Seven?"

She nods and lets her head drop back. The way she's staring up at me with that sleepy, sexy look on her face . . . the way her body language seems to be begging me to touch, to taste, to take . . . Holy God!

I nod and turn to walk away, only because if I stay any longer, she'll be coming out of those clothes. One way or the other.